The world can't get enough of Miss Seeton

"A **most beguiling**
New York T

"Miss Seeton gets into wild
of farce . . . This is a **lovely mixture of the funny and the exciting.**"
San Francisco Chronicle

"This is not so much black comedy as black-currant comedy . . . **You can't stop reading. Or laughing.**"
The Sun

"**Depth of description and lively characters** bring this English village to life."
Publishers Weekly

"Fun to be had with a **full cast of endearingly zany villagers** . . . and the ever gently intuitive Miss Seeton."
Kirkus Reviews

"Miss Seeton is the **most delightfully satisfactory character since Miss Marple.**"
Ogden Nash

"**She's a joy!**"
Cleveland Plain Dealer

Watch the Wall, Miss Seeton

A MISS SEETON MYSTERY

Hamilton Crane

First published in 2019 by Farrago,
an imprint of Prelude Books Ltd
13 Carrington Road, Richmond, TW10 5AA, United Kingdom

www.farragobooks.com

ISBN: 978-1-78842-116-4

Have you read them all?

Treat yourself again to the first Miss Seeton novels—

Picture Miss Seeton
A night at the opera strikes a chord of danger when Miss Seeton witnesses a murder . . . and paints a portrait of the killer.

Miss Seeton Draws the Line
Miss Seeton is enlisted by Scotland Yard when her paintings of a little girl turn the young subject into a model for murder.

Witch Miss Seeton
Double, double, toil and trouble sweep through the village when Miss Seeton goes undercover . . . to investigate a local witches' coven!

Turn to the end of this book for a full list of the series, plus—on the last page—**exclusive access to the Miss Seeton short story** that started it all.

*With thanks to Catherine Aird for so kindly introducing
Happy Harry to Old Brimstone.*

If you wake at midnight, and hear a horse's feet,
Don't go drawing back the blind, or looking in the street,
Them that asks no questions isn't told a lie.
Watch the wall, my darling, while the Gentlemen go by!
Five and twenty ponies
Trotting through the dark –
Brandy for the Parson,
'Baccy for the Clerk;
Laces for a lady; letters for a spy,
Watch the wall, my darling, while the Gentlemen go by!

from *A Smuggler's Song*, Rudyard Kipling, 1865–1936

The Past: Rye, Sussex, 1810

The girl in the ragged cloak went on crying. The gaoler rattled his keys, but did not speak.

"Me only brother," sobbed the girl, bundling up a corner of the cloak to dab her eyes, revealing boots far too heavy for her spindly legs. She sobbed harder. "Me poor brother! Cruel it is to keep me from him, iffen it's true he's to be taken off to Maidstone tomorrow. Oh please, sir, can't I be let see him afore he's took? They say in the town … and it's mebbe for the last time …" She dissolved even further into a flood of tears.

"If they say he'll hang or be transported, that's true enough." The gaoler offered no hope. "There's little doubt he'll suffer, caught with proof positive as he was." The girl—barely out of childhood—gulped, unable to speak for sorrow. "Your only brother? Your parents did ought to have raised him to know better, as an example to weaker vessels such as yourself if for no other cause."

"They're dead." Another gulp. "Me father took the ague terrible bad, and he died, and it was the workhouse for me mother, and just about broke her heart. She lasted no more'n a few weeks, and then there was just the two of us left on the parish, and iffen we'd then been 'prenticed apart, there'd be small enough chance of seeing each other for a long, long time …" Realising what she had said, she again burst into tears.

"Five minutes," said the gaoler. Through her tears the girl shot him a grateful look. "You tell him to pray for a kindly jury to recommend transportation, not the gallows." He picked up his keys, seized the visitor's arm, and led her through a low doorway and along a narrow stone passage. Narrow stone steps spiralled upwards from chilly flags, and the shivering girl began to struggle with her balance as she climbed, her boots being several sizes too large. The gaoler's hand clamped on her arm as he dragged her back from a tumble. "Careful! Two of you with broken necks'll be no use to anyone, and should it be transportation after all, he'd have nothing to come back for, would he, with you in the grave-yard long a-mouldered?"

She sniffed, gulped, and mumbled something incoherent that might have been thanks.

A narrow passage, a heavy door, the gaoler's keys in action; a bellowed command. "Voller, look lively! Here's your sister come to bid you goodbye afore tomorrow and away to Maidstone for your trial. Five minutes I've told her, and I'll be waiting outside. In with you, my girl."

With the door locked behind her, Ann Voller flung herself into her brother's arms as the other occupants of the slit-windowed, shadowy cell looked on. The young man bent his head. In between her heartfelt sobs Ann gasped a few quick words. Abraham wrapped his arms more closely about his sister, blundering through the tattered folds of her cloak. The gaoler watched through the tiny Judas window in the door, his eyes darting from the Vollers as they embraced and clung, to the others in the crowded room. The air smelled thick with unwashed bodies and overfull buckets.

Tomorrow, with these prisoners gone at last, he'd be able to have the mess of trampled straw cleared, and set someone to washing the floor. So far they'd stayed free here in Rye of the gaol fever that meant Maidstone couldn't take them when they should first have gone, but he must be beforehand in preparing for the next lot. The Excise men were ever on the watch for smugglers—for smugglers a-plenty there were in these parts—but the rules said he should hold no more than a dozen men in Ypres Tower and, better still, less than ten. One successful ambush on a dark night and the prison would fill again with the Gentlemen, meaning more trouble for him and a greater risk of overcrowding. And should the gaol fever flare up …

"Five minutes," he roared in alarm, realising he'd forgotten just how long he'd let the brother and sister say the goodbyes he was certain sure would be final. The lad wasn't just a smuggler, he was a traitor. Too many thought it their given right to break the law and pay no taxes, and in some ways he could understand, the price of tea and tobacco being now what they were, but the taxes were to pay for the long, weary war against Bonaparte, and aiding Boney as the guinea-boats did, carrying gold and information and spies across the Channel—the *English* Channel, and long may it so remain—was treachery, and them that built and sailed and rowed in such traitors' boats must suffer the full penalty of the law.

"Five minutes! You, girl, here! And the rest of you—one step, and she stays locked in with you till morning. There's many a sad misfortune can occur to a young wench passing the night among a crowd of men, brother or no brother. Make haste, now!"

After one lingering hug and then without a backward glance, Ann stumbled, weeping, away from Abraham. The cell door opened no wider than a crack and she had to squeeze herself through, her cloak tearing as it caught on a rough splinter. She snatched at the loosened shreds of fabric to dab again at her eyes as the gaoler locked the door behind her and began pulling her away.

"Don't forget me, Ann," called her stricken brother as she passed from his sight. He ran to the door and strained for one last look through the small window. "I'll allus remember the valiant heart of you, Ann!"

His sister was crying too hard to answer. The gaoler hurried her back along the passage and thrust her down the spiral stairs. Her hands, busy wiping away tears, groped blindly for the wall and its uncertain support. The gaoler had to grab at her more than once as her boots slipped on cold stone, and he cursed her for her clumsiness.

At last she was safely down. He pointed to the outer door of the tower, and told her to be gone. "You'll not speak to your brother again, my girl ..." But she was little more than a child. "Nor even see him," he added, "unless it's from far below the tower when they takes their final turn of exercise on the roof afore being locked in for the night." She raised her head to look at him. He swore at himself for the moment of weakness. "Oh, yes, they'll be in fine fettle when they get to Maidstone—fine enough, leastways, to stand their trial, and whatever comes to them after's no concern of mine. Be off with you!"

Through her sobs Ann managed to thank him, then turned and disappeared into the dusk. The gaoler locked the great outside door, and bolted it. His prisoners were secure for the night.

Hidden by the shadows, Ann took a hunk of bread from her cloak and, from the torn folds that had almost betrayed her, unwrapped the onion. Slowly chewing, keenly listening, she settled down to wait.

Chapter One
The Present: Plummergen, Kent, 1975

Plans for the day were being discussed over breakfast at Rytham Hall. "Louise and I," said Lady Colveden, "are invited to tea with Miss Seeton this afternoon. The birthday chocolates someone sent were delayed in the post, and you know she's not keen on the milk sort anyway. I thought we could help finish them for her before they go off." Wide, innocent eyes met the quizzical gaze of her son. She blushed.

"What happened to the diet?" Nigel, working farmer, speared bacon and egg with great relish. "Calories come, but not for everyone do they so easily go, I believe. Every time Martha gives the pair of you a lesson in baking, you and Louise gorge yourselves on cake no matter how indigestible or calorific it might be. It's clear you're trying to prove a point, even if I've no idea what it is." Licking his lips, he took a forkful of sausage balanced on fried bread and munched, happily.

Louise Colveden, the former Mademoiselle de Balivernes, turned to her mother-in-law and smiled. "Dear Belle-Mère, Nigel teases you. There is no need for diets. He knows well how the hens eat all that remains once we have sampled but a small slice each."

"Eggs certainly a more interesting flavour these days." The voice of Sir George came from behind the morning's *Times*. "Often wondered why. Mystery solved." He lowered his paper and glanced hopefully at his wife. "Talking of eggs, any chance of another?"

"Have some porridge," advised his son. "You need to build up your strength well in advance for the rigours of the evening ahead."

"Ah," said Sir George, eyeing Nigel keenly. Nigel chuckled.

"It's not telepathy. I bumped into the Buzzard yesterday and he said you'd invited him to go up to London with you to meet some Tripper who thinks he may have run across him during the war." He grinned. "Mystery solved."

"Triptolemite," returned Sir George, with dignity.

Louise looked bewildered. "Admiral Leighton, he collects fossils? This I did not know."

"No," said Nigel. "At least, I never heard that he did. It's bees, with the Buzzard."

"Nigel," said his mother in mild reproof. "George's club, Louise, is the Triptolemus—god of farmers, or something classical like that. The members call themselves Triptolemites. When Nigel and Julia were young they used to tease their father about having to walk on tiptoe all the time."

"Undue clubland confusion for infant minds." Nigel helped himself to toast, and spread butter with a lavish knife. "In and Out as well, what's more. It was years before it made sense. Every spring we imagined him dancing through fields of tulips, and we couldn't understand why he had to go all the way to Town to do it when Plummergen grew plenty of its own tulips."

He wiped butter on crust, and with the smeared knife conducted himself in muted song. "Tiptoe—to the window—by the window—that is where I'll be / Come tiptoe—through the tulips—with me!"

His mother sighed. "The In and Out, Louise, is the unofficial name for George's other club, the Naval and Military. The entrance pillars tell the taxis which way to drive—"

"As they collect the shattered remnants of various naval and military roisterers after one of their shindigs," Nigel continued. "And, trust me, Her Majesty's forces can roister with the best. Mother and I remember one occasion when the Buzzard flew his gin pennant—that's a special naval flag, inviting all officers who see it to a wardroom party—and next morning the Rytham Hall barometer ended up halfway across the garden because it kept saying Set Fair when there was a cloudburst outside. My father for some reason lost his temper with the thing."

Sir George, who remembered the occasion all too well, returned hurriedly to *The Times*.

Lady Colveden laughed. "Poor George couldn't bear the sound of tapping—I can't think why—and it was unfair to blame the poor barometer for getting stuck. Sometimes they just do. Still, if he and the admiral are off on the spree together—or do I mean on the razzle—anyway, I must check we have enough coffee. Black, strong, and in gallons, with sugar—that's how he prefers it the morning after the night before."

Major-General Sir George Colveden, Baronet, KCB, DSO, JP, ignored this remark as he coughed behind his newspaper. "Forgot to tell you: staying. Room's already booked. Chap who thinks he knows the Buzzard lives miles out of Town. Make a night of it, if he does."

"And even," murmured Nigel, with a wink for Louise, "if he doesn't."

"Not exactly a Tripper, though," went on the baronet. "One of our lodgers from the Gallimaufry. Opposite side of the square. Dry rot, you may remember. And you know what builders can be."

"My distinguished papa," said Nigel, "wants to make us feel guilty about being unable to move into our new home, Mrs Colveden." A horrified splutter exploded from *The Times*. "Mark my words, next he'll be charging us rent."

"Take no notice, Louise," interposed her ladyship. "We love having you here, though of course you'd prefer your own home, but the builders can't start until the historians have finished investigating, and in a way the delay's even helped Grimes and Salisbury. While they were waiting for Dr Braxted to tell them what was going on, they had simply ages to scout round the village for what needs doing. When the chance came to offer—or is it tender—anyway, when the time came they were able to put in by far the most favourable bid for renovating Saturday Stop, out by the Common."

Nigel took another piece of toast. "Which they've finished. Sounds as if they've done a pretty good job, too." *The Times* came down with a surprised rustle. Lady Colveden stared. Louise nodded as Nigel munched.

"*Mais oui*, Belle-Mère, it did not seem important, but we met foreman Fred the other day and he told us much about making improvements to the bungalow. Nigel explained it had been in a most—most ruinous state before—"

"*Ramshackle* was what I said, I think."

"—before," went on his wife firmly, "all was made new, including most especially the bathroom and kitchen. A bigger garage also, I understand."

Nigel grinned. "Fred said Euphemia still can't tell him how much longer she and her gang of researchers are likely to take. You could be stuck with us for a while yet."

Lady Colveden smiled. "That will be delightful. It isn't as if we've no room." Her smile widened. "And think how upset poor Dr Braxted would be if we insisted she must skimp her research so that you two could move in. She wants to write up everything properly."

The distinguished local historian, Euphemia Braxted, with a small but enthusiastic team from Brettenden Museum was currently investigating the Elizabethan house known as Summerset Cottage, into which the newlyweds had hoped to move on their return from honeymoon. This hope had been frustrated by renovating builders Grimes & Salisbury, whose discovery behind plaster of a remarkable wall painting had at once brought in the experts. Euphemia exposed the rest of the painting, realised its significance, and went on to discover a priest's hole, and a hidden cache behind a sliding panel on the stairs. Painting, priest's hole and panel dated from Tudor times, but Euphemia then expressed to the Colvedens her hopes of also finding a smugglers' tunnel or other Napoleonic survival that would put the house, and the village of Plummergen, even more resolutely on the historical map.

"Plenty of room," Sir George agreed, retreating behind his paper. He kept to himself the apprehension first roused by his friend Rear Admiral Bernard "Buzzard" Leighton, whose Mainbrace Club, like the Triptolemus, had suffered invasion of their premises by nearby victims of building work. "You know what builders are like," the admiral had grumbled. He was noted in Plummergen for being the only person ever to induce Grimes & Salisbury to finish a project on time, thereby making himself an object of both awe and suspicion. "If

I'd had the chivvying of the blighters we wouldn't have been swamped by the Catenary the way we are now, but I wasn't on the committee then. Could only make my views known, no more than that. Not the thing, mutiny. So take my advice, George. Don't let 'em slip into making the arrangement permanent! Too disruptive. Can't call our souls our own any more."

Babies, mused Sir George. Still, Meg seemed happy … "Plenty of room," affirmed the old warrior stoutly.

In Ashford police station, Superintendent Brinton read through the report from Hastings for the second time, stirring his tea with an unhappy spoon as he did so. His doctor warned about his blood pressure; his wife worried about his weight. Not that she nagged—she never did that—but she was smart. Had a way with her. How many others could have talked his sidekick into hiding the office sugar? Detective Constable Foxon was a tough young blighter, good in a scrap, quick to turn in any tight corner and stand his ground. Put him up against auburn hair, a smile, and big, blue-green eyes and he was soft as a chocolate cream.

"But I promised your wife," was all the lad could say when charged with larceny in the matter of a battered box with a picture of the Coronation on the lid, and horses round three sides pulling the celebrated Coach on the fourth.

"I take three lumps in my tea," said Brinton. "I *need* three lumps! If I don't learn, and fast, what's happened to that tin, laddie, don't even think about putting in for sergeant. There's more to promotion than just passing exams, remember. You could easily stay a plain detective constable right through to your pension—plain! Ugh. What d'you call what you're wearing today?"

"Jumbo cord's the very latest, sir." Foxon smoothed a loving hand up and down one sleeve of his new jacket, enjoying the movement of the lush pile beneath his fingers.

"Not that colour. You look like a ploughed field, or my potatoes when they've just been earthed up." He groaned. "Why did I mention food? She's got me on a diet at home, and tea without sugar's undrinkable."

"I'm sorry, sir." Foxon was gentle. He'd seldom seen the other so upset. But Mrs Brinton had been very persuasive, playing on his hidden but undoubted liking for his superior, saying that she was worried, and a decade her husband's junior, and wanted the marriage to last well into the couple's golden years …

For two days the atmosphere of the shared office had been efficient, but heavy with suffering and complaint—silent complaint, once Brinton accepted that to Timothy Foxon a promise was a promise, meant to be kept. Which in other circumstances was good, but in this particular case was not. With a scowl in the direction of his subordinate, Brinton re-read the final paragraph of the "Metal Thefts" report, closed the file, and sighed. His tea was cold. All that stirring, probably. Convection currents, he'd a vague memory from school, or was it radiation? Still, if he held his breath and drank quickly the taste wasn't too bad, because he wouldn't be *expecting* it to taste right, the way you couldn't help expect when you could see it was steaming hot. He sighed again.

The telephone rang. "Hastings calling Ashford," came a well-known voice down the line. "Hastings calling Ashford, Furneux calling Brinton. You got the report okay? What d'you make of it?"

Thankfully, Brinton abandoned his tea. "One of your motorbike patrols dropped it off this morning. Twice, I've read it." Foxon looked up. "I'd say you've got exactly the same trouble across in Sussex we've been having in Kent."

"We share a county border." There was no real need to remind the superintendent of local administrative boundaries, but Harry Furneux, the Fiery Furnace, newly promoted from chief inspector, had rather taken to teasing the older colleague who was now formally the equal Harry had secretly always considered him to be. "So, probably the same people. A local gang, you reckon?"

"Definitely local. Anyone coming from London'd be after more serious stuff—and more of it. And probably just one or two big raids and then push off to a new target area. Pros from the Smoke wouldn't take the risk of hanging around the countryside too long and giving us hayseeds the chance to nab 'em."

At his desk, Foxon still waited, but as Brinton didn't wave at him to pick up the extension he could only guess at the other side of the conversation.

"Small fry, I agree," continued Brinton. "Not even worth calling a gang, most likely. A few local low-lifes, nothing special—but a perishing nuisance all the same. They're not going for broken chunks of farm machinery or anything else that needs a big vehicle to carry it away. Garden gates, park benches, dustbins—small enough to chuck on the back of an ordinary pick-up truck that nobody would ever notice."

Brinton relented. Foxon caught his gesture, and snatched up the telephone. "Hello, sir, Tim Foxon. My gran and her next-door neighbour both had their gates disappear overnight. The beggars even went round the back and half-inched a length of railing the neighbour had removed to make room for his new shed. Hopping mad, everyone is."

"You've read the report, Foxon?" Foxon hadn't, but wasn't going to admit it.

"Much the same fun we've been having in our part of the world, sir, right?" Brinton, on his own extension, shot the young man an approving look. "And the scrap yards all struck dumb," said Foxon. "Ours don't tell us anything, either."

It was a good guess, and correct. "One lump of mangled metal looks much like another," agreed Furneux. "Not as if the stuff has a pedigree you can trace. Once it's all shredded into bales or melted down and recast, or whatever they do to make it re-usable for something else, that's it."

"And nobody's talking," chimed in Brinton. "Clams, our lot and yours both." He nodded almost amiably at Foxon. "We haven't the manpower for night patrols—not extra, anyway—and besides, who knows where the blighters might decide to try next?"

"I wondered," said Furneux, "about setting a trap." Brinton snorted; Foxon coughed. "Well," amended the man from Hastings, "more an ambush than a trap, as in putting down bait and catching whatever comes along—though on second thoughts that might be worth a try if we could only work out where to put the bait. But if there was even a hint of suspicion about one scrap dealer in particular, perhaps we could join forces to stake out the premises on likely nights and watch for anyone turning up with a load of interesting bits and pieces …"

He allowed the thought to simmer. Brinton broke the silence at last. "No good, Harry. Like I said, we haven't the manpower, even with a joint effort—and we've had no hint from anyone so we've no idea where to plant the stake—and it's not as if they're dangerous, these low-lifes, which is probably why nobody's talking. They're not killers, or even your average thug threatening the peace of the realm. They're burglars who just happen to pinch park benches and dustbins and lengths of metal fence."

"Oaks and acorns," interposed Harry Furneux darkly. "Inches and miles, remember."

"Yes, I know, let 'em get away with this and the next thing you know they'll be causing real trouble—even more trouble than they already have, that is," as he caught the eye of Foxon, and thought of Gran Biddle's gate, and her neighbour's length of railing. "You're having no better luck than us, but we'll try our scrap dealers again, if you like—" and inspiration struck. "Right. How about we borrow some of your crowd, and you borrow some of ours. If nobody recognises anyone as a copper asking questions, we might just learn something."

Plans were roughed out, and Foxon ventured one or two ideas that met with Brinton's approval. The superintendent gulped down his tea, grimacing, but without complaint. Foxon considered his superior for a moment.

"Mrs Brinton only asked me to hide the sugar cubes," he said. "She didn't say a word about peppermints. If you need a sugar fix, sir … They're still in your desk, aren't they?"

Brinton gave him a very old-fashioned look.

Chapter Two

Miss Seeton stood beside the hen-house at the end of her garden. Here one had the best view of the sunset sky: the open marshland heavens soaring overhead to curve beyond the zenith down to the slowly darkening east. It was as dramatic a red—the scarlet of flames, the jewel-flash of rubies, the richness of molten gold—as she had ever seen. One could suppose oneself to be inside a gigantic dome of burnished copper against whose fiery gleam roost-bound birds flew in drowsy silhouette. Her fingers ached to capture that drama on paper; but her talents, she knew, were all too limited. The successful capture, the prize of genius, would never be hers. Miss Seeton sighed, and continued to watch, drinking in the spectacle. Pencil or watercolour, not pastel. She smiled. A companion piece, perhaps, to that chilly likeness of dear Mr Delphick as a Grey Day her fancy had caused her to paint all those years ago …

Miss Seeton is wrong to disparage her talents. Chief Superintendent Delphick of Scotland Yard, and a growing number of police officers up and down the country, hold the little art teacher (now retired) and her abilities in very high regard, though the abilities they admire are those she herself, when she thinks about them—which is seldom, for she is always embarrassed by them—does not. Her foolish scribbles (as she calls them) she considers mere personal notes, impressions of people; character sketches only in the literal sense of sketches having come from the action of pencil at work on paper, no more. She is uncomfortable at any suggestion that these sketches give her an unusual insight into anyone's character. That would be prying. A gentlewoman does not pry; she respects the privacy of others as she would hope that others must respect her own.

Even when her London flat was broken into by a killer intent on eliminating the one witness to his killing; even when she was abducted from her garden, driven away in a delivery van with a sack over her head, making a lucky escape while lamenting the damage to her hat; even when the killer concealed himself in her cottage in sinister ambush, Miss Seeton was able to regard these intrusions into her life, these invasions of her privacy, as simple mistakes. Why should anyone wish her harm? It was true that, on her way home from the opera, she had interrupted a vicious knifing and given her statement to the police; it was true that, at the then Superintendent Delphick's urging, she produced a likeness of the knifeman that was instantly recognisable, thus putting (she was puzzled to learn) herself in some danger; but she accepted that it was her duty to assist the police, and she had assisted them. Which must be the end of the matter, as far as she was concerned. The foolish young man who tried to raid her hen-house and was interrupted had retaliated with a silly joke, driving her round the countryside in his van (and ruining her hat, which was not so silly) and would, she felt sure, have let her out soon enough, though doubtless in some place far from public transport and probably too far to walk. But there were, in the former teacher's experience, times when such thoughtless behaviour was sadly typical of the young. Of a few irresponsible young, that was to say. Others could be very responsible indeed. Whereas some … so impulsive; unrestrained. So quick to play silly jokes, too slow to think of likely consequences. Moderation came with age, and though the young man had looked old enough to know better … well, clearly he hadn't. Because if he had, she would have been spared the damage to her hat and an awkward day in court, being a witness. Which, however, Mr Delphick had rightly reminded her it was her duty to be.

Miss Seeton chooses to forget that the following year, with further sketches, she helped the police capture a vicious child-killer, as well as a motorcycle gang specialising in armed robbery and general burglary. By the time her quiet neighbourhood had become a hotbed of fake religion, witchcraft, murder and general hysteria, Miss Emily Dorothea Seeton had been recruited as the police force's Special Art Consultant, a small but welcome annual retainer giving the authorities first refusal on any drawing, painting, sketch or scribble she might produce when involved (however peripherally) in any case that baffled more normal constabulary skill. Miss Seeton believes her job is merely to provide IdentiKit drawings when photographs are difficult to obtain, and she uses the retainer to augment her pension.

It is now some years since Miss Seeton retired from a medley of humdrum teaching jobs in London to settle in the village of Plummergen, Kent, in the cottage inherited from her godmother and distant cousin (known to Plummergen as Old Mrs Bannet) who died at the age of ninety-eight. Her death caused some annoyance in the village, which lamented Mrs Bannet's failure to qualify for a telegram of congratulation from the Queen on achieving her century; it thought the old lady should have made more effort to keep going a few months longer, for the greater glory. Plummergen was thus predisposed to resent, and to harbour suspicions against, Mrs Bannet's generally unknown heir. It wasn't sure it could trust Miss Seeton. Her cousin had let the village down, and if she took after her cousin then she, too, was sure to disappoint. The fact that the opera knifing, or at least its aftermath, pursued Miss Seeton from Town and resulted in a certain degree of local mayhem before the matter was settled had (insisted Plummergen) little to do with village sentiment. Miss Seeton, for all the championship of the likes of Martha Bloomer—herself, let no-one forget, no more'n an incomer herself—and her husband Stan, local born and bred but did really oughter know better—and never mind her blood and breeding—Miss Seeton had come from London. An outsider, a foreigner, unused to village ways, and therefore unpredictable, unreliable—and untrustworthy.

Miss Seeton, settling happily into her inheritance, remains unaware of the various undercurrents that seethe around her modest person. She has her champions; seldom if ever does she see the need to be championed. Sweetbriars is her home; she is content. Martha Bloomer, who with farmhand Stan lives just across the road, cleans the cottage, cooks and bakes for its owner, and bullies her gently when organising her life on those days not blessed with the twice-a-week attentions of Plummergen's domestic goddess. Martha performed the same services for Mrs Bannet and would have been insulted had the arrangement not continued with her cousin. Stan Bloomer, too, bullies his employer in similar well-meaning ways, but as his accent is a strong one Miss Seeton misses much of his scolding, and meekly accepts what she can understand of his advice on the hen-house, which he rules, and the gardens, which he sometimes permits her to weed.

This friendly business arrangement was, like the cottage, inherited by Miss Seeton from her cousin. Old Mrs Bannet provided the wherewithal; Stan duly built suitable quarters for a small but select flock of hens, caring for them as expertly as he cared for their nominal owner's flowers, fruit and vegetables. Both households used what they wanted of the assorted produce, the surplus being sold by Stan in lieu of wages. Old Mrs Bannet, and later her cousin, was the object of much envy in certain quarters. Stan Bloomer was a noted gardener, and would have been a worthy disciple of Sir George's Triptolemus if he'd ever heard of him; although if he had, he would have had no truck with the heathen anyway.

Miss Seeton watched a rook flap its homeward way across skies beginning to darken from full-blown flame to banking fire. Ripples of sunset cloud were aglow with crimson and vermilion rather than scarlet and gold. As colours faded, so the garden began to fill with perfumes that hung heavy on the air. Miss Seeton inhaled, and marvelled as she savoured the unusual experience of a garden rich with well-tended flowers. A breeze of some sort blew from the Marsh on most days and, generally, one caught no more than a pleasurable whiff. But of course her garden, although open to the Royal Military Canal on one side, had a wall on another, which provided shelter. And the weather forecast had talked of storms, and unusual currents of air, over the Sahara; no doubt this air brought with it, as well as particles of dust and sand to redden the sky, the scents of exotic desert blooms. Miss Seeton pondered the desert exotic. Pyramids by the Nile, palm trees, camels, and oases with … orchids, perhaps? Did palm trees have flowers? Were there cacti in the desert? In the American

West, yes, but in the Sahara? She had seen cacti with flowers—or were they succulents? But if either grew in the desert, would they give off a scent? One had always understood that the scent of a flower was to attract pollinators such as bees. But there must be insects in the desert. Had not John the Baptist lived on honey and locusts? Hardly a balanced diet as one understood it, but sufficient. So unpleasant an end, after all his endeavours. Herod, weakly agreeing to the demands of Salome for the poor man's head on a charger. That vivid Aubrey Beardsley illustration, although fortunately not in colour ...

Miss Seeton awoke from her reverie to find the world almost devoid of colour, and the pale moths of evening fluttering among the flowers. More pollination. How lucky she was to live in the country in the sweet, fresh air. She breathed deeply, emptying her lungs of stale breath as that invaluable book, *Yoga and Younger Every Day,* taught her all those years ago; feeling herself relax further as she headed back indoors, still concentrating automatically on *Pranayama,* still savouring the rich fragrances of her garden, still musing on pollination, bees, John the Baptist, severed heads on plates ... Miss Seeton smiled. How fortunate that one was never troubled by nightmares. Indeed, she slept very well and seldom dreamed at all. Eight hours, in a comfortable bed, of refreshing, dreamless sleep ...

Others were less fortunate than Miss Seeton.

Dr Knight's nursing home on the outskirts of Plummergen was a private, paying enterprise, on the site of the former cottage hospital, closed during a National Health Service efficiency drive for centralisation. Henry Knight, one of London's leading neurologists, had moved from London for the good of his health, and while administering (if requested) to Plummergen in a general way, fulfilled his duty to the state by working with NHS practices in nearby Brettenden whenever they found themselves overwhelmed. Well did he know the havoc that trying to fit a quart into a pint pot could wreak on the most hardy individual. He was a firm believer in the benefits of fresh air, exercise, time for oneself, and common sense.

He was trying to apply this favourite prescription to the glamorous woman sitting in his office with a silk handkerchief to her eyes. She had dark, luxuriant hair far younger than the backs of her hands suggested she really was; he could tell nothing from her face and neck as her makeup, though skilful and becoming, was too lavishly applied for his taste.

This did not surprise him. Rumours were flying even before Catherine Earnshaw, one of the evergreen stars of the golden years of Hollywood, had been sighted in the garden of Saturday Stop, the bungalow recently refurbished by Grimes & Salisbury while the historians were making work impossible at Summerset Cottage. Catherine had arrived in a white Rolls Royce driven by a sleek young man who was not wearing the uniform, or even the cap, of a chauffeur. He was said to be her secretary; she was said to be writing her memoirs. Plummergen had its doubts.

Although it was certainly none of his business, Dr Knight harboured his own entirely understandable doubts about the relationship, as his visitor dabbed at her beautiful eyes. He couldn't charge her with artificial aids there: the world had known for years those lashes must be real. That melting velvet brown owed nothing to tinted contact lenses. No camera close-up, shot through no matter how many layers of gauze, could withstand the scrutiny of generations of envious women or sceptical men. Publicists likened Catherine to a gazelle; journalists gushed about Elizabeth Bennet, the more educated adding references to ox-eyed Hera, thus invoking classical literature of even greater antiquity than Jane Austen. Miss Earnshaw's skin, where it was allowed to show its natural self, was rich magnolia with very few, and even then very fine, lines. Never, even in the star's heyday, had it been exposed to the California sun. Poolside parties with her contemporaries always found Catherine Earnshaw taking shelter under an enormous white parasol, or a white cartwheel hat, wearing her white silk beach pyjamas or a flowing white satin kimono.

She had aged far better than most, Dr Knight conceded. Her form was almost as lissom as that of a girl, her movements almost as graceful. Dean Burscough was a lucky man if he was, indeed, more than her secretary. But unless the relationship—should there be one—affected the lady's health, it was none of his business. And as the lady complained of being unable to sleep, rumour could be wrong—or else she was playing some obscure double-bluff, which when consulting a medical man was a foolish thing to do. Yet Catherine Earnshaw did not appear to be a foolish woman.

"But I was sure you would help me." Catherine spoke in the voice that had bewitched more than one generation. "So sure you'd help me, doctor. You see, I need my beauty sleep, and I need those pills to help me sleep. It's not just the jet lag. I've always been a poor sleeper." She emitted a soft, rueful laugh. "I've spent too long being woken before the crack of dawn to fit into the shooting schedule for the producer's convenience. I'd be so tired sometimes I'd fall asleep between shots—standing up, even, leaning against a board—but it was the job, and in those days we all put up with it. They say shift workers in factories have similar problems. Won't you please think of me as a factory worker?"

"No," said Dr Knight. "I'm a good doctor, but I can't manage the impossible. Look in a mirror, and believe that anything less like a factory worker this village has yet to see." His inward eye considered Clarrie Putts, who three times a week enjoyed a gossipy, air-conditioned shift on a production line at Brettenden's biscuit factory. "You need overalls and a hair net for the next time you try to bamboozle me—" he smiled— "young woman."

Catherine flashed the far younger man a sparkling look of gratitude, and did her best to blush at the blatant compliment as she considered his suggestion. "Maybe a headscarf. One of those wrap-around triangles girls knotted over their heads in the war days."

"White, of course." Catherine famously wore nothing but white, both in private and on film, even when Technicolor had been new and all the rage. Hers was among the most scathing voices raised when Norma Shearer wore provocative red to Carole Lombard's celebrated Mayfair Ball of 1936, where the dress code had been white gowns for ladies, white tie for gentlemen. Dr Knight did mental arithmetic. Almost forty years ago.

"Just how long have you been taking sleeping pills?" he demanded.

"I need them," she repeated. "I really can't do without them."

"Too long, then. No doubt along with bottles of pep pills to keep you awake."

She did not meet his accusing eye. "But everyone did— does. It goes with the job—practically an unwritten clause of the contract. If you want to go on working …"

"When did you last work, Miss Earnshaw?"

"I chose to retire," she returned with dignity. "I didn't want to play character parts on television. I know exactly what Bette meant about the pictures getting small—"

"*Sunset Boulevard*," nodded Dr Knight, with some sympathy.

"—and a television screen gives a far, far smaller picture than would ever suit me!"

"A long-term addict, then." She winced. "Have you ever tried to break your addiction?"

"Poor Judy tried, but it never lasted long. And I ... don't have her strength of mind to even try. I remember what she went through. I—I couldn't face it. Which is why I hoped ..."

"Just how old are you, Miss Earnshaw?"

Catherine gasped.

"This is your medical advisor speaking, not a journalist."

"I ..."

"I'd like to calculate your chances of living to a ripe old age if you manage to kick the pharmaceutical habit." He smiled, very kindly. "You might be pleasantly surprised."

"I ..."

"We'll wean you off in stages. Judy Garland famously tried going cold turkey, which is never advisable. Your body chemistry doesn't like it. And your body, I would say, is in remarkably fine condition, for your age. Whatever that may be. We want to maintain that good condition for as long as possible, Miss Earnshaw. Don't we?"

"I ... guess we do. But I could maybe find a different doctor in London."

"Maybe you could. It's your choice. But this is a lovely part of Kent, and you've taken Saturday Stop for some time, I understand, for privacy and for the beauty of the scenery to inspire you while you write your memoirs. Yes?" She nodded. "A pity, then, to waste these splendid opportunities trudging to and fro from Town in the hunt for a ... less scrupulous supplier. What I prescribe for you will be properly regulated, chemically sound, medication on a graduated rate of reduction. I'd like to see you live to a hundred, Miss Earnshaw. My wife and I were always great admirers of your work."

Again he smiled. "You can whisper, if you'd prefer. These walls don't have ears." Her nervous giggle was almost a chuckle. "That's better. I'll write your notes in code, if you like—and naturally I'll keep them under lock and key at all times."

"I ... I've spent so long believing my own publicity, you see."

"Lying to yourself is never worth the effort. You aren't fooling anyone important—truly important to anyone but yourself, that is. And as the most important person in your own life, wouldn't you like that life to be as long and happy—and healthy—as possible?"

Slowly, she nodded. She hesitated, then leaned forward to whisper.

"That didn't hurt, did it? And they say confession is good for the soul."

"'Oh God, if there be a God, save my soul, if I have a soul'," quoted the actress, to the doctor's surprise. Her chuckle was full-throated and warm. "See, Dr Knight, I've done a whole heap of reading since I decided to 'rest'. Started with the autobiographies of my so-called friends, to see what they said about me so I could plot my revenge in my own book—then plain old biography, if anyone looked interesting enough. Then I got to wondering about the proper history these people lived in, and I read some more. Whatever I could find lying around without being too obvious about it." Another chuckle, rich with amusement. "Doesn't fit the glamour girl image? Well, your Sir William Wyndham caught my fancy for quoting that prayer, though I guess it was the Atterbury guy who came out of it best with the other soldier's words. I have to say, you Brits have such beautiful manners, and such a polite way of setting anybody right! And the Duke of Ormonde changing the subject the way he did—I'd love to know what he said! What a fascinating bunch they were in the old days."

Dr Knight realised that he must revise his opinion of Catherine Earnshaw. "If you enjoy history I'll introduce you to our headmaster, Martin Jessyp. He knows a good deal about this part of the country, and he's always happy to lend books to people who can be trusted to look after them, as I'm sure you would be."

"That's surely most kind of you, doctor, but there's my memoirs to write before I can take time out to socialise. Dean—my secretary, my ghost—would throw a real hissy fit if he thought I wasn't taking it seriously."

"Slave driver, eh? Maybe he's right to keep you busy. Still … Jessyp lives in the house next to the school. I thought it would make a pleasant walk for you from Saturday Stop: but as long as you take regular daily exercise and get out in the fresh air to take your mind off things—because it will be hard, no matter how gradual the reduction—I'm sure that between us we can sort you out. Now, may I see the tablets you brought with you? I'll have to check how American trade names compare with the brands we use here."

The usual crowd of gossips was clustered about Mrs Flax as she held forth in the post office. Having bought a small tin of baked beans, thereby staking her claim to floor-space while she acquired an audience, the village's wise woman set spines tingling with her views on the topic that currently exercised much of southern England, that celebrated British stand-by, the weather.

"… sandstorm fools none but fools. Mark me, them in the know is keeping from us the truth o' the matter, my reason for so saying being, there ent none as can put hand on heart an' say they've ever seen the likes of such a sky afore—leastways, not in this country. Furrin parts is different." Mrs Flax sniffed. There was a general nodding of heads. Everyone knew anything foreign was different. "I never seen nothin' like it, that's certain. Did any of you?" Murmurs; a general shaking of heads. Nobody had. "There you are, then! Tent natural, such happenings—and from an evil cause all too clear to them with deep knowledge such as mine." She wagged a menacing finger. "Atom bombs!"

Deliciously, everybody shuddered.

Everybody but one. "Atom bombs? We ent at war." Young Mrs Scillicough was among the few willing to doubt the witch to her face. "Atom bombs!" Mrs Scillicough was the mother of triplets notorious in Plummergen almost from birth. Threats against them had begun the moment they learned to toddle. How they survived to school age, nobody could understand. In their earliest days Mrs Scillicough, mistrusting London-trained Dr Knight's cheerful advice of regular habits, wholesome food, and a spot of healthy neglect, consulted the wise woman she had known all her life; but Mrs Flax failed her, ancient wisdom and herbal remedies proving ineffective. Mrs Scillicough's sister had four under five, angels the lot of them. Mrs Scillicough was disinclined to afford Mrs Flax as much credit as the older villagers, for safety's sake, still did.

"We ent at war. If we were, there'd've bin papers sent for the likes of our Trev and our Kev to be called up. And they haven't."

This logic made people look hopeful and disappointed in equal measure.

"Did I speak of war?" Mrs Flax tossed her head, and smirked. Doubting Thomasina had played right into her hands. "War? Atom bombs, is what I said. Them French bombs being tested who-knows-where, Murrey Toll or some such name." Mururoa Atoll, a French colonial possession, was in the middle of the Pacific. "Stands to reason, any place named so nearly to Murreystone ent to be trusted, be it the other side o' the world or no."

Across-the-marsh Murreystone has been rival, challenger, and competitor to Plummergen for more than a thousand years. The point was made, the argument won.

"Radiation waves," continued the witch in triumph. "Beaming high through the air, paintin' the skies in devil's colours—radiation, that's the true cause, and nothing to do wi' storms from the desert. Only, them in authority has to keep it secret, on account of they know there's nought to be done against us sufferin' horrors until the winds have blown the wickedness o' modern science away from decent folks, across the Channel to the French as began it all. But until then, take heed. We could yet be doomed to horrors should the wind change direction—as all here know, us being on the edge of the Marsh, how it does."

Heads nodded again. It was a rare day on Romney Marsh when the wind did not blow.

"An' what about them cars with sand all over 'em fell from the sky?" came the challenge of Mrs Scillicough. The tabloid press, much enjoyed in Plummergen, had carried sensational reports of gleaming white enamel turned dusty pink, of polished chrome dulled, of air filters clogging delicate machinery in vital scientific establishments.

"An' has it happened here?" countered Mrs Flax.

If it had, nobody said so. "Which just proves it's how I said, the high-ups keepin' quiet about the truth. Stories in the papers about what none have truly seen, thinking we'll be fooled. Mark my words, until the wind changes, there's nothing to be done but suffer the devil to have his way."

Behind her grocery counter Emmy Putts, who seldom thought deeply about anything, looked tearful. Mrs Stillman, who generally tried not to intervene in the conversation of her customers unless there was good reason, having no wish for a hysterical (and therefore useless) employee felt that this particular wish was reason good enough.

"Of course we've not seen it here," she snapped. "The wind blows it clear before it even has time to settle! Emmeline Putts, haven't you said yourself you've been finding more dust than usual on the shelves every morning?"

Emmy gulped that perhaps she had indeed said so.

"Didn't you need to ask for a new feather duster?" Emmy gulped again, and nodded. "And has anything terrible happened to you while you've been dusting?" Slowly, Emmy shook her head. Mrs Stillman glared at Mrs Flax. "There you are. Horrors and radioactive waves, indeed!"

Mrs Flax glared back at Mrs Stillman, but Emmy began to brighten, as did several others. Among these was Lily Hosigg, mother of the delicate toddler Dulcie Rose, asleep outside the shop in her pushchair. Mrs Hosigg, like all first-time parents, thought her baby the best, most beautiful, and most intelligent in the world, and had been worried that the voice of Mrs Flax might carry through the open door to reach sleeping ears and turn dreams to nightmares. There had been nightmares enough in Dulcie's short life. Her birth was difficult. Lily, married at seventeen to eighteen-year-old Len, was herself little more than a child. Len in panic had rushed up the narrow lane from the canal to bang on Miss Seeton's door, begging to use the nearest phone. Dr Knight, summoned from the nursing home to Dunnihoe Cottage, sent the anxious husband to boil water in the kitchen and Miss Seeton back to Sweetbriars to call an ambulance. Martha Bloomer, hearing the commotion, came to boil more water and take general charge as Dr Knight worked, Len fretted, and Miss Seeton soothed and did her best to distract.

Blue lights flashed as Lily and an unnamed, premature but breathing female infant were whisked to hospital with Len and, at Lily's tearful request, Miss Seeton in the ambulance, while Martha tidied up and Dr Knight sighed with relief. It was more than three years since this drama had unfolded. Dulcie Rose was indeed an intelligent child, quietly thriving, but still delicate; and Plummergen continued to think of her as "the Hosigg baby" when, if asked, Dulcie would insist she was a big girl now.

But the big girl had slept through the doom-laden prophecies of Mrs Flax, Lily was glad to see as she emerged from the post office with her shopping in the basket that fitted so well underneath the pushchair seat, on its own clever little shelf. Lily and Len agreed how kind it had been of Lady Colveden's daughter to say their Janie had long since grown out of pushchairs now and it was a pity to waste it. Next time they came down from London they'd bring it for Dulcie, if her parents would like it; and while the Colvedens' young farm foreman was far too sensible to refuse, so his young wife was thrilled with the gift.

Halfway along The Street, as Plummergen's main (and almost only) street is called, Dulcie wanted to walk home. Lily said she'd go on pushing until they reached the George and Dragon. Dulcie must watch for the sign with the dragon picture to tell her mother when to stop and let her climb out.

"Picksher?" Dulcie asked hopefully. "Picksher!" She waved tiny hands, and beamed.

Lily smiled. "Well maybe, if we've time. But she might be busy. We'll see. You keep a look-out for that dragon, now." Being taller, she had already spotted a moving figure in the front garden of Sweetbriars—but then it might be Stan Bloomer, though during the day he was more often than not at work on the farm, like Len.

Approaching Sweetbriars she could now make out a hat moving in the garden. Not a flat cap, or a knitted pull-on, but unmistakeably a Hat.

"Out you get," she told her daughter. "And soon we can say hello to the lady, because she's there, but we mustn't stop her weeding so we'll go straight home."

"Picksher," said Dulcie firmly. Miss Seeton, as sharpened coloured pencils grew too short for comfort, had abandoned the extension-tube she sometimes used and now passed on all her stubs to Lily, along with a sketching-block or two she insisted were bought in error. If Dulcie would enjoy playing, it was never too soon for even a small child to learn how to express herself and her ideas on paper, was it? Miss Seeton had drawn a few encouraging doodles, and Dulcie was certainly encouraged.

"Hello, Miss!" Lily saw Miss Seeton straighten, and caught a gleam of bright turquoise. "What a lovely hat." Others might have disagreed, but in Hosigg eyes Miss Seeton could do no wrong. "You been shopping in Brettenden again?"

"Birdie," cried Dulcie, pointing. "Picksher!"

Greetings were exchanged, and Miss Seeton explained that yes, her hat was a Monica Mary creation, but there had been coloured scraps left over from one of Miss Armitage's patchwork quilts, and she, that was to say Miss Armitage, had thought that she, that was to say herself, might find them fun to use as trimmings if she wasn't tempted to try patchwork on her own account, which she really felt she wasn't, because according to Miss Armitage it meant measuring carefully—which with her artist's eye she thought she could—but also the matter of sums in the making of accurate pattern-pieces, about which she wasn't at all sure.

"Not even," she added, with a smile for the impatient Dulcie, "using graph paper."

"Paper," echoed little Miss Hosigg. "Picksher." She pointed towards Miss Seeton's remarkable adornment. "Birdie— big blue birdie!"

Miss Seeton smiled again. How quick of the child to recognise the bird's-wing effect after which she had been striving when adding those few quick touches to the hat she'd bought from Miss Brown. "A bird," she agreed. "A kingfisher, perhaps," remembering the turquoise trim. "As we're so close to the canal. Rather than a peacock, which is far more flamboyant and, indeed, hardly native to these parts."

Lily hesitated. She glanced down at her daughter, gazing at Miss Seeton in expectation. Miss Seeton smiled, nodded, opened the gate, and invited her in "with your mother too, if she would care to come," dismissing with a brisk gesture any idea that the visitors were unwelcome. Friends were always welcome.

"And Martha made one of her fruit cakes only yesterday," said the temptress. "I'm sure it will be impossible for me to eat it all while it is fresh. Lily, my dear, wouldn't you and Dulcie like to help me?"

"Picksher," said Dulcie as she trotted after her hostess up the path and round the corner of the house to the back door. "Big blue birdie!"

Once the little girl was happily settled at one end of the table with a slice of cake, some coloured pencils and several sheets of paper on which to scribble, Miss Seeton looked at Dulcie's mother. "Something seems to be troubling you, my dear. May I do anything to help? You aren't worried about—" like the rest of the village, she had almost said *the baby,* so foolish when the child was now old enough to hold a pencil in her hand and eat cake while leaving almost no crumbs on the kitchen table— "about Len or—or anyone?" Lily shook her head. "You are all in good health?" Lily nodded. "You are unlikely to be concerned over Len's job," Miss Seeton went on. A gentlewoman does not pry, but the poor young thing's eyes were dark with anxiety. "Sir George and Nigel are excellent employers, as well as kind friends. There can surely be nothing to worry you there." She hesitated. "Is there, perhaps, trouble over in Rochester, with your family?"

"Oh no, Miss, thank you. My mum threw out that feller she married and the solicitor says she won't have long to wait for a divorce, provocation or something he said, on account of him trying it on with Rosie and then with me." Lily's stepfather had been taught a severe lesson by Len the instant that youthful Galahad learned what inappropriate behaviour had been displayed towards both sisters. Charges of unprovoked assault were brought, Len and Lily eloped, and with Miss Seeton's help the matter was cleared up to the satisfaction of all save the resentful stepfather. Why the fuss? Wasn't that what stepdaughters were for?

"No, Miss, thank you. It's not Mum, nor Rosie." Again Lily glanced at her daughter; saw she was engrossed in her drawing. "No, it's not them. Or—or us."

"Well, that is surely excellent news. But if everyone is— that is to say, if there is nothing—that is," determined not to pry, but Lily's tone had not convinced when she uttered that final denial, "what is the matter, Lily?"

Lily blushed. She was not so far removed from her school-days, and Miss Seeton spoke with the authority of an experienced teacher. "Well, Miss, I was—I was doing my shopping just now, and Mrs Flax was telling in the post office how these sunsets we been having …" Dulcie remained engrossed. Lily drew a deep breath. "She was saying how it's the devil's work—which I know is silly," as Miss Seeton tut-tutted and sighed, "but all that red's not normal, she's right there, and— and it *could* be radioactive, couldn't it? Monsters and such? And I don't want …" She pointed a shaking hand at the oblivious Dulcie Rose. "She's such a little, helpless thing, and if me and Len's likely to turn into something horrible who's going to take care of her?"

"I see no reason why you should turn into anything," said Miss Seeton.

"Mrs Flax said—"

It was seldom that Miss Seeton interrupted—seldom that she criticised—but now the angry gentlewoman did both at once. "Mrs Flax," said Miss Seeton, "is a foolish, ignorant woman and you are a foolish girl to listen to her nonsense. The weather forecasters and scientists have made everything very plain during the past few days." But perhaps Len and Lily could not afford a television, even a newspaper. Miss Seeton's irritation subsided. Not everyone was blessed, as she was, with a modest income and no dependants. Dulcie was young, and growing; Len Hosigg was paid well, she supposed, Sir George Colveden being a good employer as she had said, but children grew so fast. Clothes, shoes, food, toys. It was only natural that her parents should worry. And it was unfair to reproach Lily, little more than a child herself. Mrs Flax, as Nigel had sometimes pointed out when laughing over the woman's practised superstitions, could put on an act that impressed a surprising number of people. But Nigel had known Mrs Flax all his life; the villagers had grown up with her. They would naturally have a sense of perspective. Poor Lily, so shy, hadn't yet learned that sometimes people could make jokes, or rather try to, and in this case not in the best of taste, with Dungeness Power Station so close to Plummergen and radiation leaks, as Miss Seeton understood the matter, something against which precautions had always to be taken. But as to monsters …

"The remarkable skies we have enjoyed for the past few days have been caused merely by strong winds carrying sand from the Sahara Desert. Once the wind drops, and once it has rained, the air will clear as the dust settles and the beautiful sunsets will be no more than a lovely memory. I have tried several times to capture them on paper, but sadly it is impossible. The skies here are so wide, and grand, and open. One must simply enjoy the spectacle and be glad to have had the chance to witness it."

"Mrs Stillman did say," said the tentative Lily, "as the wind always blows in these parts and that's why we don't see dust all over everything, 'cepting indoors."

"Mrs Stillman is quite right."

Lily sighed as Miss Seeton topped up her cup and, with an encouraging smile, slid another piece of cake on her plate. Lily ignored it, her expression, though lighter, troubled still.

"But," she brought out at last, "but if it's not radioactive monsters—" she whispered the final words— "well, I know I dunno much about birds, sparrows and blue-tits and sea-gulls, mostly, but—well, living by the canal as we do now, I've learned a bit and Dulcie likes to watch, too, and—we both saw it, Miss, just after breakfast. Bright blue it was, like your hat, and sitting in a tree no more'n a few feet away— and honest, Miss, I've never seen a kingfisher as big as that one, and ..." a quick look at Dulcie.

"And," finished Lily with a gasp, "it was back to front as well!"

Chapter Three

Miss Seeton blinked. "Do you mean it turned round on its perch?" How strange that this should cause such obvious distress.

Lily shook her head. "Oh no, Miss. Back-to-front colours, is what I mean. Kingfishers is such beautiful birds, aren't they, greeny-blue like your ribbon, and red all down the front. Well, this kingfisher was red on the back, and greeny-blue down the front. Like I said! And with radioactive waves you never know, do you?"

Such foolish fears must be quickly allayed. Miss Seeton spoke with resolution. "What you and Dulcie saw could not have been a kingfisher. I have a bird book. Wait there and I will fetch it. We will look at the coloured plates together."

But a thorough study of the excellent volume on British birds recommended by Babs Ongar, of the Wounded Wings Sanctuary in Rye, showed nothing that resembled the over-large back-to-front kingfisher that so worried Lily Hosigg. Lily forced a tremulous smile, and crumbled cake without eating it.

"Wait there," said Miss Seeton once more. She returned with a sketchpad and fresh coloured pencils. "Now, tell me exactly what you saw."

Lily offered ideas, hesitated, corrected herself. Miss Seeton's swift movements caught the attention of Dulcie Rose, who demanded "a picksher" for herself. Miss Seeton drew a horse being shod; juvenile Plummergen loved watching blacksmith Dan Eggleden at work in his forge. As Dulcie crowed with delight, Miss Seeton doodled a large, luxurious motor car with a flat-capped chauffeur in gaiters by the open door—Martha had told her of Catherine Earnshaw's rather less formal arrangements—and added a little girl preparing to climb in. Dulcie recognised herself, giggled and, returning the compliment, began work on a stick figure with a bright blue head.

Miss Seeton and Lily concentrated on the bird sketch. "Sort of," said Lily at last, after Miss Seeton had roughed in, coloured, rubbed out. Something in her mother's voice made her small daughter look up. "Dulcie, lovey, what do you think?"

"Big blue birdie." The little girl added more squiggles to her stick figure.

Small children had sharp eyes, but short memories. But breakfast wasn't so very long ago ... "If you will excuse me, I should like to telephone a friend. Do please help yourself to more cake," Miss Seeton added. The poor young thing had relaxed now that her fears had been confronted on paper. To face up to one's fears was always the best way. Not always on paper, of course, but as a general rule. No doubt her appetite would now come back. It wasn't easy to eat crumbs in a tidy manner, which as a conscientious mother Lily would wish to do. A treat in store for the garden birds, then. Nothing wasted.

Miss Seeton left the kitchen door into the hall open for Lily to hear at least one end of the conversation. "Mrs Ongar? Good morning ... Why—yes, it is ... That is most kind

… I was hoping you might assist in the identification of a bird that has appeared in the garden of a neighbour … She described it in some detail, and I have drawn a sketch … Reminiscent of a kingfisher, but larger, and with the colours, as it were, reversed … Russet brown rather than scarlet …"

The sudden burst of electric excitement reached as far as the kitchen. Lily held her breath. A radioactive monster after all, or—what?

"Really?" Further excitement. Miss hadn't sounded frightened, more, well, pleased with what the bird rescue lady was telling her. "Did it? How very interesting! And you would be most welcome. I am always happy to see my friends and give them tea … Afterwards, yes of course, I do understand … Beyond the end of my own garden, beside the canal towards which the ground slopes to give an almost uninterrupted view across the Marsh. Naturally we cannot promise a sighting, but …"

Miss Seeton's smile dismissed the last of Lily's fears. "My dear, Mrs Ongar says you are much to be envied. It appears that the same winds that blew the desert sand all this way likewise blew several exotic species of bird far from their usual haunts. The day before yesterday a European Roller was provisionally identified on the outskirts of Rye, but by the time anyone with a camera appeared to photograph it, it had flown away. Mrs Ongar believes this is what you and Dulcie saw."

"A European Roller." Lily, giggling in nervous relief, reached for the chauffeur sketch Miss Seeton had drawn for Dulcie's distraction. "Well, this could be a Rolls Royce, right? Just like that film star."

"I know little of motors," admitted Miss Seeton. "I merely felt it went well with the horse—modes of transport, you see. The contrast between old and new."

"It's posh, innit? Posh people have Rollers and a shover to drive 'em, same as this." All apprehension behind her, Mrs Hosigg was confident. "Funny name for a bird, though."

"Mrs Ongar says it is expressive of their flight. Birds are so different, aren't they? No doubt you have observed how pigeons clatter their wings as they rise from the ground. Crows sweep theirs very slowly as they fly, while starlings seem almost to flicker and jump through the air." Lily resolved that she and Dulcie would observe this the next time they saw a pigeon, a crow, a starling. Miss must have been, still was, a good teacher. Never made you feel stupid, just that you'd forgotten and all she did was remind you.

"The Roller family—there are several varieties—has a somersaulting flight Mrs Ongar tried to describe, though no doubt it is easier when one sees it. At the moment, of course, she has no wish for us to see it. Flying, that is. Before she has photographed it. Or at least, not far. She is coming straight here, and asks if you would be so kind as to let her into your garden and show her where you saw it, although ..." There was a rueful twinkle in Miss Seeton's eye. "She might, she said, bring a friend. Or two." Miss Seeton knew her birdwatchers. "Should sufficient interest be aroused, this could in a surprisingly short time mean a small crowd. Or even a large one."

Lily, who was young and shy, looked startled. Miss Seeton smiled reassurance. "Only Mrs Ongar should be shown the exact location, I think. She will tell the others, but it might be wiser to suggest they would better serve their purpose by gathering in the National Trust pasture on the far side of the canal. They will have an almost uninterrupted view in all directions, which in a garden is not possible because of walls, or hedges, or fences."

"Or hen-houses," added Lily, recovering. Miss Seeton nodded.

"Perhaps what first attracted the bird was the sound of my hens, and then their food, although I have no idea what Rollers eat. Having travelled such a long distance—Mrs Ongar says they can come from Africa as well as Europe—the poor thing would of course be very hungry. And, naturally, very tired."

"Poor thing," echoed Lily, wondering now why she had been so unhappy. Miss Seeton and her friend between them had set her mind entirely at rest. And it didn't do to outstay a welcome. "We'll go home now, Dulcie love, and look for the big blue birdie. Ask Miss nicely and she might let you take your picture home to show your dad."

Miss Seeton was pleased to agree. She found some longer-than-usual pencil ends (green, blue, red, umber) and bestowed them on Dulcie before the child should raise any complaint at being taken away before her own "picksher" was finished to her satisfaction. Miss Seeton said that she would be passing the Hosiggs' door later that day, with Mrs Ongar; they would look in at Dunnihoe Cottage in hopes of seeing the picture of the big blue bird that Dulcie was going to draw with her new crayons.

"And perhaps you can show us the bird itself," added Miss Seeton, with a smile.

For the next few days Plummergen enjoyed an influx of visiting twitchers, as the most dedicated birdwatchers are known. They filled the George and Dragon, to the delight of landlord Charley Mountfitchet; they persuaded several villagers who'd never thought of it before to do Bed and Breakfast. They spent money on pork pies and sausage rolls from Mr Stacey the butcher; they bought ready-made sandwiches from Mrs Wyght at the bakery, or made their own sandwiches with ingredients from local shops. They bought film for their cameras, and notebooks. They lurked in bushes and shrubs with binoculars, dressing themselves in camouflage colours; they unfolded waterproofs from haversacks when it rained, and sported wide-brimmed canvas hats when the sun shone.

Then it was over. Either the Roller wearied of its perpetual audience, or else it lost its taste for the beetles and grasshoppers of Kent. One day it was perched on the branch of a tree, ready to deal sudden death from the skies; the next day—and the next—it was gone. And likewise, to the regret of commercial Plummergen, were the twitchers.

But sudden death is never far away.

On a cloudless night with no moon, the stars gave light enough for a small group of men to hurry in grim silence along a cliff-top towards a certain point marked on the map carried by their leader. It was a replacement map. The leader of the group was in a fury, and his cohorts were in despair. They were too late. They all knew it, but hours, days of planning could not be entirely wasted. There might just be something that would make all the effort worthwhile.

The leader gestured for his followers to stop, and without a word pointed ahead. He swooped his hands first outwards, then back in an encircling motion, reminding everyone of what had already been decided. Everyone signalled that they understood. No-one wanted any more mistakes. There might just be something …

There was a body.

The stars no longer gave light enough. A small yet powerful torch came into play.

The owner of the torch uttered a horrified yelp, clapped a hand over his mouth, fell back a few paces, and was sick.

Plummergen found life dull once the twitchers had dispersed. It was hard to settle back into the everyday routine of gossip, backbiting, and enthusiastic minding of everyone else's business after that brief incursion of new faces, new voices, and money. People remarked that Mrs Welsted at the draper's had sent for more picture postcards and souvenirs; sadly, they could find no reason why she should not. Mr Stillman at the post office ordered a new print run of guide books and the most popular of the Manville Henty titles that sold so well from the shelf labelled Local Author, and again this caused no particular comment.

Comments were, however, passed when Mrs Wyght at the bakery began experimenting with an Authentic Local Recipe for a delicacy to be called the Plummergen Puff. Mrs Wyght had a famously light hand with pastry, but couldn't make up her mind between sweet or savoury filling, and tried different versions on her regulars to see which they preferred. Preference was evenly divided, but there were murmurs about dishonesty from those on diets, and those who wished they'd thought of it first. This disaffection reached the ears of Miss Treeves, sister to the vicar and a keen guardian of village morals. Miss Treeves was inclined at first to take Mrs Wyght to task for misrepresentation, though she hesitated to use the word fraud. Mrs Wyght pointed out that she was Plummergen born and bred and had lived there all her life. You couldn't get more local or authentic than that. Miss Treeves conceded that you couldn't, but even so—

"Well now," broke in Mrs Wyght, "it's not as if I'd be saying it was summat traditional, or what I'd found in my great-great-grandmother's recipe book, because I wouldn't and I didn't. Only I can't make up my mind about the filling, see?"

Miss Treeves saw. Checkmate and loss of face loomed as Mrs Wyght went on to ask if Miss Treeves would be kind enough to taste a sample or two and give her (emphatic pause) *honest* opinion. The vicar's sister winced, and prayed for succour.

Succour was beside her in the form of Miss Seeton, waiting to buy a small brown loaf. Miss Seeton coughed gently. "I do beg your pardon, but I couldn't help overhearing. Might I suggest a compromise, in the manner of the Cornish pasty variant which had both a savoury end and a sweet one? I understand this was to offer miners a complete meal in a single pastry case."

Miss Treeves gave silent but heartfelt thanks, and smiled her approval. Mrs Wyght said she would give the one-at-each-end solution serious thought.

The post office gossips tried to resume their interest in Catherine Earnshaw, but as the film star was seldom encountered while out walking, and said little beyond a smiling hello when she was, speculation didn't flourish. The film star's groceries and other supplies were mostly delivered. Her secretary never drove the white Rolls Royce, no doubt because he'd found coming down from London on the wrong side of the road quite enough. Supposed to be helping her write a book, wasn't he? Well, maybe for once—nudge, nudge; wink, wink—that could be true. Which explained why you didn't see a lot of him, either. Polite enough when he was in the shops, but that wasn't often ... and thus speculation faded away. Even in Plummergen there is a limit to how long this agreeable pastime can survive when the subject remains more or less invisible to public view.

Posters appeared around the village, announcing an illustrated talk on Exotic Birds and Extreme Weather. Martin C. Jessyp, headmaster to Plummergen's Junior Mixed Infants, had sent off for colour transparencies and detailed notes. He spent some hours in Brettenden's public library, and asked Miss Seeton, part-time supply teacher, if she would be kind enough to copy a few diagrams in a format large enough to be seen and understood from the back row of the audience. Some of Mr Jessyp's pupils, growing as bored as their elders, were starting to resurrect Mrs Flax's theories about the Devil's Wind and the hellfire skies. Excitement so far was muted, but it was growing. Mr Jessyp intended to suppress incipient hysteria before it became an epidemic.

The Illustrated Talk was free, so everybody went who could: 'twasn't too late for the kiddies to stay up nor too early for anyone to have to rush their evening meal. They'd most likely not understand a word of it, but they didn't have to pay so it didn't matter.

"We will draw the blinds," announced Mr Jessyp, once people had stopped fidgeting. "Miss Seeton, would you and Miss Maynard be so kind?"

The windows of the larger of two classrooms were darkened. Children giggled as green canvas rattled down; or made ghost noises, and were slapped or scolded by their parents depending on temperament and ease of access. The more robust element, and that part of it safely out of range, giggled and ghosted even harder.

Mr Jessyp's commanding eye was less effective in the dark. He cleared a purposeful throat. Miss Maynard and Miss Seeton shushed, and shone torches in the direction of the culprits. Silence gradually settled on the room.

Mr Jessyp switched on the slide projector. A blank white square appeared on the screen in front of the blackboard. "Some of us," began Mr Jessyp, "were lucky enough to see the European Roller on the few days it was in this neighbourhood." Close-up images of a brightly-coloured bird flicked in sequence over the screen. The projector whirred and clattered. As it showed slide after slide Mr Jessyp spoke with brisk eloquence on the various types of Roller and their general habits.

"Many of us," he went on, "would like to know where the bird probably came from, and certainly how and why it came. Miss Seeton, the lights, if you please. Miss Maynard, we will have the demonstration now."

Mr Jessyp knew his Plummergen. While cheerfully willing to credit, and to monger, any amount of improbable scandal because everyone else was cheerfully doing the same, for the village when it came to hard facts, seeing was believing.

The lights were switched back on. The headmaster lifted a small, two-barred electric fire from the floor on to the desk, where an electric fan already stood. Miss Maynard set a cardboard shoebox beside them.

Mr Jessyp secured a square of metal mesh to the safety bars of the fire, and removed the lid of the box to display its contents. "Downy feathers," he announced. "We must thank Miss Seeton for having collected and sorted the smallest and lightest her hens could supply." Miss Seeton acknowledged thanks with a rather embarrassed smile. Stan Bloomer and his compost heap had first claim to sweepings, which naturally included feathers, from her hen-house. She hadn't thought to mention her modest borrowings—Mr Jessyp would hardly wish to keep the feathers, once the experiment was concluded—and she hoped that Stan wouldn't mind that for a few days the percentage of feathers added to the straw and poultry droppings had been, as it were, out of balance. After all, it was only for an evening. She would give them back. And surely a compost heap couldn't really know one of its layers was a little less, or indeed a little more, rich in feathers than usual? What happened when the birds weren't moulting—or, indeed, when they were? Miss Seeton sighed. This was one of all too many points not covered in what she still regarded as that helpful book *Greenfinger Points the Way*, of which Stan so disapproved.

She shook herself and blushed, although nobody noticed. They had been listening to Mr Jessyp while she was reprehensibly allowing her thoughts to wander. From the headmaster's change of tone it seemed the experiment was about to begin.

"... convection currents," he finished. "As heat rises, it will carry with it anything light enough to be carried, including small particles of sand, or dust. Or feathers." Once more he brandished the shoebox. "And should they rise into a prevailing wind ..."

He set down the box and switched on the fan. There was a slight popping noise from somewhere as the blades began to revolve.

Mr Jessyp scooped a few feathers from the box and allowed them to drift in front of the fan. "The prevailing wind," he said. "And now to duplicate those conditions of steady heat that are so typical of the desert." He switched on the electric fire and reached for more feathers.

He was halted in mid-reach. There came a louder pop, followed almost at once by a sharp bang under the floorboards and a shower of sparks from the socket in the wall. There were cries of alarm from the audience, and an acrid smell of burning.

"Sit still!" commanded the headmaster. "Miss Seeton, please open the door and hold it open while people leave the room—quietly," he added, "and one row at a time. Starting with those nearest the door. Miss Maynard, the fire-bucket, if you please. I said, quietly!"

With the teachers apparently so calm, any panic there might have been soon faded. Mr Jessyp was in full command of the situation, throwing sand on floorboards through which more sparks had begun to erupt, taking the long wooden window-pole and manipulating the hook on its end to drag the plug of the electric fire from its socket. He began to deliver a brief lecture on the folly of using water on electrical problems but realised his audience was staying its exodus to listen; he urged them to make their way outside. Miss Seeton held the door open; Miss Maynard guided lagging steps towards it. With a nod of approval Mr Jessyp shook the rest of the sand from the bucket, and went to his office to telephone the fire brigade.

On Friday morning, in an office on the umpteenth floor of New Scotland Yard, the telephone rang. In the tea-and-bun-acquiring absence of his sergeant, Chief Superintendent Delphick answered the call himself.

"Delphick … No, I hadn't heard … How very unpleasant."

"Very," came electronic agreement down the line. "We're not used to this sort of thing in Customs and Excise. The odd punch-up, yes. Maybe a high speed chase—at sea, on land—we can cope with that. But this is far more up your street."

"You hold the view that we have wider experience of the unpleasant and the bizarre? No doubt you're right." Scotland Yard's Oracle let the chatter of justification and apology

56

flow past him, jotting the occasional note, offering the right amount of reassurance where needed, promising he'd be on his way as soon as a car had been organised. He'd known from the first there could be no refusing an official request for help. He and Detective Sergeant Ranger had, in recent years, gained a reputation for solving the more ... distinctive criminal cases at which others might balk.

The Oracle had no need to ask why. As his gaze drifted to the office wall and the glass display case thereon, he smiled. Inside the custom-built case was a crook-handled black umbrella, very battered. He had acquired it from Miss Seeton at the conclusion of the Covent Garden murder case that first brought the little art teacher, and her remarkable talent for intuitive sketching, to his attention. He had given her an elegant black silk, gold-handled replacement for what he had, almost since the day they met, seen as an object lesson that appearances could be far more deceptive than was generally supposed—even by a professionally hawk-eyed and largely sceptical police force.

Not so long ago an eager new Civil Service broom had been brought in to reorganise, in the threefold name of progress, economy, and efficiency, the way the police worked. Fresh departments came into being. Old departments were given new names. Organisational charts (now called organigrams) promoted, demoted, and moved sideways without (as yet) altering how much people were paid, though the worst was expected, and soon. Time-and-motion theorists prowled the building and its outposts; peered into offices; inspected them for the superfluous. A tidy office means a tidy mind. The Oracle said—just once, and unmistakeably—that the umbrella in its case was non-negotiable. He then offered to move the office encyclopaedia to the floor in a corner hidden from a gaze that now could admire the less-crowded shelves and the neat files thereon. The offer was accepted.

Scotland Yard heaved a collective sigh of relief when the new broom was at last outbrushed by older and more cunning bristles back to the Civil Service, with letters after his name and a promotion. The police force thankfully resumed its normal routine.

Delphick was studying an Ordnance Survey map when Bob Ranger reappeared.

"How's your stomach, Bob?"

Detective Sergeant Ranger—six foot seven, seventeen stone and with an appetite to match—eyed the plate of fruit buns on the tray he carried in one enormous hand. "All they had left in the canteen, sir, sorry. I didn't want to hang about on the off-chance of anything fresher turning up, so I thought we might risk it for once. You're right, though, they do look a bit sad. But the tea seems okay—and there's your water, of course."

Delphick dismissed the buns but welcomed the tea, together with the hot water the Yard canteen had been trained to supply, that he might dilute the customary stewed treacle to a more acceptable colour. "Drink up, eat up, and then order a car, Sergeant Ranger. There has been a decapitation in Kent and our help has been requested."

The tray clattered on Bob's desk. He sat down with a thud that quivered floorboards several offices along the corridor. "You're not saying—you can't mean—"

"Really, Bob. Justify the faith of those who elevated you to detective status so long ago, and explain how, with my general demeanour as evidence, you could possibly deduce that the subject of this gruesome assault might be numbered among our close acquaintance."

"Sorry, sir." Bob managed a grin as he unloaded his tray. "It's only that—well, you know what MissEss is like. How things tend to … happen in her neighbourhood, sir."

"As far as I know, your adopted aunt is quietly minding her own business in her neighbourhood with nothing happening—to anyone—that doesn't normally happen in Plummergen. Our particular business is on the far side of Miss Seeton's resident county, in an area unknown to us—hence my consulting the map. The location given has already been once misunderstood, with consequences that we, at the request of Customary Excuses, are now invited to unravel."

Bob stared. "Customs and Excise? Inviting us? But they never like the Yard to get involved with smuggl—oh. Yes. Someone losing his head does sound like murder. Ugh."

"Ugh, indeed, and I must apologise. I should have said 'near' decapitation rather than implying complete, although in either case a strong stomach is required."

"Both to perform the murder and to investigate it." Bob, reassured that all was well with his son's godmother, bit into heavy dough and superannuated currants. "Ugh, again."

"Someone used a length of picture wire on a local poacher." Bob grimaced, and gulped tea. "Other wires, or rather snares, were found in the vicinity, though a detailed search of the area will naturally be left to us. Customs theorise that the victim might have been setting more snares, or checking those already set, when he interrupted someone clearly involved in that same illicit activity they had hoped to thwart, had it not been for the incorrect map reference."

"Customary Excuses." Bob grinned, and washed down more bun with more tea as Delphick began to fold away his map. Bob reached for the telephone …

The sergeant was a good driver, but after leaving the motorway the minor roads were unknown to both the London men. There came frequent oracular instructions as Bob asked for help and Delphick consulted his map.

"Didn't they take down the signposts in 1940 in case the Germans invaded?" grumbled Sergeant Ranger. "I reckon this part of the country's the land that time forgot and they never put the blessed things back after VE Day." Once more Delphick consulted his map.

At last they were bumping along a rough track across a neglected field on a shallow slope rising towards a clump of trees and a straggling, windblown hedge. "The car-pool manager's going to kill me," said Bob. "The suspension will never be the same again, and the engine doesn't sound too healthy, either."

"I agree, but it's an ill wind. The noise of our approach has produced results." From out of the trees a tall, thin man had emerged to wave at them. "Her Majesty's representative of Customs and Excise, I take it. Be kind to the springs, Bob. Stop just here and we'll walk the rest of the way."

Thankfully, Bob pulled off the track and trundled into longer grass to park. He knew there would be other official vehicles arriving before long, whose path must not be blocked. "Welcome to wild country," came the greeting of the tall thin man. "You're the first to arrive. The rest of my team's by the hut over there—" he waved towards the next field, behind the hedge— "and, local or not, the local coppers haven't got here yet—though to be fair, I warned 'em we'd be calling you lot in. Maybe they're sulking and have decided not to come." He glanced past the newcomers to the unmarked police car. "Er—you *are* from Scotland Yard, aren't you?"

Delphick introduced himself and Bob, adding his sergeant's theory about the lack of signposts. The tall thin man, who said his name was Luckham, agreed the theory was more than likely correct. This did not appear to please him.

Delphick knew there was no tactful way of putting his question. "Is that why your team went to the wrong place first?"

A wince, followed by a sigh of resignation. "It's all the fault of our new computer." Delphick and Bob guessed at once what was coming. "Not long ago some damned Civil Service efficiency-wallah decided we needed modernising. Next we knew, there was a hulking great thing installed in its own private room that's got the air-conditioning we've been wanting for years—air conditioning for a machine, I ask you! All it does is eat bits of card with holes in, and send you mad with its clanking and buzzing."

He drew a deep breath. His audience nodded in sympathy; Delphick tried to comfort him. "We, too, have suffered in the cause of progress. Much of our basement at the Yard has been invaded to provide a suitable lair for a similar monster."

"Did they tell you it was infallible?"

"They did." The chief superintendent spoke gravely; Bob resolutely held his tongue, though his eyes danced. "Which it is not—as I gather could also be said of yours."

"We queried the map reference at the time," lamented Mr Luckham, "but the bloke who punches the cards insisted it was right. We argued our case, and lost, and time was getting on, so we just had to believe what the damned thing said and off we went. With a spare map or two, in case," he added, "and just as well we did because …"

He went on to explain how, when the ambush they'd so carefully prepared had proved a wasted effort because, in the wrong place to which they'd been sent, they found nobody to ambush, they reverted to the old-fashioned methods scorned by technology buffs and re-checked their original notes, cross-referencing them against Ordnance Survey maps.

"And then, far later than we should have been, here we were." He waved an expansive arm at the surrounding countryside. "The right place for our ambush, if only we'd got here soon enough, which thanks to that—that air-conditioned postcard-chewing monster …" He broke off, lost for words. In case he recovered them, Delphick addressed him firmly.

"As there is still no sign of the local force, my sergeant will try to expedite matters by returning to the car and radioing in a rather more emphatic report than perhaps yours might have seemed to them, in the middle of the night." The Customs man grunted. "Sergeant Ranger," said Delphick, always formal when not among colleagues of long acquaintance.

"Sir," said Bob, already hurrying back to the car.

"While the sergeant is thus occupied," went on the chief superintendent, "might I be given a preliminary sight of the body?" He saw the other wince. "But I won't ask you to give me a close-up view. The fewer non-qualified people to trample over possible evidence, the better." A relieved and thankful grin greeted this reassurance.

"Yes, I see." Delphick stood looking down at a sturdy middle-aged man of weather-beaten aspect, whose clothes and boots were fastened with string rather than with buttons or laces. His head lay at an uncomfortable angle in the middle of a patch of grass stained rusty brown. "Yes. Extremely unpleasant. Your first thoughts, Sergeant Ranger?"

Bob, having despatched his get-a-move-on message to the county police and received confirmation that help was already on its way, had re-joined his superior to relay this news and stood now at Delphick's side.

"Ugh, sir," said Detective Sergeant Ranger. "Like I said in the first place." His tone was nicely calculated not to reach the ears of Mr Luckham, who while escorting Delphick to the scene of the crime had said that in present circumstances he didn't feel the least bit lucky. Again Delphick expressed sympathy, and when they drew near the body told the luckless Mr Luckham to stay well back.

"And you did warn me I'd need a strong stomach. You were right, sir."

"I also said 'near decapitation' and again I was right. Could *you* have done it?"

His sergeant knew that he wasn't being accused of murder, but being asked to consider the practicalities. "I should think so. I'm taller than him, and a decade or so younger, and at a guess I'm stronger, though with these tough country specimens you can never judge by appearances. Think of Nigel Colveden, or even Sir George. All that heaving animals in and out of lorries, chucking bales of straw about, push-starting tractors when they break down in the mud—that sort of thing doesn't half develop the muscles. But I reckon I could've garrotted the poor bloke easily enough, though I doubt if I'd've gone quite as far through his neck as this. I mean, once your throat's cut you're dead, aren't you? Talk about overkill."

Delphick bent to study the gaping slit through which the dead man's life had poured out upon the grass. "I see bone," he said, straightening. His voice was even more grave than the basic fact of murder might require. "Or rather, bones. Which, Sergeant Ranger, would appear to be out of alignment."

Bob in his turn bent to examine the gaping slit. He stood up, shaking his head. "That—that's a bit much, sir! Overkill, I said? Why, they didn't just cut the poor blighter's throat— they went and broke his ruddy neck at the same time!"

Chapter Four

"A professional killer?" Delphick set the deductive ball rolling for Bob to chase.

"Could be, sir." His sergeant frowned. "Or an ordinary bloke who didn't know his own strength, maybe. First time killing. In a panic."

"Equally plausible." Delphick nodded. "Indeed, on present evidence I'd say more than plausible, I'd say probable. If this unfortunate man was despatched by an expert, we have to ask why. The contract killing of a poacher might be considered a rather extreme reaction to the loss of a few rabbits or pheasants."

"Saw something he shouldn't, poor bloke."

"Hmm." They heard the rumble of approaching vehicles. "We have company." Delphick moved away from the body, and Bob did likewise as the newcomers—one car, one small van—rattled, bumped, and lurched across the uneven ground.

Mr Luckham, whom they re-joined as the cars drew near, thanked heaven the police were here at last, begged pardon for his unhappy turn of phrase, and said that while the Scotland Yard men had been examining the body he'd been thinking.

"We would be interested in your thoughts." The Oracle wondered how close to the Yard car the others were likely to park. He guessed that beside him his sergeant was wondering the same, already worried about the suspension and hoping there wouldn't be scratched paint and dented bodywork to add to the list of likely annoyances for the car-pool manager. That man could make life difficult for people who upset him.

The Customs man turned red. "It's only a theory, but—well, if we hadn't been in the wrong place when it happened, we'd have been here and it might not have happened at all. So I wondered if it was the same for that poor devil. He was just in the wrong place. Saw something he shouldn't have, and got himself killed so he couldn't spill the beans about what he saw."

"My sergeant agrees." Over Delphick's shoulder, Bob grinned at Mr Luckham. "The snares you spoke of earlier may be seen as corroboration, if we assume them to be the property of the deceased—"

"I'll show you." Mr Luckham was eager to leave the vicinity of the corpse. The small official team was now tramping up the field, carrying various bits of paraphernalia removed from the vehicles they had left—fortunately for Bob's nerves—several yards from their pool-car.

"Sergeant Ranger and I must first present our credentials, after which I will leave him to accompany our local colleagues about their business while I in turn accompany you."

These plans were duly carried out. Bob insinuated himself into the County team and with tact suggested additional photographs, at the same time making his own shorthand notes. Delphick was led by Mr Luckham to view the pegged-down loops of wire, agreed they looked like snares, and was then introduced to the rest of the Customs group beside the small hut in the neighbouring field. They had been waiting with impatience for several hours and, while accepting the necessity for the wait, were not in the best of humours.

Each had his own theories about the murder—after all, there had been nothing for them to do but sit and talk—and they were keen to propound them. The finder of the body claimed the privilege of speaking first. "Thieves falling out, if you ask me. Maybe it wasn't just bad luck and that bloody computer sending us to the wrong place first. Maybe there's a traitor in the camp, and we were deliberately sent to the wrong place!"

Delphick allowed some brief expostulation, then lifted an admonitory hand.

"Gentlemen—please. Before this refreshingly animated discussion goes further, perhaps Mr Luckham would be kind enough to enlighten me as to the intended purpose of the—ambush, I believe you said? Thank you—enlighten me as to its original purpose. Who was to be ambushed in this particular place at a time rather earlier than the hour at which you in fact arrived? Clearly there was an expectation of some criminal involvement, as the death of the unfortunate man in the other field has proved—indeed, has reinforced. So, Mr Luckham?"

The Customs man sighed. "Well, they *can* work according to the rising and setting of the moon, but they prefer no moon at all. Like last night. Ideal for smugglers. Clear skies, reasonable visibility under starlight, plenty of time to get things done." He sighed again. "Some things never change."

"Five and twenty ponies, trotting through the dark," agreed Delphick.

"We had a whisper there was a landing due—well, a drop from a private plane—in these parts, with the full ghostly camouflage." Luckham gestured vaguely. "Green lights, white paint, spooky noises—all the old dodges to keep anyone from getting too curious."

"The old dodges generally worked," said Delphick.

"They still do." Luckham shook his head. "Not the way they once did, but in the country there's more—more primitive survival than people in towns realise. Oh, it may be 1975, but even today not everyone has mains electricity. Or can afford to use it if they have—or are willing to trust it, come to that. Wood fires, candles, oil-lamps, shadows—the good old days never really stopped, in some places."

Most of his audience knew most of this. Some fidgeting ensued as he went on: "Over the past few weeks we've started to see the market flooded with iffy tobacco products. We'd no idea where they were coming from—you know how much coastline we've got, and we can't keep a watch on every mile of it—but then we got lucky." Further fidgeting, and a few pointed coughs. Mr Luckham hesitated.

"It's a bit complicated," he said at last. *Customary Excuses reverting to habitual secretive type*, Delphick mused. "How we found out, I mean, but take it from me that we did. We knew they'd be bringing some of the cheap stuff over from the continent by parachute drop from a small plane flying under the radar, without lights, on a particular night. The ground crew, we'll call 'em, were to collect the stuff and re-package it all in another location, to sell as a more expensive brand."

"Which brand, or rather brands, would this be?" Delphick observed the Customs team freeze into a wary silence. Surely it could harm no future strategy if he was told. After all, he didn't himself smoke; it wasn't as if he was going to take unfair advantage; but of course they had no way of knowing this …

Before he could profess his purity of intention, Luckham made up his mind. "They bring in 'Horatio' and turn 'em into 'Pyramus y Thisbe', which can retail at ten times the price. And nobody—nobody pays any tax at all on them!" His whole team groaned in unison.

Delphick couldn't decide whether it was the release of privileged information or the non-payment of Excise duty that troubled the Customs man more. He pondered the witty and highly successful marketing campaign of the Horatio brand. The slogan *But he'd be happier with a Horatio* had been attached to newspaper, television, and advertisement-hoarding images of famous smokers, including Sir Winston Churchill, smiling as he flashed his celebrated V-sign; pre-war Prime Minister Baldwin with his pipe; Brunel, the Victorian engineering genius in his stovepipe hat; and Sir Walter Raleigh, cloaked in velvet, blowing a skilful smoke-ring, and (to avoid possible confusion with Sir Francis Drake) captioned by name in elaborate Elizabethan script.

The high quality of Horatio tobacco made the fraud doubly clever, and thus more difficult to detect. Pyramus y Thisbe had no need to advertise; their excellence was a byword; but Horatio, while not in the same class, was by all accounts a reliable smoke. It would take time for the change to (Delphick hid a smile) filter through—no, that would be cigarettes. For the change to be noticed. At first, people might suppose a loss of palate, or a rare fault in cigar production from some unknown cause. They might perhaps think the change of flavour was connected with the packaging, should they be sufficiently alert to spot the differences there were sure to be between the genuine and the substitute.

Or, were they so sure? "How realistic is the substitute packaging?" he asked.

"Very," said Luckham, still glum. "Some clever blighter's got access to a colour photocopier. They're pretty new," as Delphick stirred. "We hoped to nail 'em that way, but the manufacturers and suppliers in this country say they know nothing and we've no reason to disbelieve them. We think the packaging must be coming in from abroad in much the same way as the actual cigars."

"Smuggled," said Delphick. Mr Luckham winced once more.

"I said we can't keep watch everywhere, and we can't. We haven't the manpower. And it's such a good idea. Anyone spotting the different paper—the wraparound leaflet, the cigar band—would see it's a heavier weight than usual, so they would suppose—well, they *do* suppose—it's a deliberate improvement. More for the money. Why should they complain?"

"Perhaps if they noticed a difference in taste? Reduction in quality?" offered the chief superintendent, even as he continued to ponder. It needn't be a photocopier: the smugglers could be bribing, or blackmailing, an operator in some unspecified printing works that used traditional technology. The outcome would still be the same.

"Horatio's a reliable brand, and not many smokers are as expert as they like to think," returned the Customs man. He coughed. "We ourselves only found out by a fluke."

His tone, his expression and those of his team closing ranks about him made it clear that even for Scotland Yard there would be no further information regarding the aforesaid fluke—or any details of the methods by which Her Majesty's Excise men sometimes learned of certain matters pertaining to tax evasion.

Delphick accepted this operational reticence without argument. Let Customary Excuses go after their quarry of the fake packaging, the substitute cigars.

He had a murderer to catch.

On the far side of the county that day, in Ashford police station, brooding on metal thieves rather than murderers, Superintendent Brinton drank sugared tea and muttered as he reached the last-but-one page of the final report supplied by his Sussex counterpart, Superintendent Furneux. There had been more reports, based on the notes of his own Ashford men seconded briefly to Sussex; and he grumbled to himself as, by the light of an elderly desk lamp, he now compared this Final Report with those others on the same topic the borrowed-from-Hastings crowd had written up for him over recent days.

And yet over recent days Brinton had almost become cheerful. He and Foxon reached a compromise. Rather than three lumps of pure, white and deadly per cup of canteen tea, the superintendent would be allowed to add three spoons of brown Demerara crystals, understood to be healthier. ("But *rounded*, sir. Not heaped." Foxon, while mindful of his promise to Mrs Brinton, yet had an instinct for self-preservation. Mrs B. only had to live with old Brimstone off-duty; but *he* had to put up with his boss's moods all day long. They were getting worse, and there was a limit to how many peppermints anyone could eat if a sugar boost was needed. To salve his conscience the young detective constable offered to swap the office teaspoon for a smaller egg-spoon. The offer was firmly refused.)

Now Foxon, reading and checking his own copies of the same reports, felt the same disappointment as Brinton over the lack of progress in the metal theft investigation, particularly as the severity of the thefts had increased either side of the county border; yet despite the best efforts of Kent on behalf of Sussex, Sussex on behalf of Kent, both forces were as much in the dark as ever. In the dark! Foxon glanced out of the window, and frowned. The wind was rising. Those clouds were getting a whole lot thicker. You'd never suppose it was barely eleven in the morning. He muttered something forceful.

Brinton looked up from his last page. As the superintendent, he'd had the top (rather than the carbon) copy, which made it easier to read: he'd gone through everything twice to Foxon's once. It made no more positive reading the second time around. "I agree, laddie. You'd think every perishing scrap metal merchant south of the Thames had become a Trappist monk. They none of 'em don't know nothin' and they're saying even less. They might as well be politicians."

Foxon forgot the weather as he slammed his files shut. "Too true, sir. All any of them ever seem to say is 'No comment' and the way they say it, you could almost believe 'em." But even amid the gloom, the imp of mischief was never far away. "I suppose you haven't considered that perhaps we should?"

Brinton glared. "Believe 'em? One of them, we certainly shouldn't. Trouble is, we've no idea which one. New-born lambs and driven snow aren't in it, according to this load of bumf." In his turn he slammed shut the folders over which he had been poring, and sighed. "We'll have to go on treating 'em all the same and not believing a single one of the blighters whatever they say—which means the whole damn exercise has been a total waste of time. Harry's lot might just as well have stayed in Sussex for all the good their questions did, and I might as well have kept you here in Ashford—"

"I never knew you cared, sir."

"—with the others, and saved myself the paperwork. What with travel permits and fuel allowance and heaven knows what else form-filling I've been lumbered with ... and can we just agree a straight swap of general costs? Oh no, we can't. The accountants don't like it." Glaring at his in-tray, the superintendent tore vaguely at his hair and sighed yet again. "A total waste of time all round, laddie."

"Talking of the heavens, I don't like the look of that sky, sir. And we don't usually need the lights on in the middle of the day. Did you hear this morning's forecast?"

"Heavy thundery downpours, maybe some hail. Fill my water-butts nicely, though the flowers won't like it." In his spare time Brinton cherished his vegetable patch, devoting rather less effort to the floral side of domestic horticulture.

"Yes, sir, but I only just thought. The drains. Now the blighters are moving on from park benches and chunks of railing to pinching manhole covers and—ironwork, don't they call that sort of stuff? Anyway, there could be any amount of old rubbish causing floods if it got swept right into the surface-water system rather than staying on top, caught by the metal grids. Suppose a tree was struck by lightning, or a branch broke off—"

"Always looking on the bright side, aren't you?"

"Looking ahead," amended Foxon. "But if the forecasters have got it even halfway right, shouldn't we alert Traffic to keep their eyes a bit opener than usual?"

Brinton eyed his subordinate thoughtfully. "Sometimes you're more than just a horrible fashion-plate, young Timothy." But it wouldn't do to encourage him. "I'd say you haven't looked anything like far enough ahead, though. It's the council and the fire brigade who should be on the alert.

They're the ones who'll be on the front line if anything happens—Road Closed signs, man the pumps and so on," as rain began to patter against the window. "We're lucky Ashford's not a retained service. Some of the smaller towns and villages might not be so lucky, mind you."

In country areas there was seldom the money to support a permanent fire brigade. Whereas in 1940 the wail of an air raid siren warned the neighbourhood of danger from above, thirty-five years later the sirens were used to warn farm workers and other part-time but fully-trained firemen that they were needed, at once, at the local fire station. Whatever they might be doing, they must immediately stop. No employer could refuse to let anyone desert his paid duty to perform the more worthwhile duty of saving life or property—and no employer did. Next time, the trouble might be uncomfortably close to home. Communities took care of each other, and were glad to do so. It might be their turn next for fire, flood, a road traffic accident … or a kitten stuck up a tree.

The shadows of Brinton's office vanished as the world turned suddenly white. "Ouch," said Foxon. "See how the lights flickered? Here it comes."

Brinton, reaching for the telephone, hesitated, and began to count. "Six thousand," he announced as a clap of thunder rolled around the sky. "A mile and a half away. Too late to warn anyone, the speed that wind'll blow it along." No longer pattering, the rain lashed against the office window and ran in torrents down the panes, which vibrated in their frames. Brinton frowned. "Hope it doesn't hail. We could bleed to death if a window broke and a splinter of glass got either of us."

"Another cup of tea," prescribed Foxon, rising to his feet.

"I'll come with you," said Brinton. "Good exercise," he explained virtuously, as Foxon looked his surprise. "The missus will be pleased. It's an ill wind."

"It's certainly blowing hard enough, sir. Better tidy our desks, just in case."

"As I said—always looking on the bright side." But again the lad talked sense. The superintendent cleared loose papers into a heap and weighed it down with the current edition of *Moriarty's Police Law*. "An ill wind," he repeated cheerfully, as another white flash was followed immediately by a cracking roll of thunder. "Let's get to the canteen!"

For half an hour the storm rumbled and roared across Kent. There were bursts of hail, with a few moments of golf-ball sized stones, though mostly it poured with rain that fell in vicious drops so close together that Foxon said it wasn't cats and dogs so much as stair rods. All the traffic lights in Ashford died after lightning struck an electricity sub-station and caused a massive power surge. Traffic problems were increased when the fire brigade had to pump out a major road junction flooded when a space-hopper, abandoned by a panicking child at the first flash of lightning, was blown from its front garden into the road, to roll and bump its rubbery way down the hill before drifting into, and blocking, a critical drain. A drain whose cover had been one of those lately removed by thieves, and (presumably) sold for scrap.

"A space-hopper?" Foxon had answered the telephone, and now sat gurgling with mirth as his superior digested the message he'd been too preoccupied to take himself. "A space-hopper?" The Brintons had no children. "D'you mean one of those huge bouncy balls with ears for handles, that kids sit on and—and—"

"Bounce about on? That's right, sir."

"You're telling me it blocked a drain? But those things are big enough for a child to sit on. Why didn't it simply roll away? Or even bounce?"

"It caught on something sharp and was punctured going down the hill." Foxon tried to suppress a grin, but it was hard. "Lost enough air to make it small and floppy so it could be sucked by the current partway down into the drain. Er—just the way I said might happen."

"You said a chunk of tree," countered Brinton, but his heart wasn't in it. Foxon's guess had been a good one, and he couldn't begrudge the lad his little triumph, though that smirk of his could drive a man of less even temper mad.

"I said there might be a flood, sir, and I was right. Thank goodness it wasn't market day. But that's what happened, and it's how our car got into trouble. Sergeant Mutford's going to kill those lads from Traffic when he finds out. He'll say they should've known better than to drive into water when they couldn't see clearly—"

"And why couldn't they see the hopper clearly? They're bright orange, aren't they?"

"Because it was sucked halfway into the drainage system," Foxon reminded him. "Sir."

"You forgetful old fool," supplied Brinton, almost amiably. Foxon looked startled. The superintendent grinned. "Beautiful manners you've got, laddie, but I know you. And I know Sergeant Mutford, too, and I'd say you're right. When he's finished giving those two idiots their well-deserved rollicking, he can send 'em along to me for another. What was I saying earlier about unnecessary expenses and wasting time?"

Foxon didn't rush to the defence of his hapless Traffic friends, because he saw very well the point Brinton was making. A flooded police car, a damaged engine and water-logged electrics didn't just mean one vehicle missing from the station complement until it could be repaired; it also meant that the police driver who had misjudged the situation wasn't as good at his job as he should have been, which (for Desk Sergeant Mutford) was an even greater disgrace. A member of the strict Holdfast Brethren, Mutford was duty bound by religion to maintain a rigid interpretation of the law, whether of the land, the church, or the organisation for which a Brother worked. The handbook for police drivers gave detailed instructions about dealing with hazardous conditions of weather or man-made disaster. Failure to obey the rules was, to a Holdfast Brother, a deplorable sin.

"On the other hand," said Brinton after considering the matter, "I'd better give 'em their rollicking first. By the time Mutford's finished laying down the law they'll be fit for nothing for at least a week."

"It could take that long to fix the car."

"Then while they wait they can get back on the beat like any ordinary plod. Remind 'em how the other half lives."

"And the exercise," Foxon added gravely, "will be good for them. Won't it, sir?"

Then the aftermath of the storm ceased to be a laughing matter.

With no traffic lights working, and several roads blocked by fire engines trying to pump away floodwater, council workmen in thigh-high boots set up many emergency Road Closed Ahead and Diversion signs to help Ashford's drivers navigate their various ways through the town. Desk Sergeant Mutford despatched to point duty as many beat officers as could be spared, walkie-talking to each other instructions and requests for advice as detours were made and altered, local conditions kept changing, established routes were cleared, and others were temporarily closed. Drivers with local knowledge took short cuts, though not all of them worked. The One Way Street system garnered an unwontedly vocal anti-fan club ...

The bus driver, like Mutford, was a Holdfast Brother. He realised that keeping to his regular timetable was going to be difficult, but he was duty bound to do his best. The speed limit in a built-up area was thirty miles an hour; there was little other traffic on the road; he put his foot down as he turned into a residential street, and accelerated from ten to a supposedly safe fifteen miles per hour through water that seemed only a few inches deep.

The powerful wash of the passing bus spread wide behind it, to batter the garden walls of houses on both sides of the road. While hedges and fences stood flexible and firm, brick and stone collapsed in untidy falls across pavements, and tumbled into gutters. The bus driver saw a car uncertainly approaching—checked in his mirror before changing course—saw the chaos to his rear—and, in horror, slammed on his brakes. The brakes squealed, the bus lurched, and with a loud thud and a clang the nearside front wheel threw driver, bus and passengers off balance as it skidded into an unexpected pothole. The back of the bus veered across the road ...

And the approaching car ran, head on, into it.

"She's been taken to Intensive Care," reported Brinton, after a second telephone update. "The ambulance got to her in pretty good time, considering. The bus driver's still in shock, but some of the residents who'd left their houses to curse him and take his number for demolishing their garden walls at least had the sense to phone for help the minute they saw what'd happened."

"Life before property," said Foxon with approval, through a mouthful of bun.

"Don't worry, they'll have got the number of the bus before the breakdown people came to clear the road." Brinton, older and wiser than his subordinate, maintained few illusions where human nature was concerned. "She wasn't driving fast, but the poor kid only passed her test a month or so back and she's never been out in conditions as bad as today. Only eighteen, on her way to a job interview they said, otherwise she'd have stayed at home and been safe."

"She's safe—well, in the best place—now, sir."

"She shouldn't be there at all. They'll try to throw the book at the bus driver, of course, but we know who's really to blame for the whole thing. Damn them!"

"The weather forecast? But they were right," objected Foxon.

Brinton glared, then grinned. "Sorry, laddie, you were off after tea and buns when the lad on the beat phoned in. He saw the breakdown gang towing the bus out of the pothole—and it wasn't a pothole."

Foxon, raising his mug to his lips, set it down again. "A drain," he said. "With no cover because somebody'd pinched it."

"Well deduced, Detective Constable." Brinton reached for his tin of sugar, then caught Foxon's eye. "I think I might've only had two spoons."

"You didn't, sir. I counted very carefully." Foxon was not going to let himself be—he grinned—sweet-talked by his superior. "Three. Nicely rounded, not heaped."

Brinton grunted. It'd been worth a try. "Well, never mind all that. We've got to find these blighters before they cause another accident. One young woman with suspected brain damage is bad enough, but next time—and there's bound to be a next time if we don't catch 'em—next time somebody could be killed."

"Then we'd better put our thinking-caps on," said DC Foxon.

Chapter Five

The George and Dragon, Plummergen's justly popular hostelry, is situated towards the southern end of the village's wide Street, near the church and the vicarage. The George boasts an adequate car park and comfortable bedrooms, an amiable landlord in Charley Mountfitchet and a menu of plain, wholesome fare with just enough fancy touches and no more. The kitchen is run by Charley's wife, whom nobody outside the hotel ever sees. Bertha Mountfitchet is not shy, but she knows how hard it is to maintain privacy in a village, and prefers to reign supreme in her solitary kingdom rather than risk any disturbance or challenge to that privacy.

Like Charley, head waitress Doris can turn a professional hand to many tasks; part-time staff are recruited as required from among local wives and daughters wishing for a little pin-money. The recent influx of twitchers had delighted distaff Plummergen, whose field-working menfolk had been instructed to keep their eyes open for other birds with likely commercial potential.

Apart from Charley, Bertha, and Doris (who lives in, doubling on Reception) there is one other regular member of staff. Maureen, who with her friend Emmy from the post office is regarded by Plummergen as one of its less animated citizens, is delivered to the door of the George every working day by the motor-biking Wayne, whose black leathers won Maureen's susceptible heart some years ago. Maureen can be trusted to find her way home after work—it's hard to lose your way walking from south to north along a single street— but Maureen is not a morning person. Some say she isn't at her best in the afternoon. Doris has been known to mutter that the girl is of little or no use in the evening, either. But Charley Mountfitchet is of an amiable disposition, and Maureen's family (a widowed mother and three younger siblings) is not flush with funds. Maureen (under supervision) can dust, clean and make beds as well as wait at table; there are even times when Doris, when busy elsewhere or in a mellow mood, allows her to work on Reception.

This afternoon was one of those times.

Maureen heard-without-hearing a taxi pull up in the car park. The voice of one man thanking another, and the other thanking him, did not disturb her study of the gossip column of this week's *Anyone's*, her brooding on the Jet Set lifestyle. The clothes, the jewellery, the makeup—the holiday villas, the swimming pools ... What did they have in Plummergen? The George and Dragon, and the Royal Military Canal—more like a ditch in places, full of weeds, and so slow the charity Duck Races other people ran on their waterways would never leave the starting line here.

Maureen sighed, then looked up as the rattle of the handle heralded the opening of the inside door. A tall figure carried two matching suitcases and a flight bag into the reception area and, setting them on the floor in front of the desk, looked about him, smiling broadly.

Maureen stared. She forgot to slide *Anyone's* out of sight as Doris had instructed. This young man was a jet setter if ever she'd seen one! He was tall, dark, handsome—his teeth sparkled white, and expensively straight—his clothes (*very* smart casual) fitted perfectly on a muscled but not over-bulging frame. His luggage, what she'd seen of it, was leather … and when he spoke, she was sure.

"Say, would you by any chance have a room for tonight?"

American! Rich and good-looking! A film star?

Maureen nodded dumbly. The handsome young man smiled again.

"That's great. In fact I'd like to book for two nights—no, guess we could make that three, for starters. Is that okay, ma'am?"

Anyone's vanished as Maureen opened the hotel register. She nodded again, still in a daze. "The Blue Riband Suite," she offered at last. "It's got a bathroom." At his surprise, she remembered. "The best bathroom, I mean." When Grimes & Salisbury stopped work on Summerset Cottage, Charley Mountfitchet had been there with bribes of unlimited tea and free meals to persuade the firm to make their first time-to-spare project the refurbishment of the George begun some time before, but for various reasons never completed. Charley knew that North Americans preferred en-suite to end-of-the-corridor places of personal comfort and the British were fast catching up.

"The Blue Riband Suite," Maureen repeated. "We come second in the Best Kept Village competition a few years back. Mr Mountfitchet thought we oughter celebrate."

"That's wonderful." The young man beamed. "Real local history, right? I'd be very glad to stay in your suite, ma'am—miss—pleased and proud."

Maureen collected what wits she could. "The birdwatchers weren't a bit interested," she told the young man as he began to fill in details with a gold-nibbed pen. "Out all day until it went, then they went, too. But there's a silver shield on the waste-bin up the other end of The Street tells you all about it. Near where I live." It was the only reason she recalled the little plaque's existence. She walked past it at the end of every working day.

A V Smith, wrote the young man with a flourish. He saw Maureen's fascinated gaze, and once more smiled. "My friends call me Bram," he said. "And you are …?"

"On reception for now, but I'll be waiting at table later. You want to eat here?"

Bram, who'd been about to rephrase his question, answered hers first. "If you can fit me in, I'd be glad of a table. Will I need to book for any particular time?"

"The birdwatchers have gone, so we ent so busy as we was." He didn't seem to care much about birds. In films, then. "Come to see Miss Earnshaw, have you?"

"I know nobody in the village yet, ma'am—miss—what *is* your name?"

Maureen told him, adding that you couldn't really say Miss Earnshaw was in the village because Saturday Stop, which she'd rented, was out by the Common, and she wasn't talking to anyone, they said, but perhaps he'd have better luck, being American like her.

"If it's Catherine Earnshaw you mean, I know the name, of course, but it's the locals born and bred I'd like to meet," he told her. Maureen, rummaging for the key to the Blue Riband Suite, decided he couldn't be a film star, after all.

But he knew the name. Perhaps he was a talent scout! No, those good looks and all that charm would be wasted on a talent scout. Or he might (Maureen shivered with a thrill of delighted horror) be one of those Producers with evil Designs upon innocent girls. *Anyone's* had more than once referred to the perils of the casting couch.

"Here's your key." Maureen wasn't going upstairs alone with him. Wayne's comforting image floated in front of her eyes. She drew a deep breath. "Up the stairs, there's no lift, turn right and—"

"Maureen!" A scandalised Doris appeared. "That's no way to welcome our guests. You show this gentlemen to his room, my girl—no," as Maureen's face assumed its most stubborn expression— "I'd best do it. Which room is it?"

Maureen, still mulish, said nothing. Bram Smith smiled at Doris. "Miss Maureen has put me in your Blue Riband Suite, ma'am, but I'm sure I can find my own way there. I plan to explore your charming district for some days, and this will make a grand start."

Doris smiled back. "Mr Mountfitchet, that's the landlord, wouldn't like it if we didn't make you properly welcome."

"Then after you, ma'am, and thank you." He refused with courtesy her attempt to pick up a suitcase, and followed her towards the stairs.

Maureen watched the two depart, and frowned in thought. Doris was of a different generation. Probably no need to worry about her going with this man, whoever he was. Did anyone honestly sign into a hotel as AV Smith—*Smith*? But "Bram" was an unusual name. Maureen gazed at the hotel register, shook her head, and decided to leave the matter for later discussion with Emmy Putts.

Bram thanked Doris again as she stopped by the door of the Blue Riband Suite.

"Plummergen came second in the Best Kept Village competition," she explained, "and we did really ought to have been first, so Mr Mountfitchet, he said we'd call it after what should have happened if the judging had been fair."

"Fascinating," said Bram as if he meant it. "There's surely a lot of history in this place. I'll just drop off my bags and freshen up, then I guess I'll go exploring. Your fine church is next door. You have some real historic gravestones there, don't you?"

"I suppose, but the wind blows from the Marsh something wicked, most days." Doris wasn't much interested in history. "Lots of the letters are worn and you can't read 'em."

"Even more of a challenge for me," said Bram with apparently genuine pleasure. "I've time to spare. I'm on vacation—and I enjoy puzzles."

"That was Jack Crabbe's taxi you come in, was it?"

"I believe so, ma'am. The gentleman said something about the garage and his family business as we drove past."

"Been here since before the war, right at the start of motor-cars almost. His granddad, that was, and he's still around, but it's Victor Crabbe in charge these days. Jack's his son and a clever one, all right. Makes up crossword puzzles for the papers and gets paid for them, too."

Under the name of Coronet (because he had a kind heart, really) the village bus- and taxi-driver, in his spare time, composed cryptic crosswords for the classier periodicals and produced acrostics, riddles and word-squares for less erudite publications.

Bram's smile grew uncertain. "That's fascinating, ma'am, but your English crosswords are a very different animal from ours. My ancestors may have come from this country, but I doubt I've inherited anything beyond the name." Then he smiled, more broadly. "Guess I'll be having another word with your clever Jack in any event—Rye's not so far from here, is it? Would he drive me there in his taxi?"

Doris assured him this should be possible, returned his smile, and left him to settle into the Blue Riband Suite. Revising the lecture she had planned to give Maureen once she was back in Reception, she decided that the doubts she'd observed on the girl's face might not be so far-fetched after all. This handsome, charming young American would make a very welcome guest to Plummergen, going by outward appearances.

But—was he just a little too good to be true?

"Too good to be true," said Brinton, replacing the telephone on its cradle with an irritable clatter. "If you want to believe in criminals reforming themselves, laddie, you can. I'm too old to believe in miracles."

"Leopards *might* change their spots," said Foxon, "but I agree with you, sir. Fishy's not the word. I reckon they're up to something and trying to distract us, that's what."

"But *what's* what? If we had even an idea, then we'd know what to keep an eye out for being distracted *from*, but now …"

"Now they could be playing a pretty smart game." Foxon, who'd heard Brinton's end of the hospital telephone call and deduced the rest, frowned. "Can't think what, though. But seeing the low-lifes we originally thought they were, that could mean maybe there's someone even smarter behind the whole business. Whatever it is."

"Someone with some kind of hold over the scrap dealers to keep 'em quiet?" Brinton hated so much uncertainty, and was still aggrieved that the mutual cross-border questioning had yielded no results. "Mr Big from the city handing out the threats? But nobody's reported any Smoke muscle in these parts. And," he added, "if they *have* seen 'em and not reported 'em, you tell 'em from me it's guts for garters time if I ever find out."

Foxon made a mental note to ask among his Uniform colleagues, but had little hope that routine patrols would have spotted—or been allowed to spot—anything untoward. He himself was a man of more direct action.

"I'll go to the hospital and collect the card that came with the flowers." He pushed back his chair. "Then I'll talk to the florist. They might be able to describe whoever it was put in the order."

"Ten to one it'll be an anonymous envelope of cash, and letters cut from the newspaper saying what message to send with the flowers." Brinton scowled. "Why didn't the fools tell us at once what'd happened? We might've got fingerprints off the envelope, even if off the money would be too much to hope for."

"And twenty to one they'll have worn gloves and we'll get no prints off anything." Foxon shrugged himself into the rich brown jumbo-cord jacket that had so annoyed Brinton at first sight. "But we'll soon know. I'll be as quick as I can, sir." He tried to find something to cheer his glum superior. "Still, it's good that she's starting to improve."

"Very slowly, they said, and she's still unconscious. And they don't let flowers in Intensive Care, no matter how much gush is written on the card—or how much the blighters say they're sorry and they just didn't think. Think? They never think!"

"Not often." Foxon made for the door. "But sometimes they do. You know, sir, I reckon it was the photo in the local paper that got 'em going. Her being so young, and such a looker." Brinton snorted. "And the paper gave it the full treatment," persisted Foxon. "A real sob-story. I wouldn't argue, the poor kid deserves it—and I know I called it fishy, and about leopards not changing their spots—but maybe putting a pretty face to the story, stopping it being anonymous—maybe that really *did* make the blighters think things over for once, and change their minds."

"A herd of Gloucester Old Spots just flew past the window," was Brinton's response to his sidekick's attempt to cheer him. Foxon wondered about uttering a few porcine *oink-oink* grunts as he left the office, but thought it safer to keep quiet. Old Brimstone wasn't happy about any of this; and Foxon could guess why. If the apologetic thieves were honest in their apologies, but as dishonest as ever about everything else … what were they likely to try next in their life of petty crime, in place of drain grids and manhole covers?

Miss Seeton, tidying her bureau, paused to leaf through the latest completed sketchbook, wistfully contemplating her attempts at capturing the grandeur of the Saharan-dusted sunsets, the small contrast of the wind-blown bird that had reached a haven on English shores, to remain for so short a time. She hoped the poor lost creature had flown from choice, rather than dying of hunger, and that it was now safely back in more suitable climes. Mrs Ongar of the Rye sanctuary had said that the European Roller ate insects, mostly locusts; no doubt grasshoppers or crickets made an alternative, but how good an alternative she wasn't sure, although at the right time of year there were plenty of them about. Miss Seeton had often heard them chirping and occasionally seen them leaping in her garden: the joyous sight and sound of summer at its height. After summer, of course, came autumn, the season she loved best; then winter … She considered Aesop's fable of the fun-loving grasshopper and the industrious ant. She had watched the busy little brown dots scuttle about their work, full of purpose—and annoying dear Stan, always so quick to demand kettles of boiling water. Stan didn't hold with putting down powder, which was no less than poison. Other insects, such as bees and butterflies, were useful in a garden. He'd never mentioned grasshoppers with approval; but was not this insect the badge, or did she mean the crest, of the Goldsmiths' Company? Or was it the Royal Exchange? Somewhere rich and mercantile, she felt sure. She had once taken a small class on a day trip to the City of London, explaining to the more literal-minded children that "the Square Mile" wasn't in fact square in shape, just a square mile in area; and they had all sketched the stone grasshoppers on the outside of ... which building had it been? Perhaps, after all, the Exchange rather than the Goldsmiths'. It had burned down during the Great Fire of London, she recalled, and again in the time of Victoria. Was there not an amusing anecdote about the bells ringing some foolish tune before the roof fell in?

Idly, Miss Seeton pulled another sketchbook towards her and began to doodle. Grasshoppers didn't play tunes, but they made music by rubbing their legs together—dry sticks rubbed together made fire—fire had twice destroyed the building decorated with grasshoppers ... She added a second ring of bells, smiled, and started when her own doorbell rang as she put the final touches.

The headmaster was on the doorstep, looking apologetic.

Miss Seeton smiled. "Mr Jessyp! Do come in. I was just about to make a pot of tea."

Mr Jessyp returned the smile as he followed her into the house. "You are most kind, Miss Seeton, especially when I have, as so often before, come to beg a favour of you."

Miss Seeton frowned. "Miss Maynard's mother is not ill again? You know I am always happy to help out at the school whenever she has to go away."

"Dear me, no. It's not your teaching abilities I would like to press into service so much as your artistic and organisational skills."

Miss Seeton hurried into the kitchen to hide her modest blush. Mr Jessyp, who knew her, hovered politely in the doorway as she busied herself at the sink, set the kettle to boil, took crockery from the dresser and checked in the biscuit-tin. "There is little cake left, but there are chocolate biscuits," she announced. Mr Jessyp, knowing her fondness for them, gravely thanked her and said that chocolate biscuits would serve very well.

As they settled themselves with cups and plates, Mr Jessyp coughed gently. "Of course you remember the electrical fire at the school the other evening. And may I thank you again for the prompt assistance you rendered throughout the evacuation? It was over so quickly that the fire brigade had no need to use their hoses."

"A most fortunate outcome." Miss Seeton had survived the London Blitz, and knew how water at high pressure could harm a building already weakened by fire. As for the damage to furniture, fixtures and fittings …

Martin Jessyp didn't look as cheerful as she might have expected. "The fire brigade sent one of their high-ups along later to discuss how we could prevent anything like this happening again. The school is Victorian, as you know, and from my perusal of the records it doesn't seemed to have been re-wired for several decades. The Fire Officer said it must all—he was most insistent—it must be all be replaced."

His hostess nodded again, a little puzzled. She couldn't suppose Mr Jessyp expected her to rewire the school herself, and as for recommending anyone, she felt that he, or the County Education Authority, would be far better placed than she to do so. How presumptuous of her it would seem. "There is Mr Hickbody, who works with Grimes and Salisbury," she suggested. "Or perhaps Mr Spellbrook, who has a shop in Brettenden and sold me a vacuum cleaner. I fear I can think of no-one else at present."

Mr Jessyp coughed again, with rather more force. "Oh no! That is—no, nothing like that, Miss Seeton. The CEA has its own list of contractors and will put the job out to tender, once the matter is finally settled, but ... Let's just say there is some difference of opinion as to what in fact should happen."

Miss Seeton was further puzzled—either the school needed re-wiring or it didn't—so she poured tea, and waited.

"In fact," said Mr Jessyp, "a considerable difference of opinion. The Authority has told us—myself, and the school governors—that it will fund a complete re-wiring of Plummergen School in the usual way. One hundred per cent of the cost will be met ..."

Miss Seeton knew better than to congratulate him. Another *but* was on clearly its way. "But," said Mr Jessyp, "the governors and I don't feel the CEA has made the right decision. The fire, as investigation has shown, was caused by electric cable nibbled through by mice nesting under the floorboards. You know yourself that we can't keep them out, situated in the country as we are."

"Indeed I do." Miss Seeton had heard Martha Bloomer's views on spiders. She didn't care to think what her houseproud factotum would say should any trace of a mouse ever be found in Sweetbriars.

"Traps and poison are obvious, but temporary, solutions," went on Mr Jessyp, "and some children find even the thought of them distressing. So, rather than futile attempts to render the building impregnable, Admiral Leighton proposed we should make the new wiring not only mouse-proof, but fire-proof at the same time—which ordinary wiring is not—by using mineral insulated copper cable instead."

Miss Seeton began to see where this might be leading. "Copper being metal, through which mice are unlikely to chew?"

"Exactly. The admiral explained that many warships use MICC because fire at sea can be—" Mr Jessyp recalled the Buzzard's words on torpedoed ships and the sea burning with fuel oil— "horrible," finished the headmaster, and said no more.

"I have read in the local paper," ventured Miss Seeton, "about a number of thefts, over recent weeks, of metal in various forms taken for scrap."

"That poor young woman who remains in Intensive Care. Yes. The CEA grant, Miss Seeton, simply will not run to the added cost of MICC cable—and certainly not for the burglar alarm system we feel it would be advisable to install once the re-wiring has been completed to the standard the governors and I feel is the most appropriate."

Miss Seeton, during the years of her part-time attachment to the little school in Hampstead, had heard Mrs Benn the headmistress wax eloquent on the Education Authority and its financial complexities. "Pettifogging bureaucracy," she murmured.

Martin C Jessyp, that noted paper-pusher famed for his orderly mind, looked at her with surprise, and approval. "I knew you'd understand the difficulties, Miss Seeton, which is why I've come to ask for your help with the school concert we plan as the start of a larger fund-raising campaign."

"Scenery," said Miss Seeton. "But of course. I would be most happy. And posters, naturally." Mr Jessyp smiled encouragement as she warmed to her theme. "Miss Maynard can teach the children some new songs, perhaps." Mr Jessyp did not seem to mind her tentative interference. Had he not said, on the doorstep, that he wished to beg a favour of her artistic and organisational skills? To which, it surely needed no saying, he was more than welcome. Such as they were. For the sake of the school, in particular, and for her dear village in general. Even if there was very little she could do that could not be done far better by others.

"Miss Armitage for the costumes, of course." Quiet Phyllis Armitage was the village's most skilful and artistic seamstress. The Plummergen Amateur Dramatic Society, familiarly the Padders, would have put on far less spectacular productions without Miss Armitage and her team.

"Lady Colveden is speaking to Miss Armitage," said the headmaster, "but I thought it right that I, as a professional colleague, should be the one to approach you, Miss Seeton. We—the governors and I—felt sure you would be willing, but it's hardly fair to take your co-operation for granted and the courtesies should be observed." Miss Seeton murmured that she was more than happy to help. Mr Jessyp hurried on. "Miss Maynard will join her thanks with mine, I'm sure. The school year is young; the new intake will be unused to performing in public. She will spare no effort, as you and I know, but she'll be kept very busy and it is therefore towards the older children that I ask you to direct your own attentions."

"Perhaps," said Miss Seeton, "the attentions of the more impressionable children will be diverted from nuclear fallout towards something less … unwholesome."

She and the headmaster gazed at each other, shook their heads, and together sighed. "Such a pity that your talk was interrupted, Mr Jessyp. Had you considered repeating it?"

"Once the smell of burning has blown completely away I might, but at present we have to leave the windows ajar at all times unless it is raining. Now that the bird has flown, and the rain has washed away the dust, I suspect my audience would concentrate more on the smell, or the imagined draught, and far less on my, ah, words of wisdom."

The teachers shared a wry chuckle for the oddities of human nature, and then settled to a preliminary discussion of the School Re-Wiring Concert.

The council depot foreman was always first to arrive. Elzevir Block—born and bred in Ringstave, the best-maintained town in Kent—prided himself on beating everyone else to the main gates, which he then opened with the largest key on the stout bunch he took home with him every night. There were duplicate sets, of course; Mr Block, a member of the Holdfast Brethren, took his duties seriously and knew all possibilities must be covered; but unless he was ill (rare) or on holiday (he generally refused to go, taking payment in lieu) the duplicates were never needed. He would arrive early, open up, and start to order the business of the day without interference or distraction.

This morning was different. When the next bicycle turned the corner, the gates were still closed. Elzevir stood before them, transfixed.

The bicycle braked to a halt beside him. "Someone's idea of a joke," said the bicycle after a thoughtful pause.

Elzevir stirred. "They got in over the fence round the back," he said slowly. "Chain-link is all pulled out of true, bulging summat wicked."

"We got chain-link and to spare," the bicycle comforted him. "Soon fix a bit of bulge."

"I'd like to get my hands on whoever it was," growled Mr Block. "Council property, paid for by the rates, and us doing our best to see the town gets its money's worth. Money being wasted by drunks playing damfool practical jokes!"

The bicycle looked again at the brick pillars supporting the heavy gates. On top of each was set a bright orange plastic cone, like a dunce's cap.

"Trying to make fools of us, likewise," said the bicycle after further thought. "They done any damage beyond the fence?"

Stirred into action Elzevir retrieved the keys from his saddlebag (stout leather, two straps, sturdy buckles) and opened the gates. Both bicycles were wheeled inside.

Anxious eyes darted about. "Mmph," said Elzevir. "Looks all right, on first seeming, but we best check locks and windows to make sure—no, second thoughts I'll do that. You stay here and tell who comes next to wait while I'm checking. Iffen there's anything serious to be found, the cops won't thank us for treading over likely clues."

The local bobby came in his panda car, looked for useful traces near the chain-link fence but found none, and agreed with Elzevir that the lock to the road-gang's shed, where traffic cones, temporary signs and other Highways equipment were stored, had been broken in a search for the dunce's caps. "And lucky they found 'em first crack, or it might've bin worse." As it was, everything else seemed to be in good order. No other locks had been forced; no tyres of truck, tractor or lorry had been punctured or deflated. Engines, when tested, started without trouble.

"No sugar in the fuel. That's good," was the official verdict. Mr Block shook his head at the very idea of such mean-spirited vandalism. "Like enough it was no more'n general daft goings-on after a night at the pub," decided the beat bobby. "Wouldn't be my idea of fun, but it takes all sorts."

He drove off, leaving the council workers to start work later in the day than they'd done for a very long time.

Chapter Six

Nigel Colveden stifled a yawn, and drank his coffee black. "A caffeine shot to wake me up," he explained, as his mother looked surprised. "All your fault, mother."

Lady Colveden passed his second cup. "I don't see why. It's not as if I blow hunting horns in my sleep, or tap-dance up and down the stairs."

"Good grief," muttered Sir George behind his newspaper. Louise giggled.

"If it was as you slept you would remember nothing of such disturbance, dear Belle-Mère—but Nigel has concerned himself with your problem of the school electricity." Lady Colveden blinked. "And this morning he claims to have dreamed of it also."

"And after a restless night I've found the answer," said Nigel. "Partly," caution made him add. "It was our honeymoon in France that did it, and talking of old films when we bumped into Miss Seeton the other day. She remembers seeing *The Wizard of Oz* when it first came out, did you know? And that was what gave me the idea."

"A film show in the village hall?" guessed his mother.

"A scarecrow festival," said Nigel in triumph.

The pages of *The Times* rustled as Sir George lowered them to peer at his son. He'd thought marriage would suppress much of the boy's sense of humour; evidently not.

"A what?" asked Lady Colveden.

"A scarecrow festival. They have them in France, to bring the tourists in. We drove through several places with signs up, and Louise explained." Louise nodded, but gestured for him to continue. "A village makes lots of scarecrows—comical costumes, lashings of straw, daft poses and so on—turning a somersault, falling off a wall, climbing a chimney or a tree—and then they dot them about the place and—well, people come to see them."

"Why?" Sir George wanted to know. Nigel hesitated.

"The novelty of the thing, I suppose. To be honest, I'm not really sure. But they do."

As Louise nodded again, Lady Colveden was puzzled. "But how would that help with re-wiring the school, and the burglar alarm?"

"It would bring in the tourists, of course. Look how the place filled up with hundreds of twitchers chasing that unfortunate bird. You know everyone's praying it will fly back, and they can make even more money."

"But the European Roller kept moving about," Lady Colveden reminded him. "People couldn't just dash in and out of the village, they had to book into the George or somewhere, for a better chance of seeing the poor thing. Scarecrows do nothing but stand there in fields. You could drive past and look at them and be gone in no time."

"It must work, or they wouldn't do it year after year," insisted Nigel.

Once more Louise nodded. "There is often much spirit of competition, both among the people, to see who displays the most imagination and skill, or between villages, to see who makes the most benefit from those who visit. As with the poor lost bird, they will take photographs, and buy sandwiches, and spend money."

"Murreystone," said Sir George, retreating behind his paper. "There's competition, if you like. Drop the word in the right ear and wait for sparks to fly—no," he corrected himself, "not sparks. Not with straw. But local rivals—ah. Local. Not very much arable here."

"Your father means it's mostly sheep in these parts," translated Lady Colveden. "And of course he's right. Scarecrows are for scaring crows and other birds away from arable crops. Why would anyone from these parts need to make a scarecrow?"

"The full name is *carrion* crow," said Nigel, with an apologetic look at his wife. "Sorry, Louise, but you've married a farmer. Most corvids—rooks, crows, magpies—aren't averse to stealing eggs from other birds' nests, or even eating the fledglings. They can clean the flesh from a dead rabbit in no time at all, and if they develop a taste for lambs, they first peck their eyes out and then, well ..."

"Not at breakfast, Nigel," said his mother. "And they don't. At least not very often."

"The townie tourists won't know that. Tell them we do it to save sweet fluffy baa-lambs from the evil killers that swoop out of the sky and the cash'll come rolling in, I should think. Not that we can charge them for driving into the village on the Queen's highway, but we could charge for the car park *pro tem.*, or put a collection box in a prominent position to tickle their urban consciences."

"Hmm," said the magistrate behind his *Times*. "Have to think about that."

"It's all in a good cause," said Nigel. "We'll make one special scarecrow for them to be photographed standing beside, in the same spirit as those bodies painted on boards with a hole for your head, at the seaside. I remember being an enormously fat man in a check suit when Julia was his wife, all polka-dots and a comical hat."

"When we went to the Isle of Wight," said Lady Colveden, fondly smiling. "I wonder where those photos are now? George, do you know?"

"Not many fluffy lambs at this time of year," said *The Times*, ignoring comical photos.

"Which is why this is the time we can spare for making scarecrows," his son trumped the farming expert's ace. "Ready to scare away the carrion crows in spring, when we're otherwise occupied with lambing. So, mother—what do you think?"

In another house, another man stifled a yawn and took his morning coffee black with sugar. The sleep of Matthew Bell had been even more disturbed than that of Nigel Colveden.

Matthew's companions, busy over their own breakfast, did not observe his clamped jaws and rigid bearing as a second yawn threatened to betray him. He swallowed the rest of his coffee, cursed because it was too hot, and indicated that he required more.

Matthew was a powerfully built man with a hasty temper. Those of his company who remained—several, being more or less local, had made their safe escapes after what was tactfully referred to as The Incident—knew and distrusted that temper. Throwing a punch at someone, knocking them out with a sandbag, threatening them with a gun … such methods of keeping someone quiet, they understood.

Not one of them had seen a man's head almost severed by a picture-wire snare …

Until the other night.

Matthew had given his boss in London basic details of the need to disappear, and stressed the urgency. He explained that he and what remained of the gang needed a safe place in which to carry out the second part of the job for which they'd been hired, with the idea of using it as their headquarters in the future, when the system still under trial would be properly up and running. Apart from the unexpected arrival of that poacher everything had been going well, hadn't it? Then why even think of changing a system that had worked for all those weeks and looked set to work for weeks or months to come?

At first the Boss was too startled at the death of Isaiah Gawdy, a more or less innocent bystander, to ask many questions about what had happened. He knew of a quiet farmhouse miles away across the county, but not so far they couldn't drive there in an hour at most once they'd come out of hiding. Within a day or two he had made the arrangements. Matthew Bell and his companions moved in … and the news of Gawdy's grisly murder finally broke in the daily papers, on radio and on television.

"We said no news is good news," said Matthew, "and now we've got the bad. Which is almost as good, right? But we take no notice either way, because it shows they got nothing on us, and never had, or they'd have tracked us down and we'd have heard if they'd come looking. But we didn't, because they couldn't, so they hushed it up. How it got out I dunno, but it ain't good for the cops to look like fools and that's what they look like now, with not a clue about nothing. Right?"

He glared round, and drank more coffee. "So it's safe to carry on here, same as before. Right? You lot leave all the thinking to me and the boss. We won't let you down. Reading between the lines, we've got the Yard proper flummoxed. And that's how they'll stay, mark my words. So get cracking, you lot!"

They got cracking.

After the beat bobby's departure, Mr Block undertook a careful inventory of the equipment store with the broken lock. If the original traffic-cone joke had depressed him, taking the inventory was worse. Elzevir prided himself on order and method, yet always felt uneasy about never having the time to sort out what had been done (or done with less efficiency than his) in the more casual days before he came to the depot. Even now he found that various items turned up in the wrong places far more often than they should. He accepted that he couldn't supervise every council worker every minute of the working day, and the legacy of the past didn't help, but it disturbed him that things were still borrowed and not brought back. Or brought back to the wrong place ("Well, s'all the Council, ent it?"). Things were damaged, replaced, and then repaired and returned casually to service while replacements in their turn were taken and damaged. People didn't always sign for what they took, and if they remembered to sign it was often with a scrawl of initials he couldn't decipher. Mr Block sighed for the depot's prospects once he finally retired, and was at first thankful that he had just the one storeroom—admittedly the largest, but just the one—to search, rather than the entire site.

His search of the entire site came later.

"Two pipe-cutters," he reported at last to Ringstave's small police station. "It's took longer than I'd like on account of only bein' able to ask when the blokes come in off shift, and then I had to check all the other stores in case they'd bin put down careless and forgot—but it's a funny thing. Seems just two pipe-cutters was took—the heavy duty sort, not them as you'd buy in a Do-It-Yourself, though a builders' merchant'd probably have 'em in stock."

"A builders' merchant," came a constabulary voice from the telephone, "might remember your face, buying two at the same time."

Elzevir Block was no fool. "They wanted two, means there must be two of 'em. So why not buy 'em separate? Different days? Different places, even?"

"No idea," said the telephone. "But you can bet there'll be a reason and my guess is, it ent an honest one."

"Clever," said Mr Block, "making out it was drunks playing a practical joke. Easier than a builders' merchant—us not having such good alarms," he added bitterly. Brooding over the traffic cones, he had put in a request for updating of the depot anti-theft precautions. After much follow-up nagging, he'd been told the ratepayers would never stand for any increase this year. Or next, probably.

The telephone sympathised with his bitterness, then ended the call. The loss of two pipe-cutters was puzzling, but Ringstave was unsure what to do with the information—if, indeed, it was accurate. Mr Block's orderly ways were approved by the police as well as his employers, but the best-ordered systems had their flaws. A heavy duty pipe-cutter was small enough, in general equipment terms, to be accidentally hidden under, behind, or in extreme cases inside a clutter of seldom-used council paraphernalia. Perhaps a workman had made an illicit borrowing, mislaid what he'd borrowed or just forgotten to take it back, then borrowed another for the same purpose. Whatever that might be. Which (Ringstave acknowledged) was as puzzling as all the rest …

It was Desk Sergeant Mutford's views on sin that caught Brinton's attention. The superintendent found himself pausing to listen, wondering if he'd mistaken the day of the week: he knew the regular Meeting nights and, next morning, generally kept out of Mutford's way until someone else had taken the brunt of the Holdfast Brother's enthusiasm.

This time he listened, questioned, and hurried to the office, where Foxon was already seated at his desk wearing a pious expression and—good grief!—a blackberry-coloured jacket made of crushed velvet, with lapels that reached almost to his shoulders.

But for once Brinton made no comment on his sidekick's fashion sense. "There could be trouble," he said before Foxon had a chance to greet him. "Mutford told me there was an Extraordinary meeting of the Brethren last night." Foxon brightened. "No, nothing in our line, some legal bother about a right of way across Holdfast property. But one of the Brethren comes from Ringstave, and he told Mutford that some villains broke into the council depot there. Tried to make it look like a bit of fun at first, only it wasn't." He dropped heavily on his chair. "They pinched a couple of pipe-cutters—heavy duty pipe-cutters, mark you, not the plumb-your-own-sink-in-on-the-cheap size."

"Er—did they, sir?" Foxon, clearly underwhelmed, made an effort to show professional interest. "You think the scrap metal thieves are starting up again after the lull?"

"What does anyone do with a pipe-cutter, Foxon?"

Foxon looked at him.

Brinton, to the surprise of his young colleague, grinned. "I know, laddie, I know. *Talk about the bleedin' obvious* is what you're thinking." Foxon, returning the grin, ventured a nod. "You cut pipes," Brinton answered his own question, but added in a more serious tone, "My wife has a decided fancy for Paul Newman."

"Those blue, blue eyes." Too many of Foxon's girlfriends had gushed wistfully over the star's unmistakeable good looks.

"That's right. Talks me into an evening at the flicks with fish and chips for afters every time they show one of his films." Brinton absently patted his tummy, then sighed. "A few years back I took her to see *Cool Hand Luke*." He paused. "And now for some deduction from you, young Tim, though I'd say it's been handed to you on a plate."

Foxon thought; but not for long. He too had seen *Cool Hand Luke,* and been puzzled by much of it, but he remembered the opening scene. He sat up. "You think the chummies could be planning midnight raids on our parking meters? But—"

"They could. Ours, maybe, though we've not got as many as Maidstone—but almost certainly somebody's. And if that's what they do and they end up in quod the way Paul Newman did, it'll be for vandalism and theft at the very least, and maybe causing an affray as well—civil disorder, inciting a riot, whatever you want to call it."

Foxon thought again. "Drivers in punch-ups over who gets to park where without having to pay?" It was barely a question. "But the meters can be replaced. It wouldn't take long, the rate the things are popping up all over the place. The factory that makes 'em must be working round the clock."

"Nothing to stop the chummies having another crack at the replacement meters, laddie. And another, and another. We can't watch every single meter in every single town every bally night. Empty the things of cash, take the empties to some dodgy scrap dealer to melt down so there's nothing traceable … and nobody loves a traffic warden. If someone's got into the habit of ticketing any car that overstays its welcome then, meter or no meter, we'll soon see what I mean about inciting a riot. People will take sides."

"I can just see the headlines. *Market shoppers riot on the streets of Kent.* The traffic's always bad on market day, and the parking's even more of a problem than usual."

"Foxon, I hate you." Brinton scowled. "Traffic inspector pal of mine—name of Harpe, don't think you know him—well, he says they call him Happy Harry because he never smiles. Poor bloke says he's never seen anything in Traffic to make him smile—and he's right. People have got used to tidy parking. Take the meters away, and it'll be chaos if we can't put our hands on the metal thieves pretty damn quick. I hate you."

"If that's who they are, sir. It might be another lot completely—and be fair. It was you who raised the matter in the first place, thanks to Sergeant Mutford."

"I hate him, too. The last thing I need's more to worry me than what we've got already. Thinking we may have umpteen gangs on our patch pinching manhole covers, and cutting down parking meters, and the lord knows what else, makes my blood boil. And we've no idea who the original chummies might be, never mind a second blasted lot!"

The school concert plans were modified. At first puzzled by (for nobody had heard of such a thing) and then approving of Nigel Colveden's fund-raising Festival, so many villagers were busy constructing scarecrows to attract the tourists that few of Plummergen's seamstresses could be spared for the sewing of fancy dress, even for the youngest members of the choir. Nigel's proposal having been accepted, the customary spirit of competition and secrecy was once more rampant following the (likewise customary) initial burst of free-for-all discussion. Once Plummergen had fully thrashed out a topic and decided it was for the good of the village, then that (until the appointed hour) was the end of the matter, in public terms. Nobody was prepared to tell anyone else what exactly they were individually planning. Entry forms were left uncompleted, the intention being to submit them as late as possible in case the winning idea should be stolen by some jealous rival.

The concert, however, was no competition but a performance by the kiddies, bless their little hearts. A pity there weren't the time to make proper costumes, for 'twas always good to see 'em lookin' smart and surely fancy dress wouldn't hurt, but Mr Jessyp had said no, 'twas the songs as were important and there'd be scenery to show what was going on. Miss Seeton was to paint the scenery, or leastways design backcloths and put in details, when she and Miss Maynard weren't teaching the songs and the actions to go with 'em. Props, too, given time to make 'em.

Miss Maynard rattled cheerfully away on the rehearsal piano; Miss Seeton, a long thin paintbrush in her hand as a baton, encouraged small mouths to open in unison and song. The programme was varied, to please as many as possible, though Mr Jessyp (who, busy with electricians and emergency re-wiring, still made the final choice) had rationed the pop music to make sure of Gilbert and Sullivan, traditional airs such as "Greensleeves" and "The Lincolnshire Poacher", and hearty songs of Empire. "Drake's Drum" and "The Road to Mandalay" would be sure to have the audience joining in. They would remember the words from their own school-days—and a happy audience was a generous audience.

Kipling, and proximity to Romney Marsh, made inevitable the inclusion of "A Smuggler's Song". Mr Jessyp, after numerous telephone calls, sent underlings to scrounge round Plummergen for the necessary props: Miss Seeton, willing though she was, couldn't be expected to contrive them all. Barrels being far too heavy for Junior and Mixed Infant hands, empty brandy bottles (rinsed; from Charley Mountfitchet at the George), cardboard boxes (various village stores) labelled TOBACCO or TEA (Miss Seeton and her paintbrush), bundles of fancy cloth (Mrs Welsted, draper), and bulky envelopes that looked both secret and official (paper, sticky tape, and coloured wax, again courtesy of Miss Seeton) were to be carried in regular rotation by half the choir past the other half, who stood, stifling giggles, with their faces resolutely turned to the wall behind which the scampering feet of their friends rushed, out of sight round the back, back round to the front to join in again. Mr Jessyp had firmly vetoed any idea of hobby-horses: these particular smugglers had unloaded their ponies before the song began. Now they were taking the contraband, as usual, to hiding places so secret it was dangerous to know where these places might be.

"… watch the wall, my darling, while the Gentlemen go by!" sang everyone, even those who carried the smuggled goods in their horizontal paternoster.

Miss Maynard proposed that a pinafored child carrying "a dainty doll, all the way from France" might appear as the final verse was sung, showing that the smuggler's advice had been heeded, the bribe had worked, and nobody had looked to see where the smugglers were going. Miss Seeton wondered if singling out just one little girl in this way would be entirely fair to the rest. Mr Jessyp didn't even wonder, and was firmer in his veto than he'd been over the hobby-horses. Then, all there'd been to worry him was the risk (a) to his floors and (b) of mutual bashing-up between friends, this being all too likely if children and broom-handles were brought together. But with scratched floors and juvenile violence, Martin Jessyp could cope. Let favouritism be shown to any individual child in Plummergen, however, and the place would be in an uproar before you could say "a present from the Gentlemen". Miss Maynard blushed and apologised, saying she hadn't thought it through. Miss Seeton regretted that anyone could be so foolish as to take it personally, but there had been times in Hampstead—such as when Mrs Benn cast the school play … Oh, yes, she had to agree that Mr Jessyp was right.

"Okay, so I was wrong." Superintendent Brinton scowled at the telephone he'd just replaced on its cradle. "They didn't go for the parking meters after all."

"To be honest, sir, I had my doubts." Foxon, having listened on the extension, now tried his best to be tactful, but there was no easy way to say what he thought without risk to his boss's blood pressure. "I did the sums, and—sorry, but I never was sure there'd be enough cash in even the busiest parking meter to make it worth the effort of breaking into the depot just to pinch pipe cutters they'd only be able to use once or twice without having to move on. The cost of the petrol alone would outweigh any money they'd make."

Brinton redirected the scowl to his subordinate. "A pity your sums couldn't work out that road-sign posts are worth more in scrap metal terms than any number of parking meters."

Foxon grinned. "I'm just a detective constable, sir. Only sergeants and above go in for higher mathematics."

Brinton grunted. "Well, even at your oh-so-humble rank you should be able to deduce why they left the chevrons propped against the stumps of the posts once they'd cut 'em off. Sharp bends have warning signs for a very good reason. Their consciences troubling them, wouldn't you say?"

"She's a very pretty girl, sir—young and pretty. If it's the same lot, that is. A pity we didn't learn anything useful from the florist." Foxon frowned. "Perhaps the metal the signs are made from hasn't as good scrap value as the steel poles they're fastened to."

"Perhaps an honest dealer would spot road signs were stolen, more easily than lengths of anonymous pipe—but relax, laddie. I'm not about to send you off on another tour of the local scrap yards." His subordinate brightened. "You can phone round 'em all instead."

As Foxon retrieved his notebook to begin leafing back through the pages for telephone numbers, Brinton grew serious. "This could be the thin end of the wedge, young Timothy. People will say we managed without signposts during the war—and Dover way the locals must be used to that Ham and Sandwich signpost disappearing on a regular basis, though that's more likely souvenir hunters than metal thieves—but theft, Foxon, is a crime. You're part of a criminal investigation department. So—start investigating!"

The rehearsal had ended with a robust chorus or two of "Fire Down Below," in which the audience would be invited to join. Mr Jessyp's cunning choice of encore (the children in gumboots; props to include clanking red buckets and coils of garden hose) would drive the message well and truly home, it was hoped by the School Re-Wiring Committee.

And yet, as she made her way towards the church, Miss Seeton's ears rang rather with "A Smuggler's Song" than with "Fire Down Below". Mr Jessyp, struggling with electricians and paperwork, had left it to herself and Miss Maynard to explain to the youngest children any words or phrases in the songs that they did not understand. In Plummergen smugglers needed no explanation. Tactful blind eyes and wilfully deaf ears were turned to modern rumours, but everyone knew of the fictional Dr Syn, Russell Thorndike's parson-pirate, retired to continued villainy in and around Romney Marsh. An author even more local than Mr Thorndike, the pseudonymous Manville Henty, had in Victorian times celebrated the Gentlemen personally known to himself and the rest of the village in his most famous work, *Night-Runners of the Marsh,* a title now prominent in twentieth-century paperback on a shelf in the post office, and displayed on Mr Stillman's revolving book-stand. Henty's centenary had boosted both interest and readership in gratifying numbers, and as he was out of copyright the village had profited greatly.

"If you do as you've been told," warbled Miss Seeton in happy tunelessness, "likely there's a chance / You'll be give a dainty doll, all the way from France." She thought of Miss Maynard's idea, and regretfully sighed for the vagaries of human nature. "With a cap of Valenciennes, and a velvet hood / A present from the Gentlemen, along o' being good!" It was an effort to reach and hold that long, mellow note, but an effort she was happy to make. "Them that asks no questions," sang Miss Seeton as she reached her destination, "isn't told a lie / Watch the wall, my darling, while the Gentlemen go by!"

The raised stone tomb stood on the north side of Plummergen's ancient church. Miss Seeton had heard the Reverend Arthur Treeves call it an altar-tomb, and in its day it had been a fine monument, carved round with festoons of fruit and flowers; but it had suffered much from the weather, being shaded by trees so that frosts lingered on its flat top in winter, and mossy growths took root and flourished in summer. In autumn the stone slab would be crimson with the waxy red berries of yew that, if not eaten by birds, lay there to be covered with leaves that slowly decayed and did further damage.

It might have been supposed that the Reverend Arthur would be a careful guardian of the tomb of Abraham Voller; but Plummergen's vicar, like so many of his predecessors, had an ambivalent regard for the historic monument, as indeed had the rest of the village. Plummergen's most notorious smuggler had by means unknown induced the vicar of the day to read the burial service over a coffin full of stones. The vicar had at least insisted that the tomb planned by Abraham should stand on the north, or less respectable, side of the church—but had then, with the sexton, winked at the careful placing of the massive edifice where no direct sunlight should fall on it; where the crack that might betray the sidestone's sliding movement was in almost permanent shade.

The Reverend Arthur had perforce to accept the history, but wondered if knowing the truth about the tomb and saying nothing against it was to encourage blasphemy. Or did he mean sacrilege? The question worried him, as a parish priest who had slowly but surely over the years lost his faith. He ministered to his flock according to (and often well beyond) his duty, but privately brooded on hypocrisy and could only hope, rather than pray, for the best. After all, how hypocritical had been that long-ago parson who knowingly committed those coffined stones to the grave? The stones were later removed; the tomb now stood empty, Abraham Voller having escaped death and, unwilling to push his luck, gone abroad. Yet while his dead body had made no use of the tomb, the living Voller and his cohorts had. Those convenient northerly shadows obscured the track of many a footstep approaching the heavy sliding slab, behind which could be concealed the ankers of brandy, the bales of cloth and tobacco, the tea and silk and lace brought illicitly from the Continent and, in due course, delivered to those who ordered them—including, Mr Treeves had little doubt, the parson of the time. The Reverend Arthur regretted that for historic reasons Plummergen had never been subject to the authority of a squire. Unsure of himself Mr Treeves might be, but for his calling he maintained due respect. He would have much preferred that the most important person in the village, the one who must lead by example, should be a layman of dubious morality rather than a member of the clergy with a similar human weakness. And yet ... who was he to judge? Life was different in those far-off times. Might he, too, in the same circumstances have shown the same weakness? Every autumn Arthur Treeves brushed fallen leaves and berries from the top of the tomb, and brooded.

Plummergen, like its vicar, was never sure about Abraham Voller. Village memory may endure, but in time it grows blurred. Almost two centuries had passed since Abraham's dramatic escape from prison. There'd always been questions asked about the long-gone smuggler, but answers weren't easy. Summat to do with money, Plummergen thought. Swindled his gang out o' their rights and sailed off to America without them. Mind you, he'd led them well, as needful, up to the last; nor he hadn't cheated 'em till the last, neither. Cunning, they'd called him: more than once pulled the wool clean over the Revenue's eyes, knowing the Marsh his whole life as he did. Having his own tomb built in such a way was smart work, too. Like the parson burying the stones—the same parson as let other Gentlemen use his pulpit for storage before there was anywhere else as safe. But by all accounts it was good fortune that Voller left no local girl to mourn his going. Cold-hearted, they might've said, except he took his sister with him—though that was the least he could do, seeing as how she'd played so big a part in his escape from prison as he waited in Rye for trial along to Maidstone and almost sure of execution in the near future, transportation at best. Plummergen born but never truly of Plummergen, he'd been. Allus thinking he was too good for the place, even with his mother dying in the workhouse! While the village saw no objection to any of its citizens bettering themselves, this should never be done at the expense of others. Abraham had escaped hanging when some of them caught along of him hadn't, being by ill fortune recaptured after their escape—let none say their own carelessness was to blame! All Abraham's cunning had bin used to save himself, and barely a thought for the rest. True enough, he'd left the secret of the tomb for them he left behind, only there'd bin too few had survived to make use of it …

Unpacking sketchbook and pencils, Miss Seeton pondered the story of Abraham Voller, cunning son of Plummergen. The false tomb: such an ingenious contrivance, though not unique—she'd read of something very similar in *Moonfleet*—and of course stories about smugglers, as with other figures of historical romance, were invariably exaggerated, as was the way with a good story. Or a sketch, when one developed it into a painting. The line remained true, but adding colour and depth could make the image more … real. Although one had to admit that sometimes it didn't. A pudding could be over-egged, a picture over-painted. Less could so often mean more. She had sometimes encouraged her pupils to look at an object for five minutes, and then not draw it. The results of drawing everything *but* the studied object could be dramatic. Negative space, framed by reality, allowed the mind's eye to register far more detail than the most scrupulously accurate pencil could achieve.

In the same way, negative commands could be more powerful than positive. Kipling's smuggler warned the child *not* to look, *not* to tell, *not* to ask questions. Would the warning have carried greater force had the words positively urged her to look the other way—find somewhere else to play—smile and chatter nonsense to questioners who paid her disarming compliments?

Once more Miss Seeton raised her voice in happy, tuneless song. "If you meet King George's men, dressed in blue and red / You be careful what you say, and mindful what is said. If they call you 'pretty maid' and chuck you 'neath the chin / Don't you tell where no one is, nor yet where no one's been!"

She was idly roughing out a little girl in smock and pinafore, resembling (apart from the heavy boots and the ringlets) Dulcie Rose Hosigg, as she drew in her breath for the chorus. "Five and twenty ponies, trotting through the dark—"

"Brandy for the Parson," a light tenor joined in behind her. "Baccy for the Clerk / Laces for a lady, letters for a spy …"

Miss Seeton stopped singing and looked round as the tenor completed the chorus. A tall, good-looking young man drew near, smiled, and bowed.

"I beg your pardon, ma'am, if I startled you, but that's one of my favourite songs, and to hear it sung right here—well, I couldn't resist. Abraham Smith," he introduced himself with another smile. "My friends call me Bram."

"Emily Seeton," said Miss Seeton, shaking the friendly hand outstretched towards her.

Bram glanced at her left, ringless hand. "Miss Seeton, glad to know you. Anyone who likes Kipling is surely a friend of mine." His gaze fell on the tomb she had begun to sketch. "And friends can keep a secret. It's Abraham *Voller* Smith, in full."

"Good gracious." Miss Seeton smiled, then nodded. "Of course. Americans are so very interested in family history, are they not?"

"You said it, Miss Seeton. Not that I'm in the direct line, I'm a distaff descendant. Old Abraham took his sister Ann with him when he sailed for America, and she's my grandmother I forget just how many generations back."

Miss Seeton hazarded a guess. "Did she marry a man called Smith?"

Bram nodded. "Oh, boy, is that an easy name to track! Unless you're real lucky with family bibles or shipping records, you may as well give up on the Smiths, but luckily there aren't too many Vollers in this world. Abraham himself was so busy making money he didn't marry until late in life, and there were no children, but every child on Ann's side had 'Voller' in there somewhere, and every generation had an Abraham or two, in case the old man took it into his head to make one of them his outright heir. He'd made plenty for everyone to have fair shares, but you know how families can be when money's involved."

Miss Seeton had no first-hand experience of family squabbles but had heard, and read, much. "Human nature does so often show to less advantage when it is a matter of inheritance. Particularly, one is given to understand, when large sums are involved—not that I wish to pry," she added hastily. A gentlewoman does not discuss money, any more than she would politics or religion. At the same time, a gentlewoman must follow the conversational lead introduced by her friends.

"I guess you could say it started out small by modern standards, but it ended up a pretty large sum in anyone's terms." Bram looked uneasy. "I've kept quiet about all this generally because Abraham left here under a bit of a cloud, the family always said. I wasn't sure how much people might remember, or how much they'd forget and—and embellish, if I started asking around." He grinned. "Then I thought, heck, people move out of villages as well as into them and maybe there'd be nobody left who'd know anything about it. But here you are, sketching the very tomb where he hid his contraband, singing all about him! Or that's how I like to think of it," he added cheerfully.

Miss Seeton smiled. "I myself moved to Plummergen only a few years ago, but some local families I believe have lived in the village for generations. Many tombstones are extremely weathered, but one has only to check in the parish registers to find the names. Our vicar, Mr Treeves, would be happy to assist you in your search, I feel sure, and he would respect your wish for privacy." She frowned. "But it is hard to suppose that anyone could bear any lasting grudge after so long ..."

Then innate honesty reminded her how Plummergen and Murreystone, a mere five miles distant across the marsh, have borne a mutual grudge since a Viking raid almost a thousand years ago overwhelmed the entire neighbourhood. Plummergen insists that Murreystone could have done more to help; Murreystone, closer to the coast, holds to it that they were invaded first. There had been no time to spare even to think of going to the aid of another village while their own was being so efficiently laid waste.

"Perhaps," said Miss Seeton, "you would care to join me in a cup of tea? As a friend," she added with another smile. The young man was evidently reluctant to trust his family research to the dear vicar. He might, however, find her own small library of interest. "Or, of course, coffee." Americans, according to films and television, lived on coffee and cookies. The latter was a foreign language and would feel awkward on her tongue—she could barely get by in French, though France was only just across the Channel—but would he know what biscuits were? "And a slice of cake." That must be safe in any language.

"Why, I take that very kindly, ma'am, and thank you. But surely I've interrupted your drawing? Had I better take a rain-check?"

"Oh, no. The sketch was intended purely for my own amusement. It isn't important. And naturally I have my umbrella with me." She indicated the bulky handbag acting as a support for one of her second-best brollies, on the ground nearby where they could be neither a distraction or a hazard. "Moreover, my cottage is only a few hundred yards away, and the sky does not appear in the least threatening. And Martha, who does for me three days a week, has made a Victoria sponge …"

It was a foreign language. A sponge? Was she offering him the chance to take a bath? Okay, so maybe the George wasn't the last word in modernity, but it was a fine hotel for its size and its age. And this Martha who did for people—surely she wasn't any kind of homicidal maniac! The old lady herself was living proof she wasn't.

"Why, I'd like that very much, thank you, Miss Seeton," he assured her, and bent to pick up her bag and umbrella.

Chapter Seven

They settled themselves in the kitchen as friends do, without formality. They drank tea rather than coffee: as Bram said, he was English by descent, and when in Rome …

He explained that descent in more detail. "Old Abe was a smart guy, Miss Seeton. Even being in gaol didn't stop him. His kid sister—my way-back grandmother—she humbugged her way in there crying over a raw onion, with a ball of fishing twine hidden in her cloak. Every night the prisoners were taken up to the roof for exercise—that was the tower in Rye, and a mighty tough nut it looks—and young Ann fixed for his pals who weren't in prison with him to have a coil of rope handy, and ponies waiting. The guys on the roof knocked out the guard, and Abe dropped his twine. His pals below fixed it to the rope, and he pulled it up and tied it to a drainpipe or something—those fishermen surely knew their knots—and down that rope they all went, on to the ponies and away!"

Miss Seeton was impressed. She'd visited Rye, seen the Ypres Tower, and felt sorry for those who'd been kept prisoner in that stout edifice in the far-off days when justice was considerably more robust than in the twentieth century. She said so now.

"Well," said Bram, "if conditions there were hard, you could say he deserved it. Abe was a guinea-smuggler, Miss Seeton, and I guess that's about as close to being a traitor as you can be without actually selling state secrets."

Miss Seeton had never heard of guinea-smugglers. Bram had studied history at college and was happy to enlighten her ignorance.

"You guys were at war with Napoleon for years, and wars cost money. I'm not sure of the political ins and outs, but Boney ran short of funds and tried to make up the shortfall by bringing in the doubloons from abroad. You Brits wanted liquor, and tobacco, and tea on the cheap; the Frogs wanted gold, to pay for the war. Fair exchange, I guess everyone thought it, even if your guys in charge were hoping to—well, to starve Boney into giving up. Except it wasn't food he'd miss out on so much as the spondulix. Not that it always took hard cash," he added with a grin. "Sometimes they used flour."

Miss Seeton knew when she was being teased. The young. She recalled her teaching days; her reply had a hint of kindly indulgence. "Lilies, no doubt, or, as the French call them, the fleur-de-lys—the former royal emblem."

Bram was affronted. "Hey, Miss Seeton, would I make fun of a friend? I mean honest-to-goodness flour, for baking bread. And cakes," he added hopefully.

His hostess, smiling now in silent apology for having misjudged him, cut her guest a third, generous slice. Bram grinned.

"Thank you, ma'am. My compliments to your Martha! Anyway, like I said, they didn't use the flour swap that often, because it was brandy and baccy and tea you really wanted, this side of the Channel. But, see, those French smugglers were fishermen just like you English—us English, I guess I could say. Anyways, they'd catch the fish along the French shore and trade it inland for sacks of flour—no hard currency to buy it with, remember? So when an English boat came along with gold, why, sometimes they'd take French flour in exchange, and sell it in England for a lot more than they paid for it."

Miss Seeton had to admire the practical nature of the deal, even as she disapproved of it. Avoiding unfair taxes might be (in historic terms) acceptable, she supposed, but helping to keep a despot on his throne was quite another.

"Why, ma'am, the writing was on the wall for Boney long before Waterloo! It wasn't as if he'd ever had one hundred per cent backing. People don't care for being beat, and there were attempts to assassinate him almost from the start. Plus, a good many of the spies he thought were selling him reliable information were really on our side all along. Double agents, and well paid—but he didn't always have the gold to pay them, and that's where the guinea-smugglers came in. See, the French built these special long, narrow galleys for the Brits to use: guinea-boats with a dozen oars or more. They could outrun any vessel that sailed, even Revenue cutters on the watch for smugglers—they could turn on one of your sixpences, and go against the wind where a sailboat never could. The boats were brought from Calais, loaded up with the guineas, and rowed back to France. People made special leather pockets to wear under their clothes because the gold was so heavy."

He sighed. "And this is where my namesake blackened his name, Miss Seeton—why the folk he left behind would have called him a cheat, a swindler—and why I've not been too sure of my welcome in your charming village, as a member of the family. See, what he did was to skim off a guinea or two every single time, and hide them away. And not in his tomb, either! Too many people knew about that tomb. Oh, Abraham was clever. An ordinary man would have spent the money right there and then on liquor or …" He hesitated.

Miss Seeton smiled. The poor young man was almost blushing in deference to her maiden status: so thoughtful. So unnecessary. Did he imagine those years at art school, her experience of the wartime blackout, had taught her nothing of human nature? "Or other pleasures of the flesh," she supplied neatly, with another smile.

Bram grinned in relief. "Exactly so, ma'am! But Abe was thinking ahead all the time. Big ideas, I guess—wanted something better for himself than fishing or smuggling or working on the land for the rest of his life. A sweet little hoard of golden guineas he must have built up—but he took a risk too many, and the authorities caught up with him. He was thrown in gaol and they thought he'd hang, but he got away with his ill-gotten gains and made it with his sister to the land of the free. He invested every red cent in the new transatlantic Packet Service the year after Waterloo, and—well—he never looked back."

"How very interesting," said Miss Seeton, who meant it. She wondered what more Mr Jessyp, so keen on history, or Dr Braxted, the professional, might be able to tell her about these remarkable guinea-boats and those who rowed them. Would it be tactless to ask this charming young man for his permission to make a few tentative enquiries? "No wonder," she said, "that you are so fond of 'A Smuggler's Song', Mr Smith. Bram. And of course it is only one of many songs the children will sing. I hope I can persuade you in due course to buy a ticket for the school concert ..."

The son of Plummergen, hopefully eyeing the last piece of cake, was thrilled at the chance of joining in a genuine Plummergen activity; and promised he would buy as many tickets as she could sell him.

In the post office, the regular gossips were gathered to discuss the latest doings, and to dissect the characters of the absent in a spirit of genial malevolence. After touching on the manufacture of scarecrows, and the surprising (to some) disappearance from a few local washing lines of old work-clothes deemed still wearable by the workers but seen by their womenfolk as fit only for the rag-bag, they were moving on to Mrs Newport and how much weight she did seem to be gaining, and it might be summat more, which with four already, not all of 'em at school yet and the house fair bursting at the seams as they grew, she did really oughter know better than to think of, only with that husband of hers you couldn't rightly blame the poor soul ... when the bell above the door pinged and Mrs Henderson hurried in.

"I just bin along to Mrs Wyght for a large brown sliced." She brandished her shopping basket. "And what do you suppose I saw?"

"A small white plain," said Mrs Skinner, as Mrs Henderson drew breath. A memorable dispute over the church flower rota some years ago—so memorable that the two ladies never forget, and are most unlikely to forgive—means that neither of the pair would gladly miss any opportunity to snipe at the other. And they don't.

"Miss Seeton," crowed Mrs Henderson, "busy a-luring of that poor young Yank staying at the George into her cottage!"

Plummergen opinion, as has been explained, is divided over Miss Seeton. Some see her as a decided asset to village life; others suspect her motives in settling there in the first place. Mrs Henderson is one of the suspicious.

Mrs Skinner, accordingly, is not. "Old enough to take care of hisself, I'd say. Most likely she's being neighbourly, as a kindness to a stranger. It was one of Martha Bloomer's days yesterday, so there'll've bin fresh cake on offer, I make no doubt."

"They were coming from the church," retorted Mrs Henderson. "What would the pair of 'em be doing there if it wasn't some sort of—of assignation? And she twice his age, if not more! Proper shocking, I call it."

Mrs Spice, who can never make up her mind which side of the feud to support, said she'd heard the school concert was to include "A Smuggler's Song" and Miss Seeton had probably gone to sketch the old Voller tomb, which would make a fine backcloth with the kiddies all turned to face it. Wouldn't it?

"Then what was *he* doing down there?" Mrs Henderson challenged the shop at large.

"Sightseeing." Mrs Skinner, today in spiky mood, gave nobody else a chance. "He's a tourist, ent he? That's what they do—look at things, and send postcards, and take photos with posh cameras, and tell everyone all about the place once they're home again."

To Emmy Putts at the grocery counter, photos meant cameras; cameras meant film. She thought of Maureen's casting-couch speculations. Mrs Stillman was in the storeroom, out of earshot and scolding range. "If he's here to make a movie," offered Emmy, "he might of bin looking for …

suitable locations." Even Emmy had no hope of immediate stardom, but there might just be a part as an extra, a stepping-stone to greater things …

In her haste Mrs Henderson hadn't properly closed the post office door, so that nobody had noticed the entrance of Miss Nuttel and Mrs Blaine. The Nuts, as these two vegetarian ladies are known, are among Plummergen's most notable mongers of rumour, scandal, and speculation.

"Is somebody making a film?" enquired plump Norah Blaine, "Bunny" to the friend with whom she shares Lilikot, a plate-glass-windowed, net-curtained bungalow almost directly opposite the post office, very convenient for the bus stop and an excellent location for looking out on the world when the world, thwarted by those net curtains, has no hope of looking in. "Eric, did you hear? Someone's making a film about Plummergen! Too exciting, don't you think?"

"Not so sure, old girl." Erica Nuttel—tall of form, equine of feature—frowned. "Spread the word too far and we could be overrun again. Birdwatchers, tourists, all the same—take up more space than you think. Always underfoot. Privacy completely lost."

Among her audience, grins were suppressed. During that recent twitcher incursion the Nut House (as Lilikot is irreverently termed) was one of the very last private dwellings anyone could suppose might designate itself, even in the short term, a Bed and Breakfast. The Nuts were sure to have weighed up the benefits of snooping opportunities against the risk that their guests might turn the tables by snooping on them; and while Plummergen, to make money, might cheerfully take such a risk—Mr Stillman sold a wide selection of locks and bolts; in daylight hours the twitchers would be out chasing the European Roller; and anyway they were all foreigners, easily outsmarted by native wit—the ladies of Lilikot held firm.

"Emmy only said he *might* be making a film." Mrs Stillman, appearing with a carton of tinned oxtail soup in time to catch the end of Emmy's remark, could guess at the rest. She'd heard too many of the fantasies and daydreams of young Miss Putts not to know how her mind worked, and dafter you couldn't find unless it was Maureen, only sometimes it was too much effort, on a busy day, to correct the silly girl.

"But if he was making a film," said Mrs Spice, "he'd be up along of that Miss Earnshaw trying to talk her into starring in it, wouldn't he? Which nobody can say they've seen him doing, so he probably ent. After all, she was real famous in her time, Catherine Earnshaw."

"He might want to find a local star," said Emmy, a little wistful. Then realism, coupled with a stern look from Mrs Stillman, made her add with envy: "Or he might want to film the school concert." Emmy's schooldays weren't so very far behind her.

"Then for why was he asking Miss Seeton's permission?" demanded Mrs Henderson. "By rights it should be Mr Jessyp. He's headmaster, while she's nobbut an incomer for all Mrs Bannet was her cousin—and part-time, at that."

"A part-time cousin!" Norah Blaine tittered gaily at the idea, inviting all to share the joke, but everyone else understood Mrs Henderson's meaning except Mrs Skinner, who achieved a snigger that sounded almost genuine. Mrs Henderson glared.

Elsie Stillman wanted no bloodshed in her shop. "If it's that young American you mean, it's obvious," she said firmly.

"Americans don't walk, they all have cars, which is why he's been hiring one or other of the Crabbes to take him about to see the sights, because there isn't always a bus. And in America they don't know how to drive on the proper side of the road like us, so he might worry about it, and he's here on holiday and who wants to worry about anything on holiday?" This logic could be faulted by no-one, and people began to calm down. Mrs Stillman, relieved, completed her argument. "With the school house up at the end of the village it'd be a waste of money to pay a taxi to take him, wouldn't it? Much easier to ask Miss Seeton, with Sweetbriars just across the road from the George and even an American could walk that far with no trouble."

Having, she hoped, settled whatever dispute might otherwise have burgeoned, Mrs Stillman reverted to her preferred role of neutral observer, calling Emmy Putts from behind the grocery counter to stack the oxtail tins in a neat pyramid, while she herself took Emmy's place and asked pointedly if she could help anyone.

Some customers made a half-hearted show of consulting lists, but others felt the matter of Bram Smith had not been fully explored.

"Could well be," offered Mrs Spice, "that he's more worried by them ghosts than he is by the driving …"

Recently there had been rumours concerning the northern part of the village. While only a few could claim to have seen it—and those who said they had had argued over every detail of what they'd seen—everyone knew that some sort of pale, shimmering form had manifested itself during hours of darkness before vanishing, nobody knew where, in utter silence. Or perhaps it was two forms, at different times: they argued about that, too, though it was generally felt that two silent ghosts at the same time stretched coincidence too far. But all agreed on the silence—and it was this that made Plummergen uneasy. Groans, moans, and clanking chains were to be expected when unquiet spirits roamed abroad. Silence hinted at a depth of emotion so very deep that this particular spirit (or spirits) roused from eternal slumber by the recent devil-red skies had clearly undergone terrible torment during its (or their) time on earth. Everyone knew that people could be struck dumb with terror and, as in life, why not in death? It would take a long time—nobody dared guess how long—before these memories faded and the ghost, likewise, could fade just as the red skies that first summoned it had done. After all, it hadn't faded with them. Which only proved how powerful its memory, how intense the haunting, must be.

An exorcism might have set minds at rest, but not enough villagers came forward to bear reliable witness and justify a second petition to the vicarage. Miss Treeves had been highly dismissive of the first small, shrill, quarrelsome deputation that demanded audience with the vicar but made the mistake of telling his sister why. Molly Treeves was adamant that the Reverend Arthur wouldn't dream of such a thing and even if he did—should they ever decide exactly what it was they thought they'd seen—the bishop would require details far more convincing than "summat shivery and white" before he agreed to issue a licence. They should pull themselves together and forget such nonsense. If they'd been told once they'd been told a dozen times that the strange colour of the sky had been caused by desert winds, and the devil in any case had far weightier matters to occupy his mind than stirring up ghosts near Plummergen Common.

"From what you say," concluded Miss Treeves, "it was probably Catherine Earnshaw taking a walk. Saturday Stop is beside the Common. I believe she has difficulty sleeping, and she always dresses in white." So prosaic a solution appealed to nobody, but Molly had a commanding eye and the deputation, grumbling under its collective breath, drifted away.

The Nuts, living in the centre of the village as they did, nevertheless had joined the little group of petitioners in case the revenant should tire of the Common and head further south. Now Norah Blaine lost the final traces of her smile, and shuddered.

"Oh, Eric, Mrs Spice is too right! Molly Treeves should really have listened to us instead of sneering in that cruel way. If a strong young man can show such concern for his mental and spiritual wellbeing—although as an American he probably eats steak all the time, which of course is poison to the system—"

"*Mens sana in corpore sano*," agreed Miss Nuttel as Bunny drew breath.

"—then that only proves our worries were justified! If anything dreadful happens now we'll all know who's to blame, but by then it will be far too late."

Emmy Putts dropped a soup tin. Mrs Stillman, knowing that yet again she must leave the sidelines to quell incipient hysteria, was sharp. "Nothing won't happen in daylight, you may be sure—if it's going to happen at all, which I take leave to doubt. Has anyone seen mysterious white shapes during the day? Well, there you are. Mr Smith's as safe as anyone else, he just don't fancy the walk to the school house. Emmeline, pick up that tin before someone trips over it, and straighten the one on top. Don't you dare add any more until the whole display is properly balanced."

Emmy, muttering, did as she was told. Mrs Stillman retreated again to the grocery counter, distancing herself from the hubbub of speculation that now broke out. Miss Nuttel, affronted on Mrs Blaine's behalf, remarked loudly that queer things could happen any hour of the day or night. Not as if there were rules about ghosts: midnight wasn't compulsory, just traditional. Ghosts had minds of their own. Any time, night or day. Same the world over.

"Funny. You'd never think of an American minding about ghosts, would you?" Mrs Skinner frowned. "With all them tough-guy gangsters and cowboys over there." Plummergen learns much about the outside world from films, television, and the tabloid press.

"Probably got more ghosts than we have, spending so much time shooting each other," said Mrs Henderson. "All of 'em with guns. Easy to be tough and care for nothing with a gun in your hand. Except—with ghosts—what use are guns in the dark?"

"Oh, Eric," cried Mrs Blaine. "I never thought. Just suppose he brought a gun with him from America. As Mrs Henderson says, it's hard to see what you're doing in the dark, and of course we have no street lighting. None of us will be safe going anywhere after sunset until that young man has left the George—whoever he is. I'm sure I can't think why he's stayed so long, anyway."

Mrs Henderson reminded her that he'd been seen accompanying Miss Seeton into her cottage. Both Nuts frowned, shook their heads, and looked dubious. They'd never been sure about Miss Seeton, and this only went to show how justified were their original doubts. "If she's going to start blazing away with guns in the middle of the night the way she did when she first came here," said Norah Blaine, remembering that long-ago hen-house raider who had tried to dispose of Miss Seeton and failed, "I for one will expect someone to do something about it. But we all know it's no use going to the police."

"In her pocket, every man jack," agreed Miss Nuttel.

"The vicar must speak to her," declared Mrs Blaine, above murmurs of dissent from Miss Seeton's admirers. "And we could ask again about exorcism. If the temporal powers refuse to help—as they always do when that woman's involved—then the spiritual powers must be made to do their duty!"

Upon which, the post office erupted.

While Mrs Blaine was busy slandering the constabulary, the constabulary had more serious matters on its collective mind. With Delphick doggedly pursuing, on the other side of Kent and in London, the case of the murdered poacher and finding nothing, in Ashford the office of Superintendent Brinton buzzed with a three-way telephone conversation that did little to brighten anyone's day.

"Another council depot." Glumly, Brinton echoed the words of Harry Furneux. "Yours this time, but not a repeat performance of ours with the cones and the dunce's caps—"

"Different shaped pillars to the gates," interposed the Fiery Furnace.

"—because it was obvious from the start a load of stuff'd been half-inched. Nobody had to go looking for what was taken, the way they did in Ringstave."

"Road signs and support poles," confirmed Harry. "Plus it was obvious they'd broken in by the main gate—they even had the cheek to pinch the padlock and chain!"

Foxon spluttered, and received stereo reminders that this was no laughing matter. He looked his apology to Brinton, but spoke it to Furneux. "Sorry, sir. But at least now they're leaving garden gates and railings alone."

"If it's the same lot," gloomed Brinton into his extension. "They're trying to make it look that way, but there's no definite indication that it *is* them again." He sighed. "Or that it isn't."

"You've lost sign poles," said his Sussex counterpart, "and so have we. Yes, there's a difference in our lot taking the signs as well—Road Closed, Men At Work, a couple of stop-go lollipops, that sort of thing—but they weren't out on the open road, like yours."

"She's still in intensive care, sir. Slowly improving." Foxon had become decidedly proprietorial about the beautiful young blonde, calling the hospital for an update every day.

"So their consciences wouldn't let 'em take any more roadside warnings," Furneux said, "and that's why they settled for grabbing what signs they could and packing 'em nice and flat in a truck, with the poles in a separate van. You can tell there were two, from the tyre tracks. My guess is the word's got round they're doing okay and they've recruited some help."

"So the gang's got bigger," said Brinton. "Unless, like I said, it's not the same gang."

"Whoever they are," said Superintendent Furneux, "they're growing more ambitious. This raid was better organised than yours. More stuff gone missing."

"Practice makes perfect," offered Foxon.

"Shuttup," snapped Brinton.

"Or perhaps," continued Foxon, oblivious to snubs he knew came automatically, "the price of scrap metal has gone down and they need to swipe more of the stuff to be paid the same amount of money."

"Perhaps," said Furneux, "the price has gone up and they're getting greedy. Either of you checked the financial pages today?"

"Shuttup both of you!" cried Brinton, slamming the telephone down on its cradle to free both hands for tearing his hair. Foxon, looking shocked, shook his head.

"Sorry, Mr Furneux," he told his own extension. "Once he's had his sugar fix he'll be fine—won't you, sir?"

Brinton glared, hesitated, then grinned. When next he spoke he was breathing extra-strong peppermint fumes into his phone. "Sorry, Harry. Got a bit carried away." He heard Foxon's gurgle of mirth and added, before the young man could utter one of the jokes for which you had to be in the mood: "Carried away, same as your Road Closed signs. We'll put the usual word out, of course, but somehow I don't think we'll learn much."

"Someone might just talk," said Furneux hopefully. "With a bigger gang, it all depends on how carefully they were picked. If they *have* been carefully picked ..." He coughed. "If they have, then could be—well, could be we need the—the bigger picture, as you might say, at this stage ..."

"I'll think about it," said Brinton, and once more slammed the telephone on its cradle.

Foxon was superb. He neither chortled, laughed, nor even smiled. His countenance was grave as he looked at his superior. "He might be right, sir," was all he said.

The crunch of Brinton's peppermint was the only sound to disturb the lengthy pause that followed. Foxon tried again.

"She could just have some inkling of what's been going on—or who's doing it. Everyone reads the local rag. They'll all know about Phoebe Stanley's car crash, and why it happened, and who was ultimately responsible. They might even've had their own gates or railings vanish—"

"No," said Brinton. Defiantly, he took a second mint from the bag; Foxon said nothing. "Potter has his standing orders, remember, never mind the weekly reports. If anything—anything—untoward happens within a five-mile radius of Miss Seeton, he's to let us know at once. Ned Potter's a good, honest, reliable copper. Only a constable, same as you—but unlike you he isn't going to risk getting in my bad books by not remembering to do what he's been told."

Foxon tried to look hurt, but his heart wasn't in it. He could guess why the superintendent was reluctant to consult Scotland Yard's official Art Consultant. Brinton knew and liked Miss Seeton; after a slightly bumpy start he'd come over the years to work well with her, and these days her uncanny sketches held few worries for him, apart from those of interpretation and even the Oracle, acknowledged Seeton expert though he was, boggled sometimes in the early stages. But the cases in which Brinton, or the Yard, or other official forces involved MissEss (as the police computer has dubbed her) tended to be at the heavier end of the criminal scale. Murder, kidnapping, drugs, fraud, gambling and extortion ... Old Brimstone thought so highly of Miss Seeton he was downright embarrassed about asking her advice on something as trivial as an outbreak of scrap metal thievery in a small local area.

But it was *her* local area. Brimmers must've forgotten that. Foxon tried again.

"Could be another nasty accident if anyone pinched the drains or the manhole covers from Plummergen, sir."

"The Street's wide enough that nobody ever needs to drive in the gutter, laddie."

"They've no lamp-posts, remember. Black as pitch, that place is at night. Every bit as bad as heavy rain, for visibility."

"When they go out in the dark they all carry torches." Brinton inserted his peppermint, savoured it, and then sighed. "Foxon, I hate you. Of course I know it's the most sensible thing we could do, but … to be honest, young Tim, it feels wrong even to think of taking up Miss Seeton's time with anything so—so frivolous as a few drain covers and a lorry-load of road signs."

"The thin end of the wedge, sir. Oaks and acorns, like Mr Furneux said."

"So he did, and from what he's been telling us he was right. But it still feels …" Brinton savoured again, in thoughtful silence. "The Oracle's up to his eyes with that dead poacher Customs and Excise tripped over," he said at last, "and I happen to know he's getting nowhere." Foxon was surprised. Friends of long standing Mr Delphick and old Brimstone might be, but he didn't realise they had cosy chats on the phone when the cases they were working on had nothing in common.

"Mabel Potter told her husband, who thought I'd be interested," Brinton explained. "Mabel had it from Mrs Knight, who had it from her daughter—who barely remembers what your pal Ranger looks like, the case is taking up so much time. I wonder if the Yard have any plans to visit this part of the world in the near future, to consult a certain artistic party. It'd make sense. Consultations are what she's paid for."

"Poor Anne," said Foxon, thinking of lonely Mrs Ranger and the infant Gideon. "Did she come back to stay with her parents at the nursing home? If she did, then I bet it won't be long before Bob heads this way. If the Oracle—Mr Delphick—ever lets him off the leash. Or comes with him, perhaps. Sir."

There was a further savouring silence.

"Foxon, you're not so daft as you look." Brinton crunched peppermint, and swallowed the remains. He picked up the telephone for an outside line. "We'll ask him, shall we?"

Chapter Eight

It wasn't until next morning that Brinton managed to speak with Delphick. The superintendent arrived at Ashford to find a message that Mr Delphick had called last night, and would call again today. Brinton knew it made no sense for the pair of them to be to-and-fro phoning until one caught up with the other; and waited. He felt uneasy about the whole business, and hadn't wanted to go into too much detail yesterday. Mr Delphick (the superintendent had been informed by an apologetic Yard switchboard) was out—yes, Sergeant Ranger too—pursuing enquiries in Kent. If he was sure nobody else would do, then if he left a message the switchboard would see that Mr Delphick got it.

"As, eventually, I did," Delphick said now, "but by the time I called back you'd gone home. As it didn't sound urgent I thought it best not to disturb you there when it was so late." His tone, already dry, became even drier. Bob, an interested eavesdropper, marvelled at his superior's control. He'd been with the Oracle last evening on his return to the office. "I said 'eventually', because an eager and, fortunately for him, anonymous young beaver delivering background files during our absence yesterday believed the information therein contained to be of vital importance. It was indeed important, but insufficiently so to justify the resultant … disturbance." Sergeant Ranger thought this the understatement of the year. "The beaver in his eagerness tidied away much of my desktop paperwork, on which before my departure for Kent I had been studiously working, to give to his delivery the prominence he felt it deserved. As well as throwing my investigative notes into disarray the young idiot somehow contrived to include your message among his tidying—with the inevitable result."

"These things happen. And my affair is nothing like yours. Er—how did you get on in your favourite English county, or shouldn't I ask?"

"I'd rather you didn't. Dead ends and blind alleys make a tedious recital." Delphick's tone lightened. "However, since you were kind enough to ask, let me advise you that the visits we have made in recent days, the questions we have asked, seem to achieve nothing beyond a temporary increase in our general knowledge. We are currently experts on the habits of poachers and on their lives, both public and private. We've learned the strength required to wring a rabbit's neck. Or," more soberly, "how to cut a man's throat almost to the bone as you strangle him. But none of Gawdy's associates knows, or at least is willing to tell us, anything useful. Customs and Excise have apparently been working on the tobacco-smuggling angle, but admit—grudgingly—to being in the same situation as ourselves."

"Stuck," said Brinton.

"Like glue. Against a wall of solid brick." Having given vent to his feelings, Delphick sounded almost cheerful. "A change of topic might help to clear the mental fog. What particular assistance would you like the Yard to render you?"

"It's pretty small beer compared to murder, but young Fox-on—" Foxon looked up from his notebook— "insists that great oaks grow from little acorns and we ought to be nipping this one in the bud. Something flowery along those lines, anyway."

"Inspired by his wardrobe, no doubt. His shirts—but enough nonsense, Chris. Out with it. Spill, to continue your pleasing horticultural metaphor, the beans."

Brinton told of the metal gates and railings, the drain covers, the road signs and the unfortunate Phoebe Stanley, still in her hospital bed. "And we've no more idea than you who's responsible. We're glued alongside the very same brick wall. And we wondered … It was Harry Furneux who first put the idea in my head, but … Would Miss Seeton be able to help? Would it even be right to ask her?"

"Why not? She's paid an annual retainer, Chris. She knows her duty and always does it, whether she fully understands the question or not, but I don't see her having any difficulty with the concept of theft. On the occasion of our first meeting she told me she didn't carry more than a small amount of cash in her handbag because it was unfair to tempt people. Chunks of metal in full view must present even greater temptation, to the susceptible, than a handful of coins and a couple of notes in a purse."

"I don't suppose you've thought of consulting her over this poacher of yours? I should think Customary Excuses wouldn't object if you asked her about the smuggling, either, and Foxon agrees with me—pick up the extension, laddie. That okay, Oracle? Save having to keep repeating ourselves. So, I know MissEss doesn't smoke, but neither do you—and they've been quick enough to rope you in."

"And while I'm about it, I could also be your spokes-man? She doesn't bite, Superintendent." The listening Foxon choked. "Ah, yes. If you'd prefer not to ask her yourself, send Foxon along. They've always got on well."

Brinton laughed. "Of course they get on. They even spent the night together once." Again Foxon choked. Down the line from London came a chuckle, and a laugh.

"You hear Bob agrees with me," Delphick said. "He recalls as well as I do that witchcraft nonsense, and the Satanists in the burning church. I can't deny you'd be ideal for the job, Timothy, but I fear it would be asking too much of Miss Seeton's hospitality to expect her to field two visits from the police so close together. As Mr Brinton has so cleverly guessed, having hit our brick wall and talked the matter over with Customs, we had already decided it was high time we paid a visit to a different part of Kent."

Miss Seeton was delighted to see them and said so, beaming upon Bob and reassuring him that she had been to tea at the nursing home only yesterday, and Anne and the baby looked very well, although of course they missed him … She turned a thoughtful eye upon Bob's gently smiling boss.

The smile broadened. "Have no fear, Miss Seeton. Now that Sergeant Ranger has delivered me via Ashford to your door his job, for the moment, is done. If you'll permit me to use your telephone once our own business is complete, I can rid myself of him until there is further need of his services. In this charming village he is sure to find a way of filling his time."

Bob grinned, made his grateful adieux and was gone.

"That was kind, Mr Delphick. Dear Bob has no particular interest in my little scribbles." Miss Seeton twinkled at him as she led him down the hall. "Indeed, Anne tells me he was most amusing about photographs, when I sent them the pencil sketch of dear Gideon taken from memory, after the christening. They are such a happy little family." She sighed for the pleasure of it all. "No doubt that is why sunshine seemed appropriate in the portrait when, as I recall, the day itself was rather cloudy."

Her fellow godparent nodded. "Yes, indeed, though fortunately not enough cloud for rain." Delphick, to his surprise, had experienced a flash of relief at her innocent description of the baby's portrait. Evidently the future, in Miss Seeton's view, held no particular horrors for young Master Ranger. Bob's jokes about photography had probably been relief too, rather than any lack of tact or artistic judgement.

"But you are here for an IdentiKit sketch," Miss Seeton reminded herself as they looked into the sitting room. "As you see, I have everything ready—and also in the kitchen, should you wish for a cup of tea before we begin. Martha has a new recipe for a chocolate marble cake," she added.

"Then I'll help bring the things in." Delphick cheerfully followed as she headed for kettle, tap, and teapot. "May I give you a quick précis first? The photos I have to show you aren't exactly the run-of-the-mill corpse I know you take in your stride, but I also know that you saw many unpleasant sights during the Blitz."

"People in pieces." Delphick hid a start. He'd often wondered if she might be psychic. If it was a choice between that and reading his mind, he preferred the former. Miss Seeton had a gentlewoman's respect for privacy, both her own and that of others. "In the circumstances," she went on, "it was sometimes unavoidable, but far ... messier," she frowned for a more suitable word and couldn't find one, "than the bodies I saw at the hospital. Bomb-blast and injury from shattered glass or falling masonry do more damage to the human frame—dogs and cats, too, though many had been rehomed to the country where there was more food; or put to sleep, poor things—more damage than can be achieved, I should hope, by the most violent individual."

"This particular individual almost decapitated his victim, I fear."

She hesitated. "What modern dramatists, no doubt, would call an angry young man. Or perhaps a man who does not know his own strength, when in a temper."

It was what they'd wondered themselves. Delphick nodded. "We've no idea who he is—a 'she' is unlikely, we think—but we know the name of his victim. I'd rather not cloud your judgement by telling you too much about him, but we know almost everything from his shoe size to his favourite tipple. We can guess at the reason for his presence in the place where he was killed—though again I'd rather not say too much— but we have no idea *why* he was killed. We can hazard a few guesses, some more possible than others, but we do seem to be guessing in the dark. In short, we've come up against a rather solid brick wall that, to continue the metaphor, casts a heavy investigative shadow. One of your special sketches might just throw a little light on the whole affair."

Miss Seeton shook her head over the stark black-and-white photographs of the late Isaiah Gawdy. Every detail was un-comfortably clear. "He was lying under a bush in open country," Delphick said. "The body wasn't moved after death, or at least not very far, and if it was, then it would have been very soon afterwards." There had been no drag-marks on the ground, no betraying post mortem discolouration.

Miss Seeton picked up a stick of charcoal, gazed at it, and put it down again. "Something more … colourful, I think," and rummaged for her pencils.

Isaiah had by all accounts been a colourful character, thought Delphick. One up to MissEss before she'd even started. He'd deliberately shown her the black and white prints first to lessen the impact of the poacher's appearance, tidied up by the investigators though it had been. The colour photos were his second line of approach, kept in reserve should nothing inspire her at the first time of asking. They were enough to make even such a hardened investigator as himself wish he didn't have to look at them.

"In open country," murmured Miss Seeton, and doodled a rabbit scuttling towards its burrow, tail a-bob and ears flattened. She added a male figure, surprised at the rabbit's speed, standing transfixed with a shotgun broken over his arm. "Oh, dear, I'm so sorry. It was remembering the war, I expect. He looks nothing like the poor man, does he?"

Delphick smiled at her. She'd caught on quickly that Isaiah had been a poacher; no need to blame memories of the popular wartime song. "Run, rabbit, run," he agreed. "The farmer's gun, though, seems unlikely this time to go bang, bang, bang, bang. This time he'll have to get by without his rabbit pie." And how had she known the body had been found, the murder probably been committed, on Friday as mentioned in the song? Yes, he'd prefer 'psychic' to 'mind reader' any day …

Miss Seeton was doodling again, and with more urgency. Delphick sat alert. This was the inspiration, the insight, he'd hoped she'd find. He continued ostensibly to smile over the rabbit-and-farmer sketch as he snatched glances at her reflection in the glass of the "Grey Day" picture she'd thought, so long ago, looked like him. She'd thought at the same time that Bob looked like a footballer. Anne had asked to buy that particular picture, and Miss Seeton happily gave it to her:

once the insight had been captured on paper, she seemed to have no further need for the result. Delphick wondered why he'd never dared request his own likeness from those far-off days. She had painted a picture Bob considered rather cold, but nice-looking on the whole …

"Oh, dear," said Miss Seeton again. She made to rip the completed sketch from the block with more vigour than she'd shown with the rabbit. Delphick stayed her hand. "Before you throw it in the bin, may I see?"

"But it—it's so silly! I fear I was again distracted, this time by your talk of hitting—coming up against—that is to say," blushing for her apparent rudeness, "it wasn't at all your fault. Rather, it was mine, for failing to concentrate in a proper manner."

Delphick studied the sketch. "That's Isaiah's face," he reassured her, and explained in a few words who the victim was. She was cheered by learning he'd been a poacher.

"Which may explain the rabbit—although, as you already knew, I can't see that it is of much help," she added as, enlightenment dawning, the chief superintendent uttered a quick exclamation, and beamed. "Or … is it?" she asked uneasily. "It was the school play one year, a very *modern* production—the costumes in particular, although it was the girls who protested rather than their parents, which was a surprise—but rather immoral, I always feel, to send out such a message. The happy ending is based, you will recall, on what can only be called a lie. The magic juice remains on the eyes of Demetrius long after he has woken. Poor Helena, as I see it, though of course I am no expert, even then has her doubts as to the sincerity of his affection, for she refers to him as 'mine own, and not mine own' and that is hardly the basis for a happy relationship, is it? One does expect honesty from Shakespeare himself, as a writer, even if his characters behave sometimes in most dishonest ways. Iago, for instance, although Mrs Benn never did *Othello* ...”

Delphick, for once oblivious to her courteous chatter, drew a deep, satisfied breath. “So there *is* a connection. We wondered, but now we know for certain.” Miss Seeton’s puzzled expression showed that she wasn’t at all certain, but she was too polite to say so.

The scene was unmistakeable to anyone who’d ever seen *A Midsummer Night’s Dream.* The sketch showed two male figures, one in a long, elaborate wig that half covered a heavily-masked face above sturdy shoulders; his lower half was concealed behind a wall. The other man was a swaggering, larger-than-life hero, preparing to approach the wall. A close glance showed that the hero’s face bore a likeness to that of Isaiah Gawdy; even closer inspection revealed a hand sketched lightly against the bricks of the wall, the fingers and thumb crooked apart to form a small chink. Overhead a moon rode ghostly in the sky; near the wall a small dog sat waiting, under a bush covered in spiky thorns.

“The most lamentable comedy, and most cruel death of Pyramus and Thisby,” quoted Delphick with satisfaction. “Thank you, Miss Seeton. You’ve been a great help.”

She smiled back at him. “I’m pleased to hear it,” she said, still puzzled.

He laughed. “Never mind for now. Later, perhaps. Tell me, was your modern production of *A Midsummer Night’s Dream* well received?”

It was as he prepared to telephone the nursing home for Bob that he sat back on his chair and rebuked himself. “I’m a fool. I forgot. It was the satisfaction of having a proper lead at last in the murder case—no more guesswork. Thanks to you, we know the motive wasn't personal … But I have another request for your time and talent, from Superintendent Brinton. No doubt you've heard of the recent spate of metal theft in this part of the world?"

The local paper had made it front-page news, she told him, especially after the accident to that poor young woman. She had wondered if her own metal fence might fall victim to the gang, Sweetbriars being on the corner, and thus visible from more than one direction. "But while one must deplore criminal activity, Chief Superintendent, one should keep a sense of proportion. The railings are a replacement for the fence that burned down a few years ago. The fire might well have spread to my cottage, rather than simply destroy a row of wooden palings. When compared with the tragedy of a young woman's having so nearly lost her life, at the very start of her life in the wider world—well, one feels very sorry for her, and realises one's own good fortune. It would be distressing, of course, should the thieves strike in Plummergen, but hardly a threat to my own life. Because I don't drive, you may recall."

Delphick thought back to the time he and Bob, in fascinated dismay, had watched two vans crawl erratically towards Brettenden, one hard on the heels of the other and swinging all over the road. Miss Seeton, rescued from kidnap, was at the wheel, on tow behind her rescuer and dangerously ill at ease with the concept of a brake pedal. She had (she told the jury later, at her kidnapper's trial) been a little annoyed about the damage to her hat, her head being still muzzy from petrol fumes …

"No, you don't drive," he agreed.

"So very fortunate, those packets of soap flakes and bottles of ginger beer in the back of the van. I asked Jack Crabbe about it once, and he explained what they can do to an engine and how much it would cost to repair. For a moment I did wonder if—"

"No, Miss Seeton, you should *not* have offered to pay. You could have been killed. I know you find the idea hard to credit, but believe me, that red-haired young hoodlum wasn't playing games. He was hired to do away with you, and he almost succeeded. The only recompense due him was the prison sentence he received. Besides," Delphick added more gently, "it wasn't his van. He stole it, and the owner was adequately insured." He smiled at her. "But that is in the past. It's the present that concerns us now. I've no photos to show you—after all, one drain cover differs very little from another, and you know what road signs look like—but you've read about what's been happening. Any thoughts you may have as to the identity of the gang would be gratefully received by Superintendent Brinton and by Superintendent Furneux, who's at the Sussex end where they've been having similar problems—oh, and Timothy Foxon sends his best wishes, too."

Miss Seeton beamed. "Dear Mr Foxon. Such a spirited concept of dress. These days the young have such confidence in themselves. They put colours together that would never have seemed possible, to previous generations."

"It was a plum-coloured jacket with a pale orange shirt, when I saw him—yes, I know," as she blinked, "but he seems to think it works. The male of the species is generally more colourful than the female, and young Foxon's not married. Quite the squire of dames in his free time, I imagine."

A brief argument, which Miss Seeton lost, ended with Delphick carrying the tea-things out to the kitchen while Miss Seeton retrieved last week's local paper. *The Brettenden*

Telegraph and Beacon (est.1847, incorporating [1893] The Iverhurst Chronicle and Argus) had given due prominence to the fact that Phoebe Stanley remained in hospital; reminded its readers in detail why; and demanded to know what the police were doing about it. Miss Seeton refreshed her memory, and settled down at the table with her sketchbook.

Reluctantly, she showed the result of her labours to a politely insistent Delphick. The first sketch was of a young woman, her head bandaged, lying in a hospital bed with drips attached to her arms and a medical attendant at her side, taking her pulse. Nothing remarkable here. Had the editor of a women's magazine asked for an illustration to a Doctor And Nurse romance, this drawing would have been ideal.

The second sketch …

"I'm so sorry. I was thinking of Mr Foxon, I suppose, as something of a lady-killer, and the film was on television not long ago and I watched it for old time's sake. I remember going to the cinema when it was first released, and being highly amused by the old lady with her troublesome umbrella." Delphick hid a smile.

"A film guaranteed to deter anyone from letting out rooms to paying guests," he said with admirable gravity. Miss Seeton ventured a little joke. "Or from keeping parrots." She was thankful he didn't seem too disappointed that what she'd drawn had nothing at all to do with metal-stealing gangs. Possibly the metal was already in the removal van, its weight making it roll down the hill across the road …

"A pantechnicon," said Delphick, "so heavily loaded with, presumably, stolen goods—presumably metal—that the brakes have failed. I'm surprised the springs haven't gone as well—or," knowing her fondness for old movies, "that the floor hasn't given way as it did in *The Lavender Hill Mob*."

Miss Seeton smiled. "Certainly, gold would have been far easier to transport, with so much less of it being required than its equivalent value in scrap iron or steel."

"Which would be hardly worth the effort of melting down into models of the Eiffel Tower. I forget the name of the man who in real life sold the Eiffel Tower for scrap—twice—but you can't deny he made an effort. Is this the only one?" Delphick had noted that instinctive move to close her sketchbook; her attempt to change the subject.

Looking guilty, she passed the book across to him.

"The railway bridge in *The Ladykillers*." He recognised the view at once, an overhead shot looking down on the tracks. "With the string quartet—no, you've drawn a trio—playing their instruments inside one of the freight trucks. A scene that isn't in the film, and they couldn't play more than a gramophone record, anyway. Of course, the bodies were dropped into freight trucks for disposal, weren't they? Somewhat risky, I've always felt. The authorities would surely keep records of the route of each particular train, what it carried, and where it came from. Sooner or later somebody must have made enquiries in Mrs Wilberforce's area. Hmm. I hope you don't suggest that the metal thieves intend next to uproot lengths of railway line. That would be a greater risk to the general public even than the taking of road signs or drain covers."

"I'm sorry, Chief Superintendent, but I really can't say."

"Railway lines are made of metal, as are some railway bridges, but stealing a railway bridge would be no small-time job. Up until now we have supposed the gang to be both local, and limited in number. It's possible they've been recruiting. We'll have to think about this—about these, Miss Seeton." He added all four sketches to the envelope that already held the rabbit-and-farmer drawing. Food for thought indeed; but they could now be fairly certain the death of Isaiah Gawdy was connected with the tobacco smuggling. Pressure must be put on Customs and Excise to co-operate. Pursuit of other leads, while they must remain on file, could be abandoned. As to the metal thefts …

Back in Brinton's Ashford office Delphick produced, with a flourish, Miss Seeton's sketches. "I had time to think about them as we drove here, but I'd nevertheless be grateful for your input, gentlemen." Foxon and Ranger hovered watchfully at hand as he set the rabbit drawing, and the *Dream* cartoon, on Brinton's desk. "I'd say that you and I, Bob, should now heartily twist the arm of Customary Excuses for more information on the tobacco smugglers. Pyramus and Thisbe, you see?" He enlarged briefly on the "Wall" scene in *A Midsummer Night's Dream.* "Miss Seeton said she thought my saying we were up against a brick wall inspired this, but I believe she thinks there's a definite link with the murder of that unfortunate poacher—and so should we. Isaiah Gawdy almost certainly set his snares in the wrong place, at the wrong time."

"Run, rabbit, run. I get it." Brinton hummed a few bars under his breath, then sobered. "Okay, that's your case on the right track at last, but what about ours?"

"And 'track' I sincerely hope is not the appropriate word, though I fear it may be." Delphick hesitated. "Yet I find it hard to see how even the largest gang of metal thieves could remove lengths of railway line either efficiently or safely— still, my guess is that before very long you'll have a spot of railway-related crime either in your area, Chris, or over the border in Sussex. As you told me that neither you nor Harry Furneux had manpower to spare—indeed, does anyone?—my advice would be to alert the transport police and let them keep as much of an extra eye on things as they can spare."

"All a bit vague." Brinton stabbed a finger at the freight-wagon sketch. "Does this mean there're only three people involved? But as you say, even the largest gang's unlikely to go for the big stuff. Reckon they'll go back to pinching metal fences? We'd best warn the railway cops to keep that eye on the goods yards. Plenty of fences there."

Foxon stirred. As well as garden gates, stolen metal fences interested him. "And to watch out for removal vans, sir? I'd have thought a proper lorry would do a better job."

"But more obvious," suggested Bob. "Who'd really notice a removal van broken down on the road outside? A lorry'd give the game away at once."

"*The Ladykillers* is about a bank robbery," said Brinton. "They're not stealing metal."

"The railway is a theme throughout the film," Delphick reminded him. "The soundtrack is filled with the noise of passing trains. The old lady goes by taxi to the main line station to collect the professor's trunk, and—"

He broke off as the faces of the two younger men expressed ignorance of the plot of *The Ladykillers*, that darkest of the celebrated Ealing comedies. No Fifties film buff could do anything but relish the wholesale family slaughter of *Kind Hearts and Coronets,* but there is something about *The Ladykillers* that can make the viewer uneasy.

Once again the chief superintendent enlarged on a plot. "... rent the old lady's spare room to discuss their plans ... record player prevents eavesdropping ... label on the telephone box to say it's out of order ... a runaway lorry blocks the road in front of the van carrying the cash ... only one route clear ..."

Foxon looked at Bob Ranger, then at Delphick. "With respect, sir, it sounds like an early version of *The Italian Job*. MissEss prefers old films, so perhaps she hasn't seen this one and *The Ladykillers* is the closest her subconscious can get—"

"Shuttup, Foxon!" Brinton's roar deafened them all. "Good grief, if you're right—never mind the parking meters, but if they tried that in Maidstone ..." Then words failed him.

Delphick was amused. "I take it you've seen *The Italian Job*." Brinton muttered something about his wife's preference for blue-eyed film stars. "Then you'll recall that the horrendous traffic jam in Turin was caused by expert infiltration of the computer traffic system, not by a runaway lorry. Apart from rumours of an experimental installation in, I believe, Glasgow I've heard nothing about any town in Britain with its road junctions and traffic lights under computer control. I should think you're safe, unless somebody notices three Mini cars behaving in an unorthodox manner near a sewage farm."

Brinton muttered again. This time it was more forceful.

He did more than mutter when, having waved the Yard contingent once more on its way and settled to some serious brooding, he heard his telephone ring and jumped halfway out of his chair. "If that's Harry Furneux—" he began.

But it wasn't. "Ned Potter here, sir," came the voice of Plummergen's beat bobby.

Brinton shuddered. He'd promised to pass on to Sussex the results of today's oracular visit to Miss Seeton, but he was still trying to make sense of the drawings himself, and Foxon wasn't being a lot of help. If on top of it all the old girl'd decided to throw one of her typical spanners in the works ... "Don't tell me. Someone's turned up with a van and a chainsaw and made off with Miss Seeton's garden railings."

"Er," said PC Potter. "Was you expecting summat of the sort, Mr Brinton? Because if so, then I'd better—"

"No, I wasn't!" Brinton took a deep breath as Foxon stared. Normally he was the only victim when old Brimstone needed to let off steam. "No." Brinton forced himself to speak calmly. "Has somebody abandoned a removal van bang in the middle of the level crossing with the train coming through any minute?"

"Er," said PC Potter. "Not that I've heard, sir."

Foxon continued to stare and Brinton, rolling his eyes, sighed as he motioned the young man to pick up the extension. "Sorry, Potter. What did you want to tell me? It's not your usual day for the Standing Orders report, so I know something must be up." Foxon grinned. Brinton glared. "Nothing too serious, I hope," begged the superintendent. "Just … out of the usual way of things, but not that important?" His tone was almost pleading.

Foxon crossed anxious fingers. Potter could have no idea how much stress he was putting on old Brimstone's blood pressure.

"I'm not rightly able to judge how important, sir, for it happened a few days since and Mr Burscough didn't tell me till now and iffen they'd been really worried, I should've supposed they'd not have left it so long. Only, being now official, I felt you did ought to know. This young Burscough, he's Miss Earnshaw's secretary, being the one as orders the groceries and such, when he ent busy helping write her book or keeping an eye on the hired help to make sure the lady's not disturbed. We don't hardly ever see her round the village, on account of her sleeping odd times of the day and not wanting cameras and folk staring, he says. But they've had burglars, sir, and they stole some expensive stuff as well as being a queer thing to do, to my mind. Bit unpleasant, when you think about it."

"Catherine Earnshaw? That film star staying in the renovated bungalow? Potter, it goes without saying burglary's an unpleasant experience, but what's so queer about it? Almost to be expected, sadly, with someone like her. The way these glamour girls flaunt their sparklers—"

"Nobody really sees her, sir," Potter reminded him. "But in any case, it ent her jewellery—brought with her to flaunt or no, who can say—but a couple of pure silk sheets that's been stolen." He coughed. "I'd call it a queer start bringing *them* all the way from America, never mind having 'em stolen from the line."

"The washing line? Good grief." Did Hollywood legends do their own laundry? These days perhaps they did, if the hired help—not mentioned by name, hence unknown to Potter—might demand extra money to do it. Brinton guessed the secretary had used a London agency. Londoners always expected the highest wages for the least amount of effort.

"Back from the dry cleaner's and being aired, sir." Potter guessed what had been in his superior's mind. "Always leave 'em overnight, to be sure there's no fumes left."

Foxon, that snappy dresser in velvet and cord, nodded that this course of action was routine where dry cleaning was involved. Brinton, the married man, had never thought about it. "If you say so," he said. "Well, pure silk must cost money. The thief'll be trying to sell 'em, of course. When was the theft first noticed? Why weren't you told of it sooner?"

"Miss Earnshaw, her secretary says she's had … trouble of a similar sort other times, years back admittedly, but not unknown in Hollywood, he says. At first they thought it might just be another case of some fan going a bit over the top, and her being sort of half flattered and half sorry for 'em, wanting to sleep on the same sheets as her, dry cleaned or otherwise—not that she'd have given him the chance for the otherwise, so Mr Burscough says, after it having been her …" You could almost hear the blush. "Her … well, her delicates before, sir. Only, back then the chap actually bruck into the house rather than pinch 'em from outside. Seeing as this time it was just the sheets, well, at first she didn't reckon too much of it, on account of wanting to stay quiet and private while this book-writing's going on, and with her trouble sleeping, into the bargain—"

"Why did she change her mind? Did the burglar—the misguided fan—come back?"

"Well, sir, you could almost say it was along of Sir George Colveden. You know how some Americans are impressed by a title, sir. I doubt he'd have paid much heed, else—the secretary, I mean—but he did, and he got her worried, too."

"Worried?" Brinton was astounded; Foxon, struck dumb. "Does that woman seriously believe a local Justice of the Peace would steal her blasted bedclothes, whether they're pure silk or brushed nylon or—or spun gold?"

"Oh no, sir. But like I said, Mr Burscough orders the groceries, mostly by telephone and asking for 'em to be delivered, only there's always last-minute stuff and for all Miss Earnshaw don't come into the village, the young man sometimes likes to stretch his legs after typewriting and taking dictation all day. He don't say much, just pops in and out, but he catches some of the talk going round the shops and now it's being said it's time Sir George did ought to set up the Night Watch again, well, being a stranger in these parts he got the wrong end of the stick, though I tried my best to explain when he reported them sheets. Only by then he'd gone and talked himself into worrying how it all means more trouble than I think it does, being at an educated guess no more'n Murreystone up to their usual tricks and nothing at all to do with burglars. Or prowlers, or peeping toms, sir. Sir?"

"Murreystone," muttered Brinton. Foxon suppressed a grin. "What particular tricks, Potter? This is the first I've heard of them. Forgotten your standing orders, have you?"

"But, sir, you know about Murreystone! Remember the Best Kept Village competition, and the cricket match, and—"

"Oh, yes. I remember—the same way you should remember my orders. Anything at all that's untoward, for five miles round—you tell me about it."

"Er," said the unhappy Potter. "Yes, sir, only I thought it was just the usual—"

"Dammit, Potter, tell me!"

"Well, sir, it was the scarecrow. Nigel Colveden's idea and now everyone's making them. I did tell you, sir." Brinton grunted. Potter took heart. "Well, sir, there's only posters gone up as yet, advertising, and just the one beau-boy stood alongside the sign leading into the village, waving at passing cars to catch their attention, and a sash round him saying 'Coming soon' and the dates. He's been stood there waving for a few days now about how there'll be a festival of scarecrows and All Welcome, Tea and Coffee and Cakes in the village hall and Friendly Shops and that sort of thing, sir—I did tell you."

Brinton sighed. "So you did. And I said to tell me nothing more until it all started happening." Another sigh. "Which I gather it has, even if not the way I thought you meant." He glared at the silent Foxon, who was struggling not to laugh.

"So what was it? Murreystone have kidnapped the scarecrow? Holding it to ransom, are they?"

It was Potter's turn to sigh. "Mebbe I did ought to've told you it'd been took, sir, but everyone's so sure it was Murreystone, and we'd never be able to prove anything even with arson, if—"

"What!"

"—if that's what it turns out to be, sir, and not ransom, nor blackmail, for which in any case you'd need a threatening message, and I'm not sure a box of matches and an empty petrol can would really count." Foxon clamped his hand over the telephone mouthpiece. "Besides which," said Potter, "if challenged they could allus say they dropped the matches by mistake and dumped the jerry-can because it was empty. Then the most we could do 'em for would be litter, sir." Foxon couldn't help it. He guffawed. Brinton glared. "Or the only other thing I thought of is theft, sir—of an old pair of pyjamas and a tatty straw hat and a length of ribbon Mrs Welsted couldn't sell, being as by the time she reached the end of the roll she found a flaw in it. As for the stuffing, well, straw's easy enough to lose, in the country as we are and the start of the bonfire season for such garden waste as folk can't put to compost—and Murreystone'd laugh themselves silly on our account, sir, not to mention all the paperwork and no real proof, just suspicion. Which is why I didn't think to tell you, sir. I'm very sorry."

Foxon's face was scarlet with effort. Brinton's glare entirely missed its goal: the young man's eyes were closed. Tears seeped out. Even the superintendent, after a few seconds of deep concentration, relaxed the glare to permit himself one brief chuckle of sympathy.

"A—all right, Potter." He cleared his throat. "Not really your fault. I shouldn't have yelled at you. Sorry. I understand why your scarecrow didn't seem much, in the greater scheme of things. And if Sir George thinks it's no more than Murreystone larking about, he's probably right. We'll leave the Night Watch to his judgement—and Mr Jessyp's, of course. But your silk sheets are another matter. Any strangers around?" Local knowledge would have found a likely village suspect long before Potter thought to trouble his superior with the theft: he'd have had the bloke on a charge and in handcuffs before he could blink.

"There's an American at the George, sir, but he seems rather a nice young chap for all his name's Smith—which might well be true, people often are—and Miss Seeton gave him tea at Sweetbriars," this evidently being considered further proof of niceness.

"The clincher," said Brinton. "Mind you, the old girl prefers to see the best in everyone, but she does have an instinct … She's said nothing against him? No, she wouldn't," as the listening Foxon stopped grinning to frown. "Not a gossip, our MissEss."

"No, sir." Potter hesitated. "They do say he's been hanging around the churchyard, which is where she first met him, but iffen he was looking for the ghost that would explain it." Foxon began to grin again. "And then," added PC Potter, "it's mostly been t'other end of the village where people say they've seen it."

Brinton grunted. "The white shimmering shape. Yes, you told me the other day. And I told you, if all it does is shimmer then it's welcome to get on with it. 'Lead, kindly light' and so on. But I tell you now, if it's caught with stolen sheets or found breaking into laundries, throw the book at the wretched thing."

"Not like you, sir," put in Foxon. "Encouraging sacrilege—or would it be blasphemy?"

"Shuttup, Foxon. Potter knows what I mean."

"Yes, sir," said Potter. "And I doubt we'll catch up with him, whoever it was. Most likely it was Murreystone again, rather than a—a pervert, sir." The vocal blush had returned. "Or a sneak-thief," he added with more confidence. "Should I mention it to Sir George, sir, d'you reckon? Mr Burscough didn't say I shouldn't, but—well, I dunno."

"Sir George is the man on the spot. If he decides it's worth starting up the Watch again … I leave it to you, Potter. You're the official man on the spot—and talking of men, never you mind silk sheets. But," said Brinton, "if a single manhole cover goes walkabout, or anyone's garden fence disappears overnight, or the drains do a runner—then you can tell Sir George and Mr Jessyp from me, the Night Watch has my blessing!"

Chapter Nine

It was Emmy Putts who broke the news that galvanised the village. Her mother Clarissa, for three days a week a stalwart of the Brettenden biscuit factory, was (with the rest of her production line) on a fortnight's overtime, and accordingly rose earlier than usual to catch the first bus of the day (the smaller model, driven by Very Young Crabbe) rather than her regular (driven by Very Young Crabbe's son Jack).

Victor Crabbe was puzzled as he reached the request stop. Clarrie wasn't there. Then he saw her in the distance, running from the council houses, frantically waving. When she saw she had his attention she stopped waving, and pointed as she slowed from a breathless run to a jog. Victor's gaze followed the direction indicated.

He swore. The few passengers on the bus (the garage, content for it to be a loss leader, runs it as a community service) woke from their matutinal musings and looked round to see what had upset him. They, too, saw. And swore.

Clarrie couldn't climb into the bus because everyone else was busy piling out of it. They rushed to the road sign, planted in the grass verge, that welcomed visitors to Plummergen, where a second scarecrow, carrying an informative placard, had replaced his waving colleague with the sash—but Scarecrow the Second was no longer there. Where he had been standing an ominous scatter of straw turned green turf gold around the posts that supported the Plummergen sign. The placard lay face down. *He put up a good fight but not good enough* was scrawled on the back in ominous capitals.

"I'd no time to waste going for Ned Potter," said Clarrie as, mindful of timetables, Victor hustled everyone back on board, "so I've told Emmy to pop by the police house on her way to work. And if that ent the work of Murreystone, I'll never eat another custard cream!"

Mrs Stillman, prepared to scold Emmy for arriving so late for work, bit back her scolding as the girl explained. Her narrative was very soon supported by Mrs Newport and Mrs Scillicough, who (like the Putts family) occupied council houses at the northern end of the village. One sister had spotted the glint of PC Potter's buttons as he investigated the scene of the replacement scarecrow's demise, and at once thumped on the party wall to alert the other that Summat Was Up and hadn't they better find out what it was; Ned Potter was on the prowl without his panda car but clearly, from his tunic, on official business otherwise he'd still be eating breakfast in his shirtsleeves. Trevor Newport and Kevin Scillicough, followed by or carrying the smaller members of their families, joined the investigative throng that was soon swelled by other council house tenants, including Mrs Henderson and Mrs Skinner, who arrived at a dead heat and realised with dismay that, as this outrage was clearly the work of Murreystone, there was nothing over which they could disagree.

PC Potter wrapped a large blue cotton handkerchief round the handle of the placard he knew was far too rough for fingerprints, but everyone seemed to expect him to do something and what else was there except take photos, which would be a waste of good film because they all knew 'twas Murreystone to blame. Slippery as eels they were, in the Marsh. You could never pin anything on 'em. The only thing to do was stop 'em going too far—and there was an answer to that. Solemnly, escorted by a chattering crowd, Potter made his way back to the police house and said he ought to report to Superintendent Brinton in Ashford.

"And Sir George," said Mrs Skinner.

"And Mr Jessyp," snapped Mrs Henderson.

"I should talk to Mr Brinton first," said PC Potter, heading indoors to resume his interrupted breakfast and pleased he'd told no downright lies. A little misleading, that was all. He was under no obligation to telephone Ashford: he was the man on the spot; but as soon as he'd had a word with Sir George of course he'd be telling Mr Brinton what had happened. After all, he had his Standing Orders.

Emmy, mindful of scolds, had reluctantly hurried on down to the post office, survived the wrath of Mrs Stillman, and was preparing to launch into an embellished repeat of her tale when the other witnesses burst in, clamouring to spread and discuss the news. But Emmy—thanks to her mother—had been, if not the first to know, the first to bear public witness. For a moment, Emmeline Putts was a star.

The moment passed. Mrs Stillman had cardboard cartons for her to unpack after she'd served the customers, who all had loud voices and longer experience of making those voices heard. Elsie Stillman marvelled that so many people could continue to shout each other down when everyone agreed what needed to be done. Even Mrs Henderson's support of Mr Jessyp was half-hearted: against Murreystone, a military mind was obviously best. Martin Jessyp could organise well enough, let nobody deny, but Sir George would see the overall picture and know … not just what ought to be done, but how best to do it. There was not much doubt.

The Night Watch Men would very soon be back.

Matthew Bell wouldn't have minded some advice—instructions, even, though normally he prided himself on finding his own solution to pretty much every problem that came his way. That poacher, now. Sure, the others'd kicked up a fuss about it, but what else could he have done? The old bloke had interrupted … would have talked, no question. To shut his mouth'd been the only answer, though the Boss hadn't liked it. But in the end he'd understood. And made the arrangements. He was the one with the money, after all. At Matthew's end they took the risks and did the work and got their share, sooner or later—usually later. The Boss didn't trust anyone not to skip with the job half finished, if he paid too much up front. So he didn't. Matthew had known him a long time. He'd made more of a success in his new career than he had before; no surprise to Mr Bell, who kept a closer eye on things than the Boss could do from London. Never trusted anyone, the Boss didn't. Almost his motto. And Matthew knew the man was right.

Too much relying on other people, believing in them, could sink you. Practical, that's what you had to be. After the …Incident with the poacher he'd let the locals skip without recriminations—or payment. They'd known they were lucky to get off so lightly. Matthew had flexed his muscles as he talked about the police not having a clue, and he prided himself on his strength. They could take the hint. They'd taken it and gone.

To those who stayed he kept insisting on the bafflement of Scotland Yard, reminding them there'd be good money if they waited, with more to come once it was all set up properly again. A pity they'd had to move from the old place—it had been convenient—but the Boss accepted the change was necessary. In the circumstances. And now the circumstances had changed a second time.

Village nonsense, had said those few (very few) who'd heard snippets in the shops. From the start Matthew tried to restrict the movements of his men, but despite the Poacher Incident there had been a few (minor) rebellions until the rebels learned the error of their ways. But they didn't forget. There was otherwise very little to talk about. Ghosts? Didn't believe in ghosts, though lucky for them the yokels did. Stop them wandering at night and maybe see something they'd be happier not to have seen. Nobody wanted another Incident. Kidnapped scarecrows? (This last, reported by Matthew to enliven the enforced boredom.) Local squabbles, nothing to worry about. Village Watch? (He'd been in two minds about telling them this, but felt that on balance they ought to know. They'd be even less likely to take risks than he allowed them now.) Village Watch? Let 'em tire themselves out with patrolling every night! Easier to hoodwink them when it really mattered, they'd be so sleepy. Soft as the sheep that did nothing but eat grass and look gormless in broad daylight.

But Matthew, during one of the private excursions on which he had *not* reported fully, learned of Sir George and his military training. Time spent on reconnaissance is seldom wasted. He should've been warned about Sir George, though of course it'd all happened in a rush. But now, ought he to demand that the Boss found them yet another farmhouse?

It would slow things down still more, but a Major-General wasn't to be sniffed at. Good war record, they said. Knew what he was doing. At all costs the others mustn't know. Let them go on thinking of Plummergen as a lot of peasants. If they realised the possible risks, then they'd be skipping like the others. It wouldn't be easy now to find new recruits. If they could only be left in peace, it should work out fine.

Matthew Bell visited a call-box at midnight …

And nobody answered the phone at the other end.

It happened the next night, too, although he called at an earlier hour.

On the third night, he began to worry.

Bram Smith enjoyed being a tourist by day and (he began to hope) an adopted villager by night. Depending on bus time-tables, either Jack or Victor Crabbe would drive him to take in first the local, later the more distant, sights. A day or two after meeting her, he invited Miss Seeton to share the taxi to Bateman's, nearby in Sussex. Both enjoyed themselves touring Kipling's house. They quoted their favourite bits, with Miss Seeton confessing that she always felt a tug at the heart-strings when reading "The Gardener", and could rarely bring herself to read "Baa, Baa, Black Sheep" because it made her cross. No child should ever be treated like that: it was cruel—wicked—and the mother's comfort, she feared, coming far too late for the poor little boy. As if anyone could help being short-sighted! Such a relief to know how much happier the older Kipling had been at school in Devon than with his foster-family. Bram said *Stalky and Co.* was great, but as a youngster he'd preferred *Kim.* It had been the first time he'd realised that there were two sorts of Indians; and he impressed both Miss Seeton and Jack by giving them "Gunga

Din" in its entirety on the return journey, apologising as he began the recitation for his poor attempt at Cockney.

That evening, after dinner, Bram went into the bar and Jack Crabbe not only bought him a pint, but drew him into the general conversation. Mr Smith, though struggling as ever with the accent, was discreetly thrilled. He'd made a point of dining at the George every night. While its cuisine wasn't exactly haute, Bertha Mountfitchet cooked a good hearty meal, Doris served well at table (he couldn't say the same of Maureen, but felt sure she tried her best) and Charley as mine host was straight from Dickens, though of course Dickens was long after Abraham Voller had escaped from gaol. Bram still gave no hint of his ancestral connections, but enjoyed those jokes he could understand, and tried his hand at darts, much impressed by the regular players' lightning mental arithmetic.

He had the feud with Murreystone explained to him at length, and in detail. To think it had begun four hundred years before Columbus sailed for America! On the strength of this he offered to buy drinks all round. Charley grinned, thanked him on both the general behalf and his own bar takings, but said he shouldn't make a habit of it. Once was enough, though it was good to see a guest fitting in when he stayed for more than just a couple of nights. He wished he could say the same of everyone, but it took all sorts, didn't it. Live and let live.

"Your new chap still wanting room service, Charley?"

"Better keep an eye on young Maureen, taking up all them trays!"

A comment was passed that made Charley frown and everyone else (except Bram, the non-native speaker) laugh. "There's no nonsense of that sort in this house," said the landlord sternly. "The man's convalescent after illness, in need of peace and quiet and no distractions—and I'll thank the lot of you to keep your remarks to yourselves," as there came a muted outburst of sniggering. "He gives no trouble, which is more'n can be said of some. Takes his daily paper, reads his books, listens-in to the wireless like a Christian and don't turn the knob full blast—a few more like him and I'd stop thinking about retirement and start to enjoy the job again, so I would."

There was general mirth at the very idea of Charley's ever retiring. He was a fixture at the George and wouldn't leave until it was feet first, he always said.

"Best warn the man to be careful iffen he takes the air at night," someone advised. "With this Murreystone trouble a-brewing, and the Watch on the prowl and none of us knowing what he looks like—"

"It's decided, then? Sir George has agreed?"

"The word's out for volunteers."

The speaker grinned broadly as everyone (except Bram) roared with laughter. Charley saw the young man's polite but puzzled smile, and hurried to explain.

"Whenever it's a case of Murreystone, Mr Smith, it ent so much the finding of volunteers but the choosing which of 'em to take that's the problem! The whole village would be in it if Sir George'd only let 'em, camping out on the steps of Rytham Hall to be first to give their names, but he and Mr Jessyp are grand ones for keeping lists and records. They know who was in it last time—"

"Allus another time, with Murreystone," growled someone.

"And so there is," Charley agreed. "And we all like to have a crack at the blighters as necessary, but fair's only fair.

Sir George makes sure each of us takes his turn. That way, see, nobody loses too much sleep, yet they ent left out of things."

Bram savoured Charley's words. "Sir George is the village squire?" he asked, pleased at his cunning. "I guess this Rytham Hall must be a fine old manor house."

He committed to memory the description of Rytham Hall, and its location. Mr Smith was a contented young man when he finally went up to bed.

He'd heard enough to know that Rytham Hall was a working farm, its menfolk working farmers. It was accordingly later next day that he walked up the drive and knocked politely on the front door. He knew from the movies what a loud, through-the-whole-house jangle pulling the doorbell handle would achieve: while he was enchanted by the concept, he didn't think he really had the nerve to try it here.

A graceful middle-aged woman with thick, wavy brown hair and a friendly smile opened the door to his knock. "Good afternoon," she said, and paused.

Bram, having spent the whole of his walk deciding what to say to a man with a military mind, was thrown off balance by a woman, no matter how friendly her smile.

"I'm Lady Colveden," her ladyship told one of the most handsome (if silent) young men she'd seen for ages. Apart from Nigel, of course. "You don't look at all like a feed rep, but I know my husband's expecting someone about cattle cake. Or was it sheep nuts? Some new and improved formula, anyway. You'd better come in." She glanced over his shoulder at the empty drive. "There's plenty of room. Would you prefer to move your car first? So much easier for carrying samples."

"I'm sorry, ma'am—your ladyship—but I've only come to have a word with Sir George."

"You don't *sound* like a feed rep, either." She laughed. "You're not, are you?"

"Er—no, ma'am—your ladyship—but I'd really appreciate a word with Sir George."

"How silly of me. Do come in. He won't be long, because of expecting the rep—unless it's something I could do for you, if you're in a hurry." Bram, thanking her with a profound bob of the head—he wasn't sure of the etiquette—carefully wiped his shoes and followed her indoors. "But you can't be, or you'd have come before," said his hostess, leading the way. "You're staying at the George, aren't you? And you've been there for days, so it can't be anything urgent. In here." She opened the door to the drawing room.

When Sir George turned up in search of animal feed representatives, he heard the laughter of his wife and a cheery male voice coming from a room in which he'd never have expected her to entertain a salesman. Cups and saucers, too. Not a snob, Meg, but mugs in the kitchen was the usual drill. Feed reps were always in too much of a hurry to observe the courtesies.

"Flirting again, m'dear?" He winked at Bram as that young man rose to his feet, looking awkward. Sir George waved him back to his chair. "You're that chap from the George." The baronet joined his unexpected guest, and looked pointedly at the teapot. "Recognised the accent. Seen you about, once or twice," he added, as his wife topped up from the hot water jug and stirred. "Met a fair number of Yanks during the war. Splendid chaps. Pretty good in a scrap, I remember."

"Yes, sir. I—I guess that's kind of why I'm here." Bram shot a helpless look in the direction of Lady Colveden, who gave the teapot one final stir and announced that it was stewed. She'd go and boil the kettle. She went.

Sir George raised his eyebrows at Bram's confession, heard with sympathy his bashful request, and sadly shook his head.

"Better not, but thanks for the offer. No street lighting, remember. Can't have strangers roaming about in the dark. Easily have accidents. People get excited, when Murreystone's involved. An ancestor's all very well, but you can't inherit local knowledge."

Bram was crushed. "Are you sure, sir? I've kept quiet about old Abraham because I realise how long you people can stay angry. If you don't forget after a thousand years, then Napoleon is just five minutes ago—and I guess the old guy didn't treat his pals too well, if what I've heard is true—so joining the Night Watch and going out on patrol seemed like my best chance of … well, of making it up to the village somehow."

Lady Colveden reappeared to say she'd heard an approaching car slow down outside. "That's probably your pig-pellet man at last, George. You've been too busy talking to listen." It was kinder than saying she suspected her spouse grew a little deaf with the passage of years. "Now, if you and Mr Smith have finished your business, when he knocks you can take him straight through to the kitchen. The kettle's boiled. I've put out mugs and a plate of biscuits, and your scribbling-pad and some pencils." Sir George always checked any prices quoted by a salesman against his own calculations. He could negotiate surprising discounts, but the inevitably animated discussion too often left him with broken pencil-points. The word had gone round long ago that Rytham Hall was a tough nut (as it were) to crack.

Lady Colveden smiled at Bram. "I couldn't help catching the last few words, Mr Smith. If you'd really like to do something for Plummergen, you could do worse than buy a concert ticket to support the Re-Wiring Fund and the new burglar alarm. Or a raffle ticket—or both. You could even make a contribution, anonymously if you'd prefer. You must have heard about our little explosion the other day." And her ladyship, school governor, told the tale Miss Seeton had already told, as Sir George bustled off to answer the feedman's knock, leaving the room with a gruff vote of thanks to Mr Smith but reiterating the unwisdom of accepting the American's kind offer.

He'd been sorry to disappoint the young chap. One volunteer was worth ten pressed men, and the boy did seem keen. But he'd made his decision, and in military terms you kept a decision once made. You stuck to your guns. The old warrior, recalling past decisions when real guns had been used, opened the door with so martial a look in his eye that his visitor, knowing the appointment had been for half an hour earlier, dropped the catalogues and price lists he carried, and overwhelmed the baronet with apologies.

Bram Smith thanked Lady Colveden for her hospitality, walked back to the George, and wondered how large an anonymous donation he should make.

It was market day in Ecclesham, a small Sussex town of reasonable charm apart from its roads. A mediaeval layout does not carry twentieth-century traffic without some "give" on the part of the town and a great deal more "take" by the lorries, trucks, buses and cars making their purposeful way from A to B with scant regard for the areas between.

Traffic problems were always worse on market day. There was no designated Market Square: from time immemorial sturdy wooden stalls and booths had, once a week, lined the little town's main road tempting passers-by to become purchasers. A horse-drawn cart or wagon had for centuries been the widest vehicle that could pass easily along the narrowed street; farmers tried never to negotiate a trip through Ecclesham on market day, but delivery vans often had no choice. With the coming of the motor vehicle, a compromise (stalls down one side of the road only) had seen many town council arguments but, for years, no definite conclusion. A conclusion was at last reached, enforced by a higher power— Sussex County Council Planning Department—though not without grumbling from those in Ecclesham who saw this as the thin end of the wedge. They'd be moved into side-streets next, or out of town to the old goods yard at the railway station axed by Dr Beeching more than a decade ago, which was too far for people to walk back carrying much more than the handbag with which they'd started.

On the side of a hill that overlooked a crucial main road, a small pantechnicon waited outside a house. The "To Let" board had been up for several weeks, and the neighbours were eager to see who'd finally decided to take on the tenancy: a foreigner, for certain. No local would willingly rent from the most penny-pinching landlord for miles. Cheap furniture, worn carpets, scruffy wallpaper: little wonder the newcomers had brought their own stuff with 'em! And the old skinflint keeping 'em waiting there with no keys to get in! If he wasn't so stingy as to have no phone, one or other of those on lookout would've popped to the telephone box and rung him at home to say the newcomers were waiting.

Nobody paused to consider that only one of these newcomers had as yet been seen. He'd driven the removal van himself—seemingly he couldn't afford a proper firm like Pickfords, which accounted for him being willing to rent from old Cheeryble—and parked it by the empty house. With his cap pulled close over his eyes he tried the front door, shrugged, and returned to the cab to read his newspaper while he waited. Clearly, he was in no particular hurry. He was also a remarkably slow reader. His head stayed bent over the paper from the moment he climbed back into the cab and hardly moved, although those with sharp eyes thought they caught him checking his watch every few minutes.

Then he'd had enough. All at once he folded his paper, bent to fiddle with something in the cab, opened the door and jumped out with the paper tucked under his arm, and the cap pulled even closer over his eyes. Evidently in search of a telephone box, he hurried away down the hill …

Followed by the removal van.

He had released the handbrake, and left gravity to do its worst.

Startled watchers saw the van gather speed. The hill was steep; the road was straight. The van moved faster—overtook the hurrying driver, who began to jog beside it then ran, in its rumbling wake. It reached the end of the road—thundered straight across the junction—oncoming vehicles swerved, brakes squealed, metal screamed and crumpled.

The pantechnicon bounced against a concrete lamp-post, buried its nose in a garden wall and came noisily to a halt.

The jogger ignored the damage to his cab as he reached the pantechnicon. He opened the back doors and took out a bicycle. He put his newspaper in the saddlebag, mounted the bike, and pedalled calmly away.

Behind him, he left chaos.

Stunned witnesses to that chaos roused themselves at last and hurried to see what could be done for those in the crashed cars. The road was a tangle of metal. Petrol fumes filled the air, together with the sound of curses, shouts for help, groans of pain.

There came a horrified yell from a driver who stopped clutching his battered head to point at further danger from above.

"Look out! *Look out!*"

The lamp-post was falling. As it fell it dragged with it the neighbouring wooden pole that carried the telephone wires in and out of Ecclesham. The road was blocked. The lines were down …

And it was market day.

One of the reasons always cited by stallholders to justify their refusal to move to the disused railway goods yard was the proximity of their stalls to the high street. If takings had to stay unbanked until the end of the working day because it was a long way to pop in with regular deposits throughout that day, they'd run too many risks for their liking. Nobody with any sense carried large amounts of cash on his person for longer than he must. The high street bank was close enough for everyone in turn to ask his neighbour to keep an eye on things while he deposited his takings, and he'd bring back tea and buns in exchange. It was a system that had worked for years.

It also meant that the bank became unusually full of cash as the day progressed.

Two men in anoraks, with nylon stockings over their heads and sawn-off shotguns in their hands, stormed into the bank and uttered a crisp command.

"Hands up! Nobody move!"

An exquisite young man fainted mid-signature, his deposit slip floating inkily to the floor beside him. Everyone else did as they were told.

The taller of the two stocking-masks moved against the wall by the door, and gestured with his shotgun. His partner pulled a stout canvas holdall from inside his coat, covered his colleague with his own gun and received a second holdall. The tall man resumed his overseer stance. His partner took both bags to the counter—thrust them across to a frozen cashier. He snapped an order.

"In here—fill 'em up! And I'll be watching."

There was a scuffle and an exchange of words by the main door.

"Hurry up!" The cashier hurried. The words grew louder. "Hand it over!"

Each with a bulging canvas bag, the gunmen made their escape. The market trader who had interrupted the robbery was knocked to the ground, and in a fury hurled a heavy bag of coins at his attacker. He scored a hit on one retreating back, but it was not enough. An anonymous black car screeched up to the kerb. The robbers flung open doors—jumped in—and the car sped away, heading for the one main route that was not by now a confusion of cunningly snarled-up traffic.

Market traders are not easily daunted. The view-halloo sounded even as the coin-hurler scrambled to his feet and began to run. A market trader's bellow as he cries his wares will carry many yards. Passers-by added to the uproar; so did customers fleeing from the bank to raise the alarm—but the hue and cry was already under way. Two or three traders, with perishable stock that was almost sold out, had been cutting prices to shift the rest and starting to pack things away. Trucks and vans were parked beside their stalls. As their colleague panted up from the bank, shouting, pointing, insisting, two drivers abandoned their property, leaped into their vehicles, and as the winded coin-hurler clambered up into the leading truck, still pointing, the hunt was on.

The black car scorched along the road ahead of the market traders, whose vans were built more for sturdiness than speed, but it hadn't yet gained the distance advantage the robbers might have expected. While the traffic around town had come to a virtual standstill, the coin-hurler had surprised them by the speed of his reactions. One of the robbers rubbed the small of his back, and cursed.

"Done my back in, he has. Let me just get my hands on him and he'll be sorry."

"Cool it," advised his colleague, shaking his bag of stolen money and grinning. "We got no need to take it out on 'im—and we won't be here to do it, neither. It's the life of Reilly for us in future!"

The driver kept glancing in his rear-view mirror. "Not if that lot catch up with us. Who'd have thought they'd get after us so quick?"

"We're dead on time, right?" said Reilly with the bag. "Then shut your trap and do the necessary, and they won't be able to catch us. We'll be in clover!"

The car roared on, towards the railway line and the level crossing. As it drew close, the passengers could see that the automatic half-barriers were down.

The pursuing market traders looked on in horror as the car, swerving and lurching from side to side, rounded each half of the barrier in turn and continued its escape just as a train rattled ponderously down the line, blocking their view—and the crossing—for five hideous seconds. By the time the train had passed the black car was out of sight, heading for the county border and the convoluted byways of Kent. The traders knew they had lost.

"We got to keep going," wheezed the man who had hurled the coins. "Got to find a phone box—tell the cops where they went."

"Barriers won't be up for a bit yet," said the driver. "There's a train due the other way. Have to stay down till it's gone."

"Planned the job well," said the wheezer, with grudging admiration. The driver didn't argue. It would be a lifetime until the second train went by …

The black car slowed a little as it left the main road for the maze of side lanes in which the driver hoped to lose any pursuit. He tried to drive in a less noticeable manner, but he'd been made nervous by the unexpected chase. He checked again and again in his mirror for any sign of the two market vehicles, and when at a crossroads he spotted a small white van approaching, he was convinced the driver wore a peaked uniform cap.

"Bloody hell—how did they find us?" He put his foot down again.

The postman in his temporary van (his own red Post Office vehicle being in dry dock after failing its MOT test) was surprised at the way the black car took the crossroads corner on two wheels. Not so much dangerous, as downright stupid—or a guilty conscience, perhaps? Curious, he decided to follow. He had, he felt, an official duty to the community he served, just as the forces of law and order had.

The driver of the black car was making his colleagues more than uneasy.

"Slow down, you stupid bastard!"

"That's not the fuzz—there's no chequerboard down the side!"

"He's after me, whoever he is," growled the driver, and pressed hard on the accelerator.

It was bound to happen. He didn't so much misjudge the bend as miss it entirely. He saw no speed chevrons to alert him now that the supporting poles had gone: the grass had grown too high.

The local postman, confidently rounding another sharp bend, could do no more than watch as the strange car disappeared at speed straight through the hedge, tipped into a ditch, and rolled over to hit an oak tree with a very, very solid trunk.

"Two dead. One critical, not expected to live." Superintendent Brinton and his Sussex colleague had caught up with each other at last. At first Harry Furneux had been too busy with the aftermath of Ecclesham's bank raid for the right penny to drop. The staff were hysterical, the customers even more so. The traffic men from Hastings said the snarl-up in the little market town was about the worst they'd ever seen; the railway transport police bent everyone's ears on the subject of Automatic Half Barrier crossings and the risks run by those who ignored them—didn't the fools stop to consider the shock to the train driver? Telephone wires hummed, sounding a permanently Engaged tone to anyone who dialled.

"Metal theft is one thing," said Brinton. "It's manslaughter, now. I can't say I'm breaking my heart over your bank lot, but I'd prefer to catch 'em honestly and chuck 'em in the nick to having the perishers end that way."

"And your girlfriend with the sketchbook wasn't able to help? Not at all?" The Fiery Furnace was almost pleading.

"She ... did her best." There was, even at such a time, a faint chuckle in Brinton's voice. "She warned us your bank was going to be done over by three men, though even the Oracle didn't realise at the time that's what she meant."

Foxon looked up. The would-be sergeant, without mentioning it to his superior unless the results were likely to impress, had decided to tackle the Metal Theft file in a new way. He would read each report (and there were many) in date order backwards. He'd heard somewhere that authors often tackled their page-proofs like that, thereby spotting all manner of mistakes and errors of plotting they wouldn't otherwise have seen. He wondered if some strange connection, an unnoticed clue, might leap at him from the much-thumbed pages and suggest a different—a correct—line of investigation. It wouldn't hurt his chances to have a star (or maybe two) added to his personal file …

But "she" in this context could only mean Miss Seeton. He looked up. Brinton nodded.

"Young Foxon," the superintendent informed the telephone as he waved Foxon to the extension, "has a contribution to add. Okay, Harry?"

Foxon demurred. "It isn't exactly—"

"Stop havering, laddie." Brinton was impatient. "If you've got something to say, say it."

Foxon was unusually hesitant. Brinton glared. The younger man coughed. "Well, sir, she was right about the *Ladykillers* trick of blocking the road with a lorry, wasn't she?"

Brinton explained. Furneux sighed. "She was right."

Foxon pressed on. "And the railway side of it—she got that, too."

"So it seems. We don't go in for computer-controlled traffic in these parts."

"And Mr Delphick made a joke about *The Italian Job* and the Mini cars …"

Brinton groaned. "Yes, he did. I forgot. I was more worried about Maidstone and the parking meters."

"Go on," urged Furneux as the detective constable fell silent.

"Sorry, sir." Foxon coughed again. "It was just that I thought—it's worked at least three times, sir—in those two films and now in real life. It's pure chance they didn't get away with the loot this time, isn't it? And that blonde is still unconscious in hospital."

"We're hard at work on the metal thieves here," Brinton told Furneux, again with that hint of a chuckle. "There's a young Galahad on my team who takes it very seriously."

"My gran's front gate—" began Foxon, then subsided at Brinton's grimace.

"Go on," urged Furneux again.

"The trouble is, sir, I don't know there's much to be done about it beyond, well, asking MissEss what she thinks, because—" over Brinton's groan— "with her—with us with her—it's hindsight that works best. But she might *just* see something before it happens—and I could be wrong," modestly, "but if the newspapers make the connection— can't you just see the headlines? *The Gridlocker Gang,* or something of the sort—"

"Shuttup, Foxon! I hate you!" Brinton had paled. He knew what was coming. A catchy name like that ... copycat crime was almost inevitable, and their hands were already full.

"What's happened to this lot should put anyone else off trying the same game," he said, with desperate optimism.

"Doesn't follow." Furneux saw no reason to be optimistic. "Foxon, you could be right. In theory it should have worked, and a workable idea soon catches on. Just their bad luck they ran out of road—and road signs. Of course we've got to get those metal thieves before they cause a far more serious accident—might be an ambulance next time, or a fire engine—but stopping anyone else trying the same choke-the-town-with-traffic dodge is a damn sight more difficult. I don't see how even your Miss Seeton could do anything."

"She'd wave her brolly at the railway timetable and that would be that," said Brinton.

"Doesn't have to be anything to do with trains, does it? Blocking the right roads would be enough." Furneux sounded regretful. "If there was only time for someone to sit down with large-scale maps of every town—"

"There isn't," said Brinton, and Superintendent Furneux couldn't argue. It might not (he pointed out) necessarily be in Kent or Sussex—it could be Scotland next.

Foxon cleared his throat. Now for the tricky bit. "I only thought it *might* happen, sir. My feeling is there'd need to be another, er, gridlocker robbery before the papers got on to it and the idea took off." He looked at the Metal Theft file on his desk: it had grown over recent days. Either the thieves had resumed their conscience-interrupted career, or publicity had inspired others. (A workable idea soon catches on.) Or, possibly, both. The bank robbery had come at a convenient time, for his burgeoning theories. The Gridlockers notion had struck him as a bit of a joke, then he'd seen the possibilities. Old Brimstone was always uncomfortable about asking Miss Seeton for help, while he himself didn't feel he could go to Plummergen and ask her without official sanction.

"I've been doing my best with the metal thefts, sir, and I'll bet the Sussex lads were just as busy, until this bank business—" Furneux said he'd made sure of that— "but I wonder now about … well, about looking at it from the other end, sir." He wouldn't mention reading backwards: too much of a distraction to explain, when it had taken long enough to work it out for himself. "MissEss said she'd read of the early incidents in the local paper, Mr Delphick gave her the details, and then she drew the *Ladykillers* sketch for him—for us, that is. And after today she'll have more—more dramatic consequences to read about—" Brinton cursed him, in a half-hearted way— "but suppose, at the same time we asked for her thoughts on the bank robbery, we asked for drawings of the scrap dealers themselves, at the end of the chain? And not just the—the results of the scrap metal thefts?"

There was a thoughtful pause.

"Bank robberies," said Brinton, breaking the silence, "happen anywhere, at any time."

"Not easy to predict," rejoined his Sussex counterpart.

"John O'Groats to Land's End, sir," chirped Foxon, thankful that *sir* was an indefinite mode of address. "Miss Seeton knows me," he went on. "After all, we once spent the night together—" ("Tell you later, Harry," interposed Brinton)— "and I thought I might take one of the unmarked pool cars and give her a guided tour. She'd be my dear old auntie wondering how much she'd make if she had a wooden fence instead of railings, or replaced her ancient kitchen range with something modern—and she'd clock the faces of every dealer, sir, and just maybe something might—might do the trick. Sir."

"Hmm." Brinton brooded. Foxon held his breath. "You won't be working on today's affair, of course. The robbery itself is a Hastings job, and they already know who the chummies are, or if they don't they soon will—that right, Harry? Okay, they crashed on our patch, but it'll be Kent Traffic that's most concerned and you aren't Traffic, laddie. Although," he added with one of his scathing looks at the young detective's sprightly attire, "stand you on a street corner in those clothes and you could pass for a traffic light any time."

"Sir," protested Foxon, delighted. Looked as if Brimmers was coming round to the idea. "Mr Brinton has no sense of current fashion, sir," he explained to the telephone, which was uttering sounds of puzzlement. "It's not as if I've gone psychedelic yet."

"Shuttup, Foxon. Anyone unlucky enough to work with you needs sunglasses. Heaven only knows what Miss Seeton will think," said Brinton. "I feel sorry for the poor old bird."

"Sir," protested Foxon happily; and, after some discussion about ways and means, the conversation drew to a close.

Chapter Ten

Having geared himself up for action it was frustrating for DC Foxon that Miss Seeton's telephone rang unanswered next morning. Not one of Martha Bloomer's regular days, then. He tried the police house. If Ned Potter wasn't there (as he probably wasn't) he might still catch Mabel, who knew most of what went on in the village.

"Could be off with her sketchbook," suggested Mrs Potter. "That bird's here again—the back-to-front kingfisher as does somersaults in the sky." Plummergen's wayward fancy had been caught by Lily Hosigg's turn of phrase. That girl (the village had begun to feel) might just about be considered local, though coming from Rochester (which was at least in Kent). She'd lived here a number of years, with that sickly babby of hers even born in Plummergen and, when the time came, likely to go to school there. "The whole village is filling up again," said Mabel. "Ned's watching for folk trying to park in the wrong place. Dunnamany there'll be this time round, but there was hundreds before."

"At this rate you won't need scarecrows to attract the tourists. The money's going to come—wait for it—rolling in. Rolling." Mabel groaned, then laughed, and Foxon rang off cheerily. He glanced at the superintendent's empty desk. Brinton had been buttonholed by Desk Sergeant Mutford over his, Mutford's, powers of arrest in the matter of civil trespass when the trespasser threatened, but did not in fact punch, a Holdfast Brother on private Holdfast property. Foxon grinned. While on desk duty, a member of the Brethren would consider attendance behind that desk to be compulsory. The superintendent mountain (smaller, thanks to the diet, than he once was) had perforce left his office to talk to the Holdfast Mahomet and discuss relevant paragraphs in the latest edition of *Moriarty's Police Law.* Foxon had no idea how long the discussion might last.

He scribbled a note, left it on his superior's blotter, and with his jacket slung over one shoulder and a set of car keys in his pocket, headed for the yard at the back where pool vehicles waited. It had all been arranged the previous day. Foxon whistled a happy tune as he headed for Plummergen.

In Plummergen Miss Seeton was, as Mrs Potter had guessed, out with her sketchbook. Late the previous afternoon Lily Hosigg had knocked on her door, with Dulcie Rose in tow, saying that the "big blue birdie" was in their garden again. Miss Seeton thanked them, and accepted an invitation to tea and biscuits once she'd telephoned her friend Mrs Ongar, who was sure to be interested. Miss Seeton duly admired Dulcie's sketches of the returning Roller and drew several of her own, before the bird somersaulted away to the far end of the village, pursued by a group of twitchers on serendipitous tour with bicycles and binoculars. Miss Seeton pondered her own bike, and decided against its use. Birds, naturally, flew. It was unreasonable to expect them to stay in one place long enough for people to catch up with them, and after all she'd already seen the exotic visitor. She hoped

Mrs Ongar wouldn't be too disappointed if she missed it this time around.

Miss Seeton had been delighted to see Lily and the small Dulcie Rose. Her afternoon had until then been—well, somewhat fraught. At another concert rehearsal, the matter of hobby-horses had been raised by the child of someone who'd made a scarecrow and been left with sufficient fabric and straw to put them to another use. Mr Jessyp said no. The child cried, the hobby-horse was confiscated until going-home time, and the mother stamped peevishly into the school to complain of wasted effort. Miss Seeton was thankful for the relative quiet of her mile-long walk back to Sweetbriars from the far end of the village, and the prospect of a cup of tea: the unexpected change of scene, and a closer sight of the equally unexpected European Roller, had done her a great deal of good.

Next day her services were not required at school. Prompted by the concert, she felt drawn again to the tomb of the Napoleonic guinea-smuggler. Having heard Bram Smith's tale she had borrowed one or two books on the period from Mr Jessyp. So very interesting. And, understanding the history a little better, she felt bound to agree with the young American that his collateral ancestor had been something of a rogue, though she would hardly call him a traitor: a harsh judgement. He might easily have been one of the many double agents employed by prime minister Pitt and his successors. Which would somehow make it better, even if it didn't explain why he'd been thrown in gaol and had to escape.

Unless, of course, the authorities had connived at so very daring a venture; which she supposed they might have done. If he was a double agent it would have been unfair if they hadn't. They could have given him money to leave at once for

America on condition that he never spoke about it; except, of course, that he had. Otherwise Mr Smith—Bram—and his family wouldn't have known all about it, and he, Bram, couldn't have told her. And yet it was so very long ago. She wondered if Bram's concern as to the collective memory of Plummergen could really be justified …

Then she thought of the Murreystone feud, and had to concede that it might well be so. There were, she must admit, some … over-enthusiastic individuals in her dear village. But it was not her place to criticise. While never a rich family, and of recent years little more than comfortably off, no Seeton had ever been close to the breadline. No shadow of the workhouse had loomed over them. She, last of her line, had been so fortunate as to find employment in London in a (mostly) enjoyable job, and on her retirement, thanks to the generosity of her godmother and the retainer fee from the police, could support herself without having to worry about, well, anything. So very different a life from the heavily-taxed farming poor and the fishermen of the early nineteenth century. What was that saying about having to walk a mile in someone else's shoes?

It was barely a furlong—one-eighth of a mile—from Sweetbriars to the churchyard across The Street, and the tomb of Abraham Voller. There had been a descriptive passage about this tomb in one of Mr Jessyp's local histories. The side panel could be moved and replaced without (it was claimed) attracting notice, for the position of the tomb meant that direct sunlight never fell upon it. Always in shadow, it could tell no tales …

Except that, to the trained eye of an artist, it did. There was—something—that didn't look right. A slight distortion from the vertical, perhaps? A glimpse of carving that, from the wrong angle, stood out further than it should? The mason who assembled the great stone chest had carved his ornately draping festoons intending them to distract the non-observant populace, but Miss Seeton was not fooled by distortions of shape or shadow. She considered the mason a most skilful man, and smiled as she sketched his work.

There was nobody to hear. She raised her voice in untuneful song: another memory from the rehearsal. "Boot, saddle, to horse—and away!" Perhaps Mr Jessyp—although it wasn't her place to criticise—had been a little strict with his hobby-horse veto. There were so many horses and ponies about which the children would sing; and, supervised with care, they were unlikely to go to war with their broomsticks. The Civil War. Roundheads and Cavaliers—besieged castles—Gertrude, honest and gay, laughing, waiting confidently for her husband and his men to come to the rescue ... Browning also, of course, wrote of galloping horses when he told of how they brought the good news from Ghent to Aix. Such a puzzle as to what the news had been, but then much of Browning could be a puzzle. *Sordello*—wasn't there a joke that the only lines anyone ever understood were the first, and the last? *Ghent to Aix* was different. She recited the stirring lines quietly to herself as she drew three horsemen—Joris, and Dirck, and the anonymous narrator—in a furious rush down a dusty road set in the flat Flanders landscape. As flat, perhaps, as Romney Marsh, famous for its smugglers. "Five and twenty ponies," she suddenly sang.

There was a rustle in the undergrowth. Miss Seeton, turning back to the tomb to continue her original sketch, in an awkward key celebrated brandy for the parson and baccy for the clerk. Ponies, she felt, were rather more her style today than prancing war-chargers and exhausted post-horses. She'd often pondered the ultimate fate of Joris and Dirck and their mounts. Had they carried bad news then such a great hurry might have been justified, but good news would keep for a few hours, surely. Unless it was to prompt further action that couldn't wait. But if one had no idea what the news had been …

"Baccy for the Clerk!" Miss Seeton found a more comfortable key. She must be distracted no more by literary conundrums. She set sketchbook and pencil on the ground beside her umbrella, and made a frame with her hands. The drape of the festoon—similar to the branch of that tree—could she fit them in the same sketch, a pleasing echo?

"Oh," she said.

In the frame, in the trees beyond the tomb, she could make out the figure of a man. He did not move, but although he wore camouflage clothing Miss Seeton saw him.

"Oh, good morning." She lowered her hands. "I'm so sorry, but I believe you're too late. The bird, I fear, has flown."

"The bird has flown." The man emerged warily from the bushes. "Some kind of password? Who says so? Why?"

"Because it has. It did. Yesterday. To the northern end of the village, near Plummergen Common. It may of course have returned by now, and you might be lucky after all—but probably not here. You should be closer to the canal." She pointed. "Down there."

The camouflaged man stared at her. "Go past my cottage," she told him, "where The Street narrows to a lane over the bridge, and there you are."

"Your cottage." The man sounded as bewildered as he looked; and he did not look as if he was accustomed to uncertainty. Here was a man of decision, of action. Elderly spinsters delivering cryptic utterances seemed to make him nervous. He took a step backwards.

"Sweetbriars, on the corner. You can't miss it. The garden wall runs alongside the lane—or should I rather say the lane runs past my wall? It was in the garden of some young friends—" at this he looked even more bewildered— "and you know how they fly, so it would be wrong of me to promise you will see it, because if it has moved on again, you won't. And there will be no-one to ask, because they have gone in search of it—excepting myself, of course, or how could I be telling you all this?" She smiled for her folly. "There aren't as many this time, having already seen it. I understand they—you—even take time off work." Another smile, highly sympathetic to enthusiasm. "And as I explained, that was yesterday."

"Oh," said the man. He took another backward step.

"I made several sketches, and felt there was really no need for more, when the tomb is of more immediate interest. The concert is tonight, of course. Most gratifying, so many of your colleagues having bought tickets." She regarded him, the embodiment of twitchers, with approval. "But," remembering her manners, "before you set off on what may be a fruitless chase—one hesitates to refer to wild geese because, well, it isn't a goose—but you might be interested to see my sketches."

"Of the smuggler's tomb?" He looked startled.

"Of the Roller," she corrected gently, flipping back through the pages to find the quick likenesses she had drawn. "Such wonderful colours, as of course you know." Again he was startled. She didn't notice. "Yes, here we are." She held out the sketchbook. With automatic courtesy he took it from her. "It has stayed for an encouragingly long time in this area. I do hope it hasn't now gone for good. After your splendid efforts to disguise yourself that would be most unfair, when the rest of us have been so fortunate."

"Right," said the man. "Er—thanks." He closed the sketchbook and returned it. "By the canal, you said?"

She nodded. "What a pity you forgot your binoculars. I understand from Sir George Colveden that these days there are some very compact models, for military use and, I imagine, if one is willing to pay the high price I'm told they command, for people keen on birds. Or other wildlife. One can even see with them at night, which of course in the case of the Roller would serve no particular purpose as in the dark one cannot be entirely sure of colours. And one sleeping bird must closely resemble another, don't you think? *With her head tucked underneath her arm*," carolled Miss Seeton, with no warning and little tune.

"Er—right," said the man again, and was about to beat a hasty retreat when a cheerful voice rang out across the churchyard.

"Calling Miss Seeton! Hi, MissEss, are you there? It's Tim Foxon!"

A delighted smile broke on Miss Seeton's already contented face. "Mr Foxon; how very nice. I wonder how he found me here? But of course, he's a detective." The man halted his retreat to stare at her yet again. "A charming young man, and an old friend," she explained, as Foxon appeared and began making his way round the gravestones towards her. "I hope there's nothing wrong. Superintendent Brinton usually keeps him so busy he has very little time for social calls."

"Hello, MissEss." Foxon, dapper in velvet jacket, kipper tie and flared trousers, merrily shook the hand she held out to him. "Sorry to intrude," as the man in camouflage gave him an uneasy smile, "but how do you fancy a ride in a police car?"

The uneasy smile faded. The man's stare became frozen. Foxon saw his expression, and laughed. "Don't worry, you aren't consorting with a dangerous criminal. Miss Seeton is one of our most distinguished colleagues." He turned back to the blushing Miss Seeton. "Mr Brinton knows all about it, in case you were wondering, and says hello."

"As I greet him in return. Do I infer the chief superintendent does not?"

"Know?" Foxon, unlike the twitcher, did not need a translator. "He wouldn't much mind if he did, but he doesn't. It's to do with the matter he came to see you about the other day—one of them—and I can explain better in the car. If I'm not interrupting?" He glanced at the man in camouflage.

"This gentleman was looking for the Roller, only in the wrong place." Miss Seeton began to collect bag, umbrella, and sketching things together. "The search is now better directed towards Plummergen Common, as I explained." Gentlemanly Foxon, who'd been about to claim her impedimenta and carry them, stayed his hand. The translation this time was not so simple.

"An ordinary unmarked car, MissEss. A Roller? The force can't run to luxury models, even for you. If it was up to me, of course, you could have a dozen Bentleys if you wanted."

She laughed for the extravagant compliment. The young. How they loved to tease. Mr Foxon could always make her smile. "A rare bird, not a motor car. The poor thing was blown here from the Sahara during that very dusty weather we recently had. Those sunsets, if you recall. I managed a few sketches, but it flew away before this gentleman saw it."

"If Miss Seeton told me to look round Plummergen Common, I'd go there and look," was Foxon's advice. "Or anywhere else. She knows."

"Er—thanks." The man in camouflage shook his head. "So—not the canal?"

They sent him on his way at last, still puzzled. Foxon escorted Miss Seeton back to Sweetbriars, where the not-Rolls-Royce unmarked car waited outside. He opened the passenger door, and Miss Seeton settled herself in the front seat with her brolly on the back, and her bag and sketchbook beside her.

"It's about the scrap metal thefts again," began Foxon, starting the engine. "It's got a bit more complicated, and then I had a sudden brainwave …"

Foxon had been wise to escape market-day Ashford before the streets became as clogged as they usually did. Locals knew the short cuts and escape routes, but tourists and other visitors didn't. Matters today weren't helped by a van that broke down as it delivered the latest selection of French vintages to a small but exclusive wine shop down a narrow side-street. A traffic warden, unsympathetic to clouds of steam and a smell of burned rubber hose, slapped a ticket on the windscreen and told the driver to get his nearside wheels off the pavement or there'd be more than just a fine. The wine shop owner, unlike the driver, could speak English. When sweet reason failed, he adopted English of a forceful nature. What the **expletive** (he asked) did the **censored** silly bovine expect Pierre to do—pick up the **colourful** van in one hand and carry it away? They'd already phoned the garage for a breakdown truck, and the **sanguinary** woman ought to be helping redirect the traffic rather than blaming the poor illegitimates who were doing their best—and if she couldn't see that for herself, she really ought to have her **highly emphatic** eyes tested …

The deployment of a number of Road Closed signs and barriers went unnoticed.

The armed bank robbery and subsequent getaway in a fast car came as a shock.

In theory, the illicit road closures should have provided a clear route out of Ashford. It was only when the narrow side street was found to have a cluster of uniforms at the main junction—all engaged in heated argument—and a breakdown truck half blocking the entrance, that things went wrong.

The thwarted getaway driver slammed on his brakes and achieved a handbrake turn that pointed him in another direction, but drew the immediate attention of the arguing uniforms. The dark blues were on the point of addressing their walkie-talkies when the walkie-talkies spoke first.

"Armed robbery, high street bank, four men, grey saloon heading east, report at once if sighted."

The traffic warden found herself abandoned. "You sort it, luv," yelled one of the beat bobbies whose routes had converged at the junction when concerned Ashfordians reported to the police that trouble was brewing near the wine shop. Desk Sergeant Mutford heroically refrained from delivering a temperance lecture, and sent all the men he could spare. That particular traffic warden had never been the most popular woman in town.

Breathless messages alerted the despatch room. Every car patrolling to the east of Ashford adjusted the radio handset within closer reach. Cars at other points of the compass did likewise: everyone knew how easy it was to double back on your tracks, or lose yourself in a network of narrow roads.

Brinton, cursing the absent Foxon, pored over large-scale maps and calculated. "If the original idea was to cut through past the wine shop, then he'd have come out *here* and in a couple of minutes he'd be heading straight for the motorway. We'll assume that's where he still wants to go. We've got to stop him before he reaches the junction. All he needs to do once he's gone for London—or Folkestone—is reduce his speed to a nice, steady sixty-five and take care not to draw attention to himself. Nobody'd notice him until too late. A blasted nuisance, two cars short, what with Foxon gallivant-ing and that other car flooded."

"He'll have heard the radio chatter," someone tried to soothe him. "He'll know what's happened—and Foxon's a good driver, sir. If they head his way they won't escape."

Brinton clutched his hair. "He's got a passenger with him." He drew a deep breath and crossed mental fingers. "They could be out of the car visiting scrap metal dealers and know nothing about it—or they could be heading for a round-the-corner smash-up in five minutes' time, heaven help 'em."

"Someone mentioned it was Miss Seeton with him, sir. It should be okay."

Brinton groaned. "One day even that woman's luck will run out, and there could be one hell of a mess when it does. All the close shaves and narrow squeaks she's built up over the years letting rip at once—it doesn't bear thinking about."

He abandoned the maps and strode back to the despatch room. "I need to talk to DC Foxon in whichever car he's driving. Anyone heard from him yet?"

"No, sir."

"Everyone else knows what's happened?"

"Yes, sir, but nobody's radioed in a report since the beat men here in town. It hasn't been very long, sir. And if the chummies have slowed down to think things over, with their chosen route blocked and nobody having got the number plate anyway—"

"Try again," snapped Brinton.

No answer from Foxon. Repeated, though muted, calls were made to him as the superintendent waited with the others in the despatch room for news.

A crackle across the airwaves: not Foxon. "Grey saloon, four men inside, driving within the speed limit in a westerly direction." Details of the road being travelled, and the number of the car. "I'm following."

"Hmph," said Brinton. "Bit sooner than I thought, but still—well spotted, that man." He had little doubt this was the getaway vehicle. On a normal working day, most able-bodied men are at work. Four of them at once apparently doing nothing was suspicious in itself, while close observance of the speed limit had to be the clincher. A quartet of office workers on their way to a business meeting or some other innocent destination would be far more relaxed about travelling above thirty miles an hour.

He consulted the large-scale map on the wall, and moved a numbered pin. "They're hoping to double back, of course. My money's still on the motorway. Are enough people moving into place?"

"Yes, sir."

"At least we have the number now, in case they give our lad the slip. Which, if they do, proves they're a bit dodgy even if they aren't our bank lot—though I'll bet they are."

"No takers, sir."

"Foxon here," came the welcome voice from the loudspeaker. "What's up?"

"Mr Brinton wants to talk to you," said the successful despatch officer. "Hang on."

"I'm hanging," said Foxon. "I make a lovely picture, I do."

"Foxon," barked Brinton, "where are you?"

Foxon told him. Brinton looked at the map, and sighed. "Miss Seeton with you?"

"Yes, of course she is. Sir," he added, just in case. A funny note in old Brimstone's voice. "Everything okay your end, sir? We're both fine."

"You're not planning to go anywhere near—?"

"He's spotted me!" burst from the loudspeaker. "Bloody fool—he's put his foot down! Gave the game away. Tally-ho!"

Above the clamour that now erupted as every car demanded to know in which direction the chase was heading, Brinton was unable to put the rest of his question. He'd have to wait for the noise to die down … but if he drove like fifty bats out of hell there was no way Foxon—and Miss Seeton—could encounter the Ashford gang before they were caught. Assuming it was them, which he still believed it was—it was, or they were? To hell with grammar at a time like this. Now, thank heaven, he wouldn't have to tell the Oracle he'd let one of his men go joy-riding through Kent with the Yard's special art consultant and got her squashed to a pulp by the chummies she hadn't even been asked to find.

"Seen enough scrap metal yards, have you?" he enquired of Foxon once explanations for all the fuss and furore had been made.

"Yes, I suppose so." Foxon didn't sound as cheerful as he had. Brinton grinned. The lad was missing out on the action and didn't like it.

"MissEss happy to go home?"

A brief exchange. "She says yes, sir, because it's easier to draw when the paper isn't joggled about, though if you're in a hurry—"

"No, that's fine." His mind now at rest, Brinton had briefly forgotten the reason for Miss Seeton's whistle-stop tour. "We've another bank robbery to deal with, and it's not over yet. You take her back and wait while—" He remembered where he was, and who could be listening. Miss Seeton and her doodles too often threw him off balance.

"Take her home, settle her in, and report to me as soon as you can," he finished.

"Willco," said Foxon, and was about to sign off when Brinton's conscience pricked him.

"And for pity's sake drive carefully!"

"You can trust me, sir," said Foxon, hurt; and left the airways free for another burst of hot pursuit as the grey saloon sped towards the motorway junction.

One of the first things learned by any police officer assigned to a new station was where the best chippies, cafes and tea-shops were located. Foxon had been a quick learner, all those years ago.

"We're about halfway through, and a few miles to go before the next place," he'd told his passenger as she strapped herself in her seat. "You must be getting hungry."

"Martha made a hotpot that requires no more than heating," offered Miss Seeton, who wasn't sure how far they were from home but suspected her young friend had a hearty appetite. So busy and hardworking, the police: naturally they would try as far as possible to eat at regular hours. "And fruit cake," she added. Dear Bob Ranger, although of course he was rather larger than Mr Foxon—no, Tim—always enjoyed Martha's fruit cake.

Foxon sighed. If her hotpot was only half as good as the cake he already knew, Martha's cooking was worth a detour. But (with a glance at the dashboard clock) he couldn't justify it. "We're some way away, and I'm afraid we need to get on. Now, even for you we can't run to caviar, but there's always fish and chips—shepherd's pie—bangers and mash—all on the firm. This trip justifies expenses, so what's your fancy?"

Miss Seeton deemed it wise to opt for scrambled eggs on toast. Quick (he was clearly in a hurry) and sustaining, but not costing a lot. A gentlewoman did not discuss money—and she didn't—but Mr Foxon was a young man and she had no idea how well he was paid. He had made his little joke about expenses as if he meant it—so tactful—but she would hate to think of him as being out of pocket on her behalf.

The tea had been stronger than she liked, but Mr Foxon—Tim—had asked for another pot, with plain hot water, and she thought again how kind the young man was. She hoped she wouldn't disappoint him. Almost the only "impressions" (which was what he wanted) she'd received while visiting the scrap yards had been … depressing. The motor vehicles, all with their broken windows and crumpled bodies that spoke of accident, injury, death; tyres piled in tottering heaps; squat, ugly pyramids of old refrigerators, cookers, baths and water-tanks; wash basins, lead pipes and flashing from demolished houses; cast iron fireplaces and rusty garden railings for which there was no further use …

She had politely demurred at his proposal that she might hint at selling her own front railings. Stan kept them in excellent condition. Sometimes he even allowed her to apply the undercoat, though she didn't care for the smell of gloss and he wouldn't have let her anyway. But she had no such thought in her head, and pretence was always so difficult, even in the line of duty. She supposed it might be allowable to say she could be looking out for a brass fender to suit her sitting room fireplace. It had indeed once crossed her mind that it would save Martha the effort of black-leading the one already there, with its elaborate curlicues, though Martha had laughed at her employer and said brass needed polishing—unless it was lacquered, which she didn't really like—and it would be swings and roundabouts, wouldn't it? Miss Seeton abandoned the idea, but she *had* had it. One did so much prefer to be truthful.

The greatest impression (she decided as they arrived back at Sweetbriars) had been made by the scrap dealer who'd done rather more than take lorries, cars and vans to pieces and sort those pieces accordingly. Kidman and Gallop—she hadn't been sure which had welcomed them, but he'd greeted Mr Foxon by name—boasted on their signboard that *Urns, tubs, garden furniture* were sold on the premises as well as *Garden ornaments*—these being concrete gnomes of extreme ugliness, classical female forms with chipped noses and no arms, and odd bits of pipe welded strangely together with nuts, bolts, and springs from old mattresses or chairs. Modern art, of course, or a layman's guess at it. The "furniture" was large barrels cut at right-angles, with planks nailed in for seating; she'd been interested to see that many of the flower-tubs were made from motor tyres of varying sizes, white-washed and fastened with copper strips.

"We tell the punters it kills the slugs," said Mr Kidman (or Mr Gallop) with a wink. Miss Seeton, who had watched Stan attach cut-and-hammered copper pipes round the pots that contained his—or indeed her—most cherished specimens for just such a purpose, nodded. She had no need to ask if it worked: she knew that it did.

"Unless one allows the foliage to droop over the side and reach the ground," she said, "when the slugs can use it as a bridge. Especially when the leaves are heavy with rain."

The scrap dealer laughed aloud. "Your auntie's got a head on her shoulders," he said to Mr Foxon—to Tim. Another adopted nephew; in the circumstances, one could permit the subterfuge. Had they not for some years been able to tease each other about having spent the night together? Such a likeable, cheerful young man.

Which made it so much worse that she had indeed, against hope, disappointed him. Over a second, more acceptable cup of tea he made while she sketched, she'd produced recognisable but, she had to admit, sadly dull portraits of almost every dealer she had met today. But some had been real characters, such as the one who kept a shaggy but contented pony ("Costs a small fortune in shoes") and a gaily-painted cart in a field beside his yard. For her entertainment he had delivered the traditional totter performance, a roar of "Henyole dahn, rags, bolls, bones?" *Any old iron, rags, bottles, bones?* and a deafening peal on a brass hand-bell. "Give 'em a goldfish," he said, as Miss Seeton nodded and smiled at recollections of her own childhood. She had, just once, been allowed to ring the bell herself while the family's cook-general disposed of unwanted bones from the joint. "Allus offer a goldfish when there's kids in the house—but most times they're only too glad to have stuff took away and don't want no more than a thank-you …"

His portrait was most lifelike, she thought. His smile, his energy as he swung the bell, and in the background the shaggy pony pulling the cart—ah. Not so lifelike, perhaps. Such a very large glass bowl, with an enormous goldfish happily swimming, grinning a gigantic grin. How The Whale Got His Throat. Kipling, again. And a pony—but of course the school concert was tonight. Her pencil darted next to show Mr Gallop (no, he'd said his name was Kidman) on a throne made of rubber tyres, holding like Neptune's trident one of the welded pipe ornaments that, on closer inspection, more resembled a road traffic sign. *Cattle crossing*. A foolish distraction: beef bones from the Sunday joint, and she really hadn't been able to avoid hearing the police car radio give details of the bank robbery, and how the Ashford streets had been so cleverly (one had to admit) blocked off to aid the high-speed escape. Mr Foxon—Tim—had done his best to look as if it didn't matter, but she could guess he would have much preferred to be chasing criminals rather than escorting a spinster art teacher from place to place—from face to face—with so little apparent result.

Kid-man. A young goat capered in the enthroned-as-Neptune background; Miss Seeton thought of Capricorn, the sea-goat. Perhaps the goldfish was really Moby Dick? No, that was the other sketch. Kidman—Neptune—goldfish … ponies, carts, and cattle—rag-and-bone men … Bones. At least she hadn't drawn a skeleton. Once, when she was still teaching at Mrs Benn's school—but that was long in the past. She mustn't be distracted further, by thoughts of the concert, into reminiscence, amusing (in retrospect) though the incident had undoubtedly been. Children could be so mischievous.

She added a crown of gracefully curved spare ribs to Kidman Neptune's head, and gave Moby Dick a necklace of bells.

And that was all.

Detective Constable Foxon thanked her for her help, gave her a receipt for the sketches she'd torn from her block, and drove thoughtfully back to Ashford.

Chapter Eleven

Juvenile Plummergen, over-excited, gobbled or gulped or shovelled down its evening meal to rehearse its lines with a fervour that induced near desperation in familial audiences who'd heard it all a hundred times before. It felt more like a thousand. Threats of straight-to-bed-with-no-supper were pointless. Clips round the ear might drive words and music from young skulls. "Go round Mrs Thing's and watch her telly" worked (to a degree) on those Junior Mixed Infants whose parents couldn't afford colour television and still had only black-and-white; but most adults gave up the unequal struggle and sent their offspring out to play. Better risk indigestion than have everyone driven mad by repeated enquiries as to whether Captain Drake was sleeping there below, or what should be done with the Drunken Sailor.

Though the backcloth design included in one form or another most of the song titles, the children had begged for "some dressing-up, sir, *please*," and Mr Jessyp had agreed, so long as their parents did. The hobby-horse contretemps had warned him he'd better not push his pedagogic luck too far. Mothers had duly been coaxed, nagged or otherwise chivvied into leaving scarecrows unfinished as they stitched hurried green jackets (for "Greensleeves") that, with the addition of red caps with white feathers, could be worn by the Little Men who lived up the airy mountain and roamed the rushy glen. Piratical black eye patches (Gilbert and Sullivan were Plummergen favourites) and hanks of raw wool begged from local farmers ("All in the April Evening") were much in evidence. Miss Maynard had collected as many of these props as she could, labelled them, and locked them away until required.

Participants and audience alike carried torches as they left home and made their way to the village hall, it being more central and easier for strangers to find than the school, almost half a mile distant. The car park wasn't as full as might have been expected. The European Roller was back in Rye, but this time as a guest of Babs Ongar at Wounded Wings, after a too-close encounter with Amelia Potter's Tibs. Tibs had never before met a bird that moved in such a way, and for once in her marauding life had missed, with a pawful of tail feathers her only reward for the pounce-and-grab manoeuvre that usually worked so well. The whole episode having been watched by horrified observers, Mrs Ongar was at once called to the rescue and returned to Rye with a subdued passenger in a cardboard box, and an escort of outriders on bicycles and in cars.

There remained enough of an audience to encourage Mr Jessyp to believe the Re-Wiring Fund would benefit hugely when raffle tickets were sold. He made an explanatory speech—Plummergen tried not to fidget—and announced the first song. Children wearing incoherent draperies and waving paper flowers tripped on-stage, inviting nymphs and shepherds to come, come away as this was Flora's holiday.

The concert progressed as planned. Kipling's smugglers were a great success, Bram Smith being so impressed that he resolved to purchase all the raffle tickets that remained, as well as giving the anonymous donation on which he'd already decided. In fact, he'd double the amount! "Early One Morning" gave the descant section an opportunity to shine, as they begged to be never deceived or leaved, and asked in plaintive tremolo how could a poor maiden be so u—u—used. The British Grenadiers stamped their stuff in a glorious tow, row, row that encouraged audience participation. The floorboards shook.

The final song before "God Save the Queen" was a spirited rendition of "The Mermaid", with actions. As the raging seas did roar, everyone waved blue, green and white streamers up and down. When the stormy winds did blow, the descant added "ooooh, woooo" noises and swayed on its feet. Sir George Colveden, sitting with his wife on one side and his friend Admiral Leighton on the other, observed the latter glance at the seats directly in front, close his eyes, and shudder audibly.

"Making me seasick," he moaned. "Give me a nudge when they stop."

"You'll hear when they stop," muttered Sir George.

"Can't bear to think about it." The Buzzard put his fingers in his ears. Sir George and Lady Colveden smiled wryly at each other. Nigel stifled a gurgle of mirth; Louise, rather pale, looked back with eyes full of sympathy. She'd loved every moment of her honeymoon—except the ferry to and from the Isle of Wight.

Outside in the lampless Street, keeping to the shadows and lurking by hedges, a furtive shape moved in a northerly direction from the southern end of Plummergen.

The National Anthem saw Admiral Leighton rise to his feet, assisted by Sir George and, leaning from the row in front, a grinning Nigel. The Buzzard stood to attention, and as Miss Maynard crashed out the final chords on the piano opened his eyes to applaud with added fervour.

What he said when Mr Jessyp announced an encore of "The Old Superb" made Nigel blush. Louise was sure to ask for a translation. She did. "Oh—just something nautical," he hissed as the choir began to bellow of sailing westward, ho, for Trinidad, with more waving of streamers and deafening cries of ship, ahoy! "My pa was in the army, so I wouldn't know."

Outside in the lampless Street, keeping to the shadows and lurking by hedges, a furtive shape moved in a southerly direction from the northern end of Plummergen.

A final encore of "Fire Down Below" and then the lights went up. Raffle tickets were called out, prizes distributed. Martin Jessyp thanked everyone for coming, Miss Seeton and Miss Maynard for their help and, most of all, the children, for their splendid efforts. The admiral nodded and cried *Hear, hear!* The doors of the hall were opened and empty fire buckets positioned on either side; few people dared to pass by without tossing in a few coins. The admiral handed a five-pound note to Mr Jessyp, congratulated him, and said how about "The Ruler of the Queen's Navee" next time?

His spirits were evidently restored. As chattering crowds emerged from the hall, those with raffle prizes already doing swaps and arguing over the exchange rate, Admiral Leighton stood loudly inhaling deep, refreshing breaths of cool night air. "You okay, old chap?" Sir George was concerned for his friend.

"Fine, thanks." The admiral dismissed all hint of fuss with the stoicism typical of a naval officer who'd taken hurricanes, torpedoes, and minefields in his stride.

"But indeed, one does understand," said Louise, as colour returned to her cheeks. "The visual effects were ... most realistic."

"Rather too realistic for a man my age," said the Buzzard cheerfully. "I blame it on my new specs—spectacles to you, Louise. Glasses. Bifocals, in fact, and they're still settling down. But you're young, my dear. Have Nigel pour you a stiff brandy when you're safely home, and you'll be right as a trivet in no time."

"Does poor Louise feel a touch under the weather?" Miss Seeton, flashlight in hand, brolly and bag over one arm, had come up beside the group where it stood bathed in the pale golden glow from the open hall door. She had modestly accepted praise for her versatile and multi-titled backcloth but insisted to well-wishers that she had been very lucky in Mr Jessyp's planning, which left her little to do beyond sketch the charcoal outlines and explain to the children where the appropriate paint should be applied. The older, neater children had filled in the words: she was delighted it had all proved such a success.

"The motion of the sea," said Louise, rocking her outstretched hand from side to side, "I do not much care for, but I will survive. It is soon over."

"Not *that* soon," said the admiral. "Very lifelike stage effects, Miss Seeton. For some of us, possibly a little too lifelike."

"Oh dear," said Miss Seeton. "The children did so enjoy themselves, but—"

"Fresh air's the thing," the Buzzard hurried on before she could apologise, although it was hardly her fault. Jessyp had stage-managed the affair; on the whole he'd made a thundering good job of it. "Fresh air. Let me escort you home, Miss

Seeton. A gentle stroll the length of The Street would be as good as a tonic—as well as giving me the pleasure of your company, which of course goes without saying."

"Oh, of course," replied Miss Seeton gravely, though her eyes danced.

The admiral's beard was seen to twitch as a chuckle was suppressed. He met gravity with gravity, bowed, and took her hand upon his arm.

"All the nice girls," chanted Nigel, "love a sailor."

"And you know what sailors are," promptly returned the admiral. "Come along, Miss Seeton. We'll leave that impudent young hound to be driven back to the Hall like the idle fellow he is, while we energetic old folk stretch our legs."

"But Nigel farms," began Louise, "and rises early—"

Lady Colveden patted her shoulder. "English humour, my dear. I shouldn't worry."

"My mother," said Louise, catching on, "was a Scot."

PC Potter directed traffic from the car park, uniform buttons flashing as quick movements of his torch warned of an inattentive pedestrian, a bicycle with no lights, or (by far the greatest danger) old Mr Meredith in his motorised chair. As deaf as a post but always ready to join in any village escapade, even a concert, this long-term resident at the nursing home had been warned on more than one occasion that hot-wiring was illegal. The purpose of the wheelchair's speed limiter was—well, to limit the wheelchair's speed. Mr Meredith would sadly shake his hearing aid, and complain that it needed new batteries.

As Miss Seeton passed by on the admiral's arm, and a chuckling Mr Meredith sped northwards up The Street, PC Potter revived his failing *amour propre* with one of the smartest salutes he'd achieved in years. "Good night, Miss

Seeton—sir!" Admiral Leighton kindly returned the salute—magistrate Sir George and the other Colvedens were driving—as a darkened bicycle clattered past, its bell trilling in derision and its wheels only just missing PC Potter's regulation toecaps. A mocking whistle echoed through the night.

The close of a typical Plummergen evening, nothing more.

As the concert audience dispersed and the crowds grew smaller, two dark, furtive shadows moved and melted into even darker shadows. Watching.

The admiral delivered his prize to the southern corner of The Street and waited for her to find her key. He took it from her, walked with her up the short front path, and inserted it in the lock as she shone her flashlight to make things easier for him.

"Thank you very much, Admiral Leighton. So kind," said Miss Seeton.

"A very good night to you, ma'am." He saluted again; watched her inside the cottage. He heard the key turn on the other side of the door, and nodded. George had told him how long it took the authorities to persuade Miss Seeton that, living alone as she did, with her house in full view of anyone who passed, it was as good as issuing an open invitation if she didn't take sensible precautions. Scotland Yard once arranged the installation of an alarm system, but she'd blown it up—fused it—scuppered the thing, anyhow, in that way she sometimes had of turning everything topsy-turvy without meaning to. Fearing a rather more widespread power blackout next time—there was bound to be a next time—they'd decided to let well alone, appealing instead to her sense of duty. It wasn't fair for someone who had everything in life she wanted to present temptation to those who had not. The argument was persuasive. Miss Seeton understood what they meant, regretted that it really hadn't occurred to her before, and promised she would always lock her door at night.

"During the day, of course, there is no need," she said. "I have so many friends in the village, who would be sure to notice should anyone enter my house without permission. People are always going in and out of shops, and of course the George is just across The Street—but I am most grateful for your concern."

The admiral heard no shooting of bolts. Perhaps, like old Meredith, he could do with a hearing aid as well as bifocals? No, most likely she hadn't bothered. Still, from what he knew of Miss Seeton she could repel any number of boarders without trouble. He wouldn't say anything to George, fellow clubman or not. She was captain of her own ship, bless her, and by all accounts managed to set a pretty straight course under her own steam. He set his own course towards Ararat Cottage, halfway up The Street, and the kye—strong naval chocolate shredded into hot sweetened milk, with a tot or two of rum for extra flavour—that was his regular bedtime noggin.

He was so busy making up his mind whether it should be a two-tot night, after all the excitement of the concert, that he did not observe how one of the watching shadows had melted away at his advance, and was drifting in the direction of Sweetbriars.

Nor did he notice the second watching shadow following the first.

The kettle was ready and waiting, should Miss Seeton decide on a cup of tea before bed, but her mind, too, was busy. Images of the concert still dazzled her inward eye, even after that pleasant walk in the fresh air under the admiral's escort.

Such a gentleman. And a great surprise that he should suffer from seasickness, though she knew that Nelson had suffered likewise. Or maybe he'd been teasing. Poor Louise, it seemed, had not. He could have been putting her at her ease, as befitted a gentleman. And another Horatio—Hornblower, CS Forester's midshipman who'd been sick off Spithead. All the nice girls love a sailor. So naughty of dear Nigel. She remembered a music-hall act where they'd sung "gulls" instead, and danced a comical hornpipe in feather costumes, playing the kazoo and penny whistle to sound as birdlike as possible. Miss Seeton smiled. Not that she would use it herself, of course, but everyone knew the admiral's nickname: he was Bernard "the Buzzard" Leighton. Perhaps it was something to do with his beard. Bearded like the pard, as Shakespeare put it, although wasn't that the soldier rather than the sailor? All the world's a stage …

She had no idea how long she'd been lost in thought, but she hadn't made a cup of tea or even removed her hat. She found herself seated at the bureau in the sitting room with an open sketchbook before her, looking back through the concert rehearsal sketches and adding details of the finished performance on the stage of the village hall. The weary lambs of the April evening—the booted Cavaliers riding to the relief of Castle Brancepeth—the smugglers with their bales, boxes and barrels—oh.

To her dismay, she realised that she'd included the hobby-horses to which Mr Jessyp had raised such an objection. Oh, dear. Five and twenty ponies: such an insistent phrase, being the first line of the chorus. Mr Jessyp had been too busy as the producer to take photographs: he was skilful and painstaking with a camera, and disliked a hurried job. She had promised a series of coloured pictures of each song just as it was performed, to be hung on classroom walls after the children had chosen their favourites.

She turned to a blank page, and started again. In firm black letters, to remind herself, she wrote *Smugglers* and underlined it. How very foolish. What was that seagull doing there? All the nice girls ... Did smuggling fishermen count as sailors? She supposed they did. The Merchant—rather than the admiral's Royal—Navy, of course. And of course they would never be seasick, because if they were they could be farmers instead, and never go to sea, as advised by the Ruler of the Queen's Navee. She hummed a snatch of Gilbert and Sullivan, and drew another bird, with a hooked beak and beady eye. A buzzard. Oh, dear. Perhaps she was a little tired. After all, it was late. A seasick sailor ... *Horatio*, she wrote beside the elaborate curl of a French horn, adding first a trombone and then a trumpet, in lieu of a penny whistle. She wasn't sure she knew what a kazoo looked like. The "Punch and Judy" squeaker, wasn't it? No, that was a swizzle—or was it a swozzle—but an equally curious name, for another instrument that made such a curious sound ...

A sound. Curious, Miss Seeton turned to listen.

It was late. Martha? She'd seen Martha leave the hall with Stan almost immediately the raffle prizes were announced: farm workers rise early, as dear Louise reminded the admiral—a gentleman, but such a tease—and Martha had waved goodbye, and said she'd see her tomorrow. She'd said nothing about coming today—except that perhaps it already *was* tomorrow. A glance at the sitting room clock—yes, tomorrow—but all the same, a most unusual time for Martha to be at the kitchen door, as it was evident somebody was. The concert audience would surely have gone to bed by now; guests and those like Doris and the Mountfitchets, who lived at the George, would be in bed too. Moreover, Martha had her own key, both to the door and to the gate in the side wall that made it so convenient for popping across from the Bloomers' little cottage down the narrow lane.

Any visitor at this hour—a lost traveller, no doubt, seeing her light still on—would come to her front door, not the back. Miss Seeton rose, and went into the hall.

She stared. The man she'd met by the tomb of Abraham Voller, still in his camouflage, was coming out of her kitchen.

"Good gracious. What are you doing here? Really, this is—"

"Shut it," he told her. She glanced round at the sitting room door through which she'd just come. "Get back in there, right? And keep quiet."

She stared at him. Were she to shut the door as he wished, how could—?

"Hurry up," he said.

"I don't underst—"

"Hurry up," he said again. "And don't talk rubbish. You've found out where it is, and—" He hesitated. "And you've got to keep quiet about it—a couple of days should be enough."

"I have no idea what you mean." Miss Seeton was firm. "Nor do I know why you are here where really you have no business to—"

She broke off. Some birdwatchers, she knew, could become a little … unhinged in their enthusiasm. He still wore his camouflage outfit, which proved it: what use was camouflage in the middle of the night? Most birds, apart from owls, would be asleep. Besides, as she had suggested to him before—only now she knew that it was true, because Mrs Ongar had told her so—the bird had definitely flown. Or

216

had flown as far as Plummergen Common, then gone on in a cardboard box to Wounded Wings.

He was glaring at her: frowning. Almost scowling, like a child. Well, there had been tantrums enough at the concert tonight, soon brought under control: but she was tired. There was a limit to how far even the sulkiest child should be humoured, no matter how over-excited.

"I fear you may be acting under a misapprehension." She would try reasoning with him as an adult; the wisest course would be to let him down gently, if she could. "The bird has indeed flown, and there is little point in my agreeing to keep quiet about its whereabouts because everybody knows." She smiled. "Mrs Ongar said she had almost a police escort as she drove to Rye."

The frown—the scowl—changed to a narrow-eyed glare. "The police?"

"Mrs Ongar's little joke." Humour, of course, was a very individual matter, and she knew that once it was explained in detail any trace of humour tended to be lost; but he did appear to be worried. "So many of your friends went with her, you see."

The glare turned to an open-mouthed stare. "She assures me it is safe," she went on. Naturally, so keen a twitcher would be anxious to know the fate of the unlucky Roller. "Tibs missed it—so fortunate, apart from the tail—and that of course will grow back in time."

Worry turned to bewilderment. "Sit down," he told her, indicating the chair by the open bureau, "and shut up. I haven't a clue what you're talking about. I just want you to—"

He grabbed the sketchbook on which she'd been doodling her thoughts on Hornblower, Nelson and musical instruments, on seagulls and buzzards.

217

He uttered an exclamation Miss Seeton didn't recognise, although she knew from his tone that it was ... forceful. To say the least.

"I see no need for bad language." The automatic rebuke from an experienced teacher.

"Oh don't you, you daft **blank**!"

"No," said Miss Seeton.

They stared at each other. The man in camouflage brandished the sketchbook under her nose. "First you try kidding me you don't know nothing about it, then you talk a load of gibberish—then you show me this."

"I didn't show—"

"And you talked so much tripe I was starting to believe you!" The protest reminded her again of a child, thwarted in its intentions and not quite knowing what to do next. "Look, I know you know about it—God knows how—but all I want is for you to keep shtum for a day or two, right? You've got to promise. Or else," he added.

Yes, very like a child. "I've already told you," she began; then wondered. Had she?

No, she hadn't. Of course, he wanted the full address. "You must go to the Wounded Wings bird sanctuary in Rye," she explained apologetically, and gave details. No wonder he'd been so annoyed at her forgetting to tell him what he most wanted to know. "Mrs Ongar is a very kind and helpful person," she went on, "although I would strongly advise your waiting for the official opening time, which I believe is nine o'clock. It may be ten. No doubt you will find your friends there, too. But one shouldn't really take advantage of the kindness of another. It is hardly fair, when she is always so busy."

She smiled at the muscle-bound child with the puzzled expression. Too old for sweets. "How would you like a cup of tea?" she asked. "There is fruit cake in the tin. Mr Foxon— you will recall meeting him, the young police detective with such a—an individual sense of fashion—ate only one slice, because we had already lunched together and he was in something of a hurry to return to Ashford." She rose to her feet.

"A cup of tea," he echoed.

"The kettle is already filled. It won't take long."

He dropped the sketchbook on the bureau shelf, and followed her into the kitchen.

The whole evening was a thrilling experience for the young American visitor in search of his Plummergen roots. Everyone in the village (he thought) must have been at the concert—as had he! Sir George Colveden, the only local who knew of the family connection, greeted him with a friendly nod but didn't say much beyond the usual courtesies. Lady Colveden smiled at him; Nigel and Louise chatted for a while. Others who had met Bram Smith in shops, or at the bar of the George and Dragon, or just generally about the place, said rather more; Jack Crabbe and his father Victor, tourist taxi-drivers, engaged him in cheerful conversation and introduced him to Old Crabbe, Victor's grandsire and founder of the garage that bore their name. Old Crabbe and his wheelchair-bound crony Mr Meredith were laughing together over some internal combustion mischief they planned, and cheerfully invited Bram to join them when neither Jack nor his father would. At Jack's warning look Bram thanked them for the invitation, but said he didn't know how much longer he'd be staying.

After the concert, his spirits high, he walked up The Street as escort to Maureen-from-the-George (who'd been given the night off by Charley Mountfitchet, two of her younger siblings being concert performers) and her friend Emmy Putts. Maureen's Wayne, wheeling his motorbike, glowered suspiciously all the way to the corner of the road where stood the gateway sign welcoming people to Plummergen. Mr Smith solemnly shook hands with the third scarecrow on Welcome duty, then tipped an invisible hat to the ladies, grinned at Wayne, and said he guessed he'd be heading back to the George now in case Mr Mountfitchet forgot he'd given him a key and had shot the bolts across the door.

But he wasn't yet inclined for bed. He walked past the George, where the only light was above the door and every room was dark. He walked on down the narrow lane, over the bridge to the canal; he strolled some way along the Rhee Wall, then wandered back past the Bloomers' cottage and past Sweetbriars, where the light was still on. Miss Seeton had helped organise the concert, which had been such a success. She'd be sitting with a cup of tea, or perhaps a glass of sherry, enjoying a peaceful gloat, he decided. He hesitated on the corner before making for the churchyard and another private look at Abraham's tomb. Was the old guy laughing, wherever he might be? Did he approve of his how-many-great grand nephew's interest in his smuggler past? What did sister Ann think of it all?

He didn't stay for long amid the leafy shadows from a starlit sky, but he stood so still that when an owl hooted close by he jumped, and felt the air stir as the bird flew from tree to tree on white, silent wings. The moon was setting. Perhaps it was time for bed after all.

Not knowing the correct procedure he left the outside light on as he entered the George, secured the door behind him and headed for bed. Within minutes, he was asleep.

What woke him? His dream certainly hadn't disturbed him—there was no harm, surely, in flocks of sheep grazing on fresh green April grass beside the sea, with ponies trotting freely among them and, in the background, a ship in full sail. The Old Superb, or a smuggler? An owl hooted. The same owl he'd encountered by Abraham's tomb, or a signal from the Gentlemen? He blinked his way out of bed and went to the window. By the gleam of the porch light he could see, in the distance, a man creeping through the shadows with a dark, narrow shape slumped over one shoulder. *Laces for a lady*. He went back to bed.

What woke him? This time, he woke properly. That hadn't been a bundle of lace, or a sack of letters for a spy the man in shadow had carried. It had been … human.

Murreystone! The scarecrow. Only—why bring it all the way from the far end of town? He peered into the night. Where were the Watch Men who hadn't let him join? What had happened to the scarecrow? How long ago? Did he have time to do anything about it? Should he rouse the landlord?

No, he might have dreamed the whole thing after all.

But if he hadn't … and if modern Plummergen couldn't put things right, historic Plummergen would sure as hell give it the old home try.

He was dressed, down the stairs, and out of the George within minutes. He looked in all directions as far as he could see, but saw nobody. The owl hooted in mockery. Was that all it had been? He'd wondered before if old Abe might be laughing, and maybe …

He turned his steps towards his mischievous collateral's tomb.

It wasn't easy, in the middle of the night, to see exactly where he was going, even with the torch he'd quickly adopted as a proud Plummergen custom. Shadows were deceptive, and there were rough bits of ground and clumps of grass to catch his feet. There was the owl again—no, it must be another night-bird. Did they have screech owls in this country? A kind of high-pitched, trilling call—

Calling for help.

In a human voice.

He almost dropped his torch—recovered himself—stood and listened.

"Help!" There it was again—muffled, weak, but distinct. She wasn't far away.

He slowly revolved where he stood, listening. It didn't seem right for him to shout out loud, so close to a church.

"Help!"

Now he had the direction. He pointed his torch to give him the line …

The cries for help were coming from the tomb of Abraham Voller.

Bram Smith didn't believe in ghosts, not even ancestral ghosts. Old Abe had survived many years beyond that phony date inscribed on his tomb. If he haunted any place at all, it would surely be somewhere on the other side of the Atlantic.

"Help!"

He was closer now. "I'm coming," he called softly, hoping she'd hear him through the heavy stone walls—but of course, if he could hear her she must be able to hear him. "I'm here!" He stopped. *But how the hell do I get you out of this?*

"Hang on!" he told the captive, and began to rack his memory for what he'd read about the smuggler's—the stonemason's—clever trick. The front panel—or was it the back—could be pushed to one side and free the longer side to be slid along …

He pushed, shoved, changed sides and pushed again. There was a grinding sound. The panel moved. He sniffed, leaned in, sneezed, and shone his torch.

"Miss Seeton! That can't be you!"

"Yes, it can," said Miss Seeton. Her hat was squashed over her eyes. "Oh, my head."

"Holy cow!" Bram took a closer look. Miss Seeton's hands were tied. The battered hat made a blindfold she couldn't remove. More rope was tied around her ankles. Every knot looked both efficient, and strong.

"My head," said Miss Seeton again. "Is that you, Mr Smith?"

"It surely is, ma'am. I won't ask what you're doing here— let me help you, first."

"He knocked me out, I believe." Now that rescue had arrived, and brought fresh air, she could breathe deeply and start to recover her senses. "I was making him a cup of tea, and … and I'm sure my hat must be ruined."

"Wow," said the admiring Bram. "Do you Brits know how to keep your cool, or what!"

"What?" In less uncertain moments she would have begged his pardon and said she didn't quite understand.

"Forget it. Let's have you out of there. I don't have a knife, so I may have to take a few liberties, but I guess in the circumstances that's okay with you."

"That's okay." Miss Seeton tasted the word on her tongue. Slang could be most expressive, and she was suddenly too weary to care overmuch for the Queen's English.

Before beginning his work he removed her hat, and shone his torch on the wreckage. She sighed. "It could be worse," she said faintly.

Bram was a tall, well-built young man; Miss Seeton weighed seven stone fully clothed. It was more the awkward angle than her physical size that made liberation rather slower than he would have liked, but at last she was out in the open air, thanking him.

"I'll take you to the George," he decided. "They'll have knives in the kitchen for these ropes, and a stiff brandy for shock."

"But my cottage—" she began. He cut her short by sweeping her into his arms. "And you ought to see a doctor. Can you hold the torch while I carry you?"

He rose to his feet and strode through the night, feeling secretly proud. The long-lost son of Plummergen had scored a greater hit than any official Night Watch Man.

This time Bram Smith had no qualms about disturbing the landlord. Charley Mountfitchet was horrified at the sight of Miss Seeton. Bram had raided the kitchen for a suitable knife—even in his horror Charley suffered a fleeting twinge about what Bertha was likely to say—and lengths of sawn-off rope littered the floor of the bar, where Mr Smith had settled Miss Seeton in a comfortable chair while he raised the alarm. Charley poured a generous dollop into a brandy glass and, as Miss Seeton uttered a faint protest, added a splash of soda. He poured more of the same for Bram, and said he would call the police.

"Oh, dear," protested Miss Seeton, pale but rallying, as she sipped.

"And the doctor," said Bram. Charley waved acknowledgement and vanished towards the entrance lobby, and the telephone at Reception.

The landlord of the George and Dragon cherished a desire to live in California and wear a trilby and a trench coat, to smoke cigars and talk from the corner of his mouth, to flash his private eye's licence at all and sundry as he prowled the mean streets. In true British style he compromised by helping the police with their enquiries on every possible occasion. With anyone other than Miss Seeton he would have called the doctor first; but Charley knew Miss Seeton of old, and how quickly she could bounce back from the most startling misadventure. He therefore telephoned PC Potter and waited eagerly for the call to be answered. Only then did he telephone Dr Knight.

The doctor arrived to find his patient being interrogated with some urgency by a half-buttoned PC Potter, who'd even forgotten his cap in his excitement. As Dr Knight, like all her friends, knew Miss Seeton well he allowed Potter five minutes for the basic story, then chivvied everyone out of the bar in order to check for concussion, memory loss, cuts, bumps, and bruises. He said she wasn't to hit the booze too hard, shook Bram Smith warmly by the hand—the young man glowed with pride—and went home to bed.

Potter, meanwhile, in obedience to his Standing Orders had telephoned Superintendent Brinton in Ashford ...

The aftermath of the bank robbery had taken longer to resolve than Brinton expected. As Foxon, fresh from his Scrap Yard excursion with Miss Seeton, turned up with her sketches in a large brown envelope, intent on opening an artistic discussion, he found the superintendent at his desk drinking strong tea, with the coronation sugar-tin defiantly in front of him and its owner glaring at his approach.

Before Foxon had done more than greet him: "Don't ask," snarled Brinton. "Shakespeare, isn't it, who says we first kill all the lawyers?"

Foxon took the hint, and dropped the envelope without comment into Brinton's already full in-tray. He made a swift deduction. "The chummies have smart briefs, already on tap. They're not new at the game and they know when to keep quiet," he said.

"As advised by their lawyers, who took an age to get here and gave the blighters even longer to rehearse No Comment in a dozen different voices."

"But, sir, from the radio chatter I thought we'd got 'em bang to rights. By all accounts, I missed a pretty good show."

Brinton grunted. "Tell that to Traffic. Chased the blighters halfway to the Smoke before they caught up with 'em, then tried the pincer trick and found the damn getaway car'd been fixed so the engine was at the back. Complete rebuild—a more powerful engine—and from the outside you'd never know. They bashed our leading car kerwallop up the backside straight into the central barrier—braked—a quick reverse giving our other two the chance to bash into the first—skipped merrily round the carnage and carried on regardless. Of course, we got 'em in the end—it all happened too far from the next junction to get off the motorway in time, and the damage made 'em conspicuous—but it was lucky nobody was badly hurt. Before we got 'em back to the station, they claimed it was panic that made 'em bolt. Admitted stealing the car but said they'd no idea it worked like that, dearie dear how sorry they were for everything. Then they shut up like clams, and now the lawyers say it was shock made 'em say as much as they did."

"Silence is golden," observed Foxon dryly.

Brinton picked up the office *Moriarty* to wave the twenty-second edition of the standard work on Police Law under the younger man's astonished nose. "How I'd love to throw the book at the blighters. One of the smartest smart-alecks quoted Section 249 of the Highways Act on experimental vehicles undergoing road trials. Said just because they didn't *know* it was a new design didn't mean the law shouldn't still apply. Claimed the car was *Not subject to the Regulations* and not subject to the speed limit, either. Kill 'em all, I say. It's not so much the bank job—the oodle was right there with 'em, there's no way they can deny it—but those three cars will be off the road for weeks and that annoys me, Foxon. When I think of the cost of repairs—not to mention the one those other idiots drove into a puddle and flooded—and the crooks we wouldn't be able to chase now if they committed multiple murder on the station doorstep—my blood boils." He tore vaguely at his hair, and poked angrily at the heap of papers in his in-tray. "And now you want me to look at pretty pictures, with this lot hanging over me. Oh, we'll get 'em in time, but where's the time to come from?"

He rubbed his eyes, grimaced, and drank more tea. "Mutford wants to do 'em for litter in a public place," he went on. "Of course they'll deny it, and you can bet we won't find any prints on those Road Closed signs and they'll swear it was nothing to do with them anyway, but it's a start. I suppose. Only—where do we go from there?"

"One step at a time, sir," said Foxon encouragingly.

Brinton's gloom was such that he didn't even tell Foxon he hated him.

Chapter Twelve

The afternoon and evening stretched almost beyond endurance. Questioning was slow. Too many questions went unanswered, or were answered with studied ignorance. Relays of police officers varied the questioning; villains smirked at each new visitation. Lawyers began to speak of Habeas Corpus, and how much longer did Brinton think he could drag this out. Why not just bail their clients and let everyone go home to bed?

"They're stringing us along for laughs, sir. We could be here all night. Can't we kick 'em out now and bring additional charges later?" Foxon, leaving Brinton alone with his in-tray, had taken his own turn at questioning and been the recipient of a particularly exasperating smirk.

Brinton looked up from the scrap dealer portraits he was studying. "Ten to one they'd skip bail and that'd be the last we'd see of 'em. Even with this lot of oodle impounded for evidence—ha bloody ha—you can bet there's enough cash knocking around elsewhere for them to manage without it. Those smart-Aleck briefs don't come cheap, laddie. They need to know they'll be paid, one way or another. They wouldn't be here otherwise."

Foxon, who in common with the rest of Ashford station knew and liked the three Traffic men now in hospital, sympathised with his boss. Shakespeare hadn't been wrong. The lawyers had (with strong reservations) eventually conceded the presence of shotguns and stolen money in the car—but their clients had known nothing about them. (When this stout denial was reported to Brinton he turned purple, giving Foxon several anxious moments.) They'd admitted to Taking and Driving Away. They'd been joy-riding, but that was all to which they'd admit, and joy-riding didn't merit hours of interrogation and loss of freedom. Bank robbery? They'd been as surprised as anyone at the police claim to have found stolen money in the vehicle—and such a vehicle! No wonder its remarkable performance had unnerved the joy-riders into fleeing the scene when they were ambushed …

"Any minute now," growled Brinton, "they'll say we planted the oodle and the shooters in that humbugged car and it's all our fault for having spoiled their nice day out."

As he hadn't yet been asked to give his ideas on Miss Seeton's sketches, Foxon tactfully left Brinton to his brooding and looked instead through *Moriarty's Police Law* in hopes of finding a way to break the legal stalemate so they could all go home.

"Reckless damage to property," he said at last. "It doesn't specify *whose* property, and by all accounts they were driving recklessly and you said yourself, sir, it'll be ages before those three patrol cars are back on the road. Would that do?"

Brinton emerged from his thoughts. "Not bad, laddie, not bad. We'll have to chance the bail, I suppose. Enough is enough and I've had it up to here with the runaround we're being given. As it is we'll be stuck in this place past midnight, tidying up the paperwork."

They were.

Brinton was a responsible officer, and wouldn't ask his men to do anything he was not prepared to do himself. He might delegate—in a busy police station that was inevitable—but he didn't go home and leave them to it. He stayed until the last completed form had been submitted for his approval, and he read every one. His blood was still simmering at the wily arguments employed by the legal team from London.

"If I took a good-sized hatchet to those perishers as they deserve," he told a yawning Foxon, "I'd let one of 'em live so I could brief him for the defence. Scot free and snow white I'd be, with him to argue the case." He sighed. "But it makes my head hurt. Is there a connection, or is it a copycat job and your Gridlockers idea is catching on? One lot blocks the road with a removal van and then gets killed because the road signs have been pinched—which is their bad luck, but gives somebody else a better idea. Somebody who? Did they know the first lot—or is it just coincidence? They raid a council depot, pinch more road signs and rig it so there's only one quick way out of town for them, too. Maybe one lot saw *The Ladykillers* on telly the other week, and the other prefers *The Italian Job.* MissEss seems to think there's an answer of some sort to *something* with these two blokes—" he indicated the Moby Dick goldfish, and Neptune with his trident— "but does she mean one for each gang, or something else altogether?"

Foxon hesitated.

"Come on, young Timothy." Now that he'd let off steam, Brinton was almost amiable. He gazed thoughtfully at his in-tray, then glanced at his watch. "You've had longer than me to think about what she meant when she was doing these scribbles—and fruit cake into the bargain, I'll be bound." Foxon grinned. "Well, then."

"She did seem to take rather a shine to—"

The telephone rang. Brinton, muttering something expressive, snatched it up. "Potter?" Foxon froze. Brinton listened. "What?" He indicated the extension. Foxon, very much aware of the lateness of the hour, with some apprehension picked it up. "Dr Knight's happy about her, is he?"

"Yes, sir, though she ent too happy herself," reported Potter. "Keeps apologising for getting everyone out of bed, and complains about her hat and says tent even as if they was real feathers—"

"Feathers?" chorused the two in Ashford.

"Seems he's very keen on birds, sir. Obsessive, she called him. Said he weren't best pleased when she told him it'd been took to the sanctuary in Rye and—well, lost his temper and thumped her when she said she couldn't see the point of keeping quiet about it because everyone knew where it was. Sir," Potter ended, on an apologetic note.

"Stay there," commanded the superintendent. "And keep her there—and the bloke who found her, too. We're on our way."

He looked towards his subordinate, shrugging himself into his jacket. He drew a resolute breath. "Hurry up … Detective Sergeant Foxon!" Again Foxon froze, one arm stuck in a sleeve. Brinton pulled a small brown envelope from his in-tray and threw it across.

"Came earlier, but with one thing and another …" One being that, in between dealing with the bank robbery, he'd had time to worry about what he would do should Foxon want to move on. "Ought to have told you before. Sorry—and congratulations, laddie. You may not believe me, but I think you deserve it. As to what happens next … that's up to you."

"I drive us to Plummergen, yes?"

Foxon was grinning broadly; but the superintendent's grin almost split his face in two.

Before hurrying from the office Brinton collected Miss Seeton's scrap dealer doodles and returned them to their envelope. If there was time, if she was okay, he'd ask about them after they'd looked into this other business. He then took Foxon the long way round to the car park so that he could address him as "Sergeant" when they passed Sergeant Mutford at his desk.

"It was the reckless damage that clinched it," the superintendent explained, as Mutford regarded the pair in apparent surprise. "Your littering wasn't at all a bad notion—but reckless damage deserved a pat on the back, I thought. So I promoted him."

"Yes, sir," said Mutford, who had little sense of humour but knew everything that went on in Ashford police station before anyone else did. He'd recognised the envelope as soon as it arrived, and Brinton knew that he had. "A great surprise, sir—and well merited, Foxon." He gave the young man a solemn look. "You'll be able to buy a more suitable wardrobe with the increase in pay, won't you." It was not a question.

"Oh. Will I?" Foxon's indignant response was.

Brinton hurried him away. "Save the sartorial discussion for tomorrow—for later today, I mean. We're off to Plummergen now, Mutford," he announced over his shoulder.

"Yes, sir," said Mutford, who knew that, too.

When they arrived at the George and Dragon they weren't surprised to find Charley Mountfitchet, would-be sleuth, standing guard with PC Potter over Miss Seeton. Likewise it didn't surprise them that she looked embarrassed by all the attention. She felt so much better now—Dr Knight had

232

said there was no need to worry—it was really only her hat, and Mr Mountfitchet had done his best, though she hated putting people to so much trouble—but of course one could not condone burglary even when nothing had been taken and, while enthusiasm was always to be encouraged, there were times when she felt it might go a little too far, and she feared that this had been one of them …

To set her at her ease Brinton told her Foxon's news. She was delighted on behalf of her newly-acquired nephew, and lost all awkwardness. Introductions were made; Brinton thanked Bram Smith for his quick-wittedness before saying his statement would be taken in due course, but for now would he mind if they spoke first to Miss Seeton.

"The Residents' Lounge," suggested Charley at once. "You and me, sir," to Bram, "and Ned Potter if the superintendent will turn a blind eye, we'll have a nightcap here in the bar."

"We'll be back," said Brinton, and ushered Miss Seeton from the room.

She was about to remind him that Sweetbriars was within diagonal sight across The Street from the George when she realised how very selfish of her this would be. Asking to go home when he'd said he wanted to talk to that charming Mr Smith (who'd been so very kind) and would have to come back here in order to do so. She'd tidied herself as best she could—Mr Smith had gone to his room and fetched his clothes brush, while Mr Mountfitchet really had tried his best—Miss Seeton sighed—but she knew how important it was to help the police with their enquiries, even if there was very little she could tell them except that the man was probably in Rye by now, and she was sorry they'd had to come all this way just to find that out when they could have gone straight there in the morning.

"And I trust," she finished, "that he will act with rather more restraint towards Mrs Ongar than he showed towards myself. The smell, you know—although I did find it less oppressive than some of the painting supplies one sometimes has to use—but I have never smoked in my life, and to be confined in so small a space—"

"Smoke?" burst from Brinton. "I'm sorry, but—you mean tobacco? In that tomb?"

"Mr Smith is a non-smoker. He tells me he is very keen on sport, and I know Sergeant Ranger does not, either."

Brinton stared at her, then at Foxon. The same incredulous light was starting to gleam in both pairs of eyes. She'd even mentioned the Oracle's sidekick …

Brinton coughed. "This bird-man of yours, Miss Seeton. Can you describe him? Better still," he produced her envelope of scrap dealer portraits, "could you draw him on the back of one of these?"

Oh, dear. Miss Seeton sighed again. She'd been afraid her sketches would be of no use to Tim Foxon—how splendid that he was now a sergeant, like dear Bob—and she could tell they hadn't been. Of course, Mr Brinton was in a hurry, so perhaps … And if she'd been in her cottage she could have used fresh paper and her own pencils, but …

"I will certainly do my best," she said, "if someone could lend me a pencil, but Mr—that is," with a smile, "Sergeant Foxon can describe him far better than I in words, and at once. They met earlier today, or I should perhaps say yesterday." Brinton stared. Foxon frowned. "When I was sketching the smuggler's tomb."

"That was him?" Foxon wasn't one for grammar in moments of urgency, any more than Brinton. "The bloke in the camouflage outfit?"

"Some birdwatchers pursue their hobby with great intensity, as I know. Several of my friends—" Miss Seeton broke off. "But very few, I trust, would be so—so extreme as to treat anyone with the great discourtesy shown to myself." She looked a little cross. Her audience couldn't blame her. To be hit on the head, tied up and shoved inside a cold stone box until someone came to the rescue was a good deal more than discourteous, by police standards. Not to mention (Foxon silently added) the reckless damage to her hat. The hat was probably what had annoyed her most.

"To say to one's face that one's word is disbelieved," went on Miss Seeton, "is not the behaviour of a gentleman. At least the other man didn't try to approach me. To be accused once of speaking an untruth is annoying enough, but I managed to keep my temper. One does not wish to be rude, but had he—the other man, that is—said anything of a similar nature to me I fear I would indeed have spoken to him sharply. But as he so obviously had no wish to be seen as he began to follow the other man, no doubt that is why he didn't."

Brinton untangled the number of men who might, or might not, have called Miss Seeton a liar. "Someone's been following this chap who hit you on the head? You're saying there were two of them up to monkey tricks at one and the same time?"

"There were a great many strangers in the village, Superintendent. Sharing the same interests, their paths were bound to cross, and on more than one occasion." Mr Brinton, she knew, was a gardener rather than a naturalist. "People sometimes travel the length of the country to view a rare specimen, and from what Mrs Ongar told me the European Roller very seldom reaches these shores. For which reason, once it had flown away they went away too, and on its unexpected return there weren't nearly as many who came back before the poor thing was attacked by Tibs. So lucky that it was reported to Mrs Ongar and rescued, as I tried to explain— to the man in camouflage, that is, not the other, who wears dark clothing of a … a casual style." Her gaze wandered to Detective Sergeant Foxon, and lingered for a moment. "They always try to merge into the background—twitchers, that is—and, while camouflage is intended to break up the outline, I noticed him almost at once. He must have moved at just the wrong moment, and brought himself to my attention."

She glanced again at Foxon, and smiled. "Shortly after our little chat began you arrived, dear Sergeant, and invited me to go with you. It is clear now that he supposed I must have more information on the bird's whereabouts than I had given him, in which of course he was mistaken, but as you and I were out of the village for much of the day he would have wasted his time knocking at my door. The only surprise is that he waited so long to ask me, but that must have been because he wasn't sure when the concert ended. Which was foolish, as the time was on the posters. Or he could have asked someone." Her brow furrowed. "I can't think why he didn't, unless he was hoping to prevent the other man from finding out, which could be why he—that is, the other man—was following him again tonight."

"The man in dark clothes was following the bloke in camouflage," Brinton translated.

"Yes, and *he* was following *him* at the same time." Miss Seeton chuckled. "It was most amusing to watch as they … dithered to and fro in the shadows all along The Street. Like children playing Grandmother's Footsteps, but then of course I had the impression that he—the man in camouflage—was in some aspects of his behaviour little more than a child. Impulsive, with no thought for the consequences."

Brinton shook his head; it didn't clear. He looked at Foxon. Let the lad earn his stripes.

"MissEss, even if I've seen the first chap the boss hasn't, and a picture would be a big help. And neither of us has any idea at all about the other bloke in—" he grinned at her— "the boring duds. Could you give us a picture of each?"

"I've only got a pen," apologised Brinton. Foxon was on his feet. "They'll have pencils on Reception, for when people keep changing their minds." He was gone and back with a handful of pencils before anyone could blink. "Would it be easier to concentrate if you were alone, Miss Seeton?"

She hesitated. Foxon winked.

"Mr Brinton's left Ned Potter in the bar with your friend Mr Smith and Charley Mountfitchet. Just because we can't hear any singing doesn't mean they're not tuning their tonsils this very minute. We ought to go and check up on 'em."

Miss Seeton was smiling as the two policemen departed barwards. Timothy Foxon was always so pleasant and cheerful. Mr Brinton teased him a great deal, but must be very glad of his company when working on a difficult case. Not that one could call the present situation a case, exactly. Perhaps a quiet—no, better a stern—word with the camouflage man about the need to grow up and learn to curb his stronger emotions might be all that was required. Indeed, it seemed hardly worth troubling the authorities with something that she herself, an experienced teacher, could have dealt with had the man only given her the time. But he hadn't. Grandmother's Footsteps, always looking over one's shoulder …

She trotted into the bar with a sheaf of papers, two portraits, and the pencils in her hand to find everyone drinking coffee. "Make sure us don't drop off to sleep," said Charley Mountfitchet, knowing her preference for tea. "I'll have the kettle boiling dreckly minute, unless you'd care for more brandy."

The kindly offer so startled her—spirits, at this time of night! It wasn't as though she were ill—that in handing her sketches to Superintendent Brinton she dropped them and the pencils together. As the Scrap Dealer drawings were underneath the rest, the papers drifted in a modest avalanche, and the pencils rolled, in several different directions.

"Oh, dear, I'm so sorry." Everyone was leaning down to scrabble on the floor. There was a general attempt at guessing which way up the drawn-on sheets should go before the papers were passed to their intended recipient.

"Ent that Mr Castringham?" Charley paused mid-guess to admire the likeness of a well-built man of military bearing but in plain clothes, smoking a large cigar. "Never knew you'd met him, Miss Seeton. Keeps himself very much to himself, that man, on account of having bin ill and here on a rest cure. Room service every time, and only goes for walks in the fresh air when it's quiet, on account of not wanting to be disturbed."

"Let's see that." With a curt apology Brinton seized the portrait from the landlord. "Miss Seeton, is this the man who hit you on the head?"

"Oh, no. As I was about to explain to Mr Mountfitchet, I did catch several glimpses of him yesterday, when he was trying to conceal himself from the other one who did—but that hardly counts as meeting him, does it? Even again last night, when he was following him. Hit my head and spoil my hat, that is. So vexatious, although thanks to Mr Mountfitchet—"

"For pity's sake tell me," begged Brinton, "which man is which?"

"Blood pressure, sir," murmured Foxon, leaning over his shoulder. "That's not the bloke I met chatting to MissEss, so the birdwatcher isn't Castringham—and he's not staying here." He shuffled through the stack of loose leaves to find the other portrait. "Right, Charley?"

"Don't know him from Adam," confirmed Mr Mountfitchet, thrilled to be yet again Helping the Police with Their Enquiries. "Might have seen him around the place when all them birders were staying—but not to notice, as such."

"Potter?" snapped Brinton.

"Seen him around, sir, same as Charley, not to notice, with so many of 'em here and me more worried about 'em parking in the wrong place and so on."

"How about you, Mr Smith? Do you recognise either of these two men?"

Bram Smith shook his head. "I've seen a whole heap of folks during my visit, but you could say there are too many to remember. I'm sorry, but I can't tell you who either of these gentlemen is."

"No," said Brinton, "but it seems clear from what you've told us, Miss Seeton, that they each of 'em know who the other one is. They'd have to, to make it worth the effort of playing peek-a-boo up and down The Street in the middle of the night."

Bram looked doubtful, but was too polite to speak. Nobody else for an instant doubted that Miss Seeton had seen the men she said she'd seen, where she said she'd seen them, behaving as she described. The trained eye of an artist might see things in a different way from the lay person—and in

Miss Seeton's case, that could be a very different way indeed—but the trained eye *saw*.

"Which room's he got?" Brinton asked the landlord.

Charley told him. "It's official business," said Brinton, consulting the clock he was pleased to see the landlord kept five minutes fast. "He'll just have to put up with coming down in his pyjamas and dressing-gown, if Miss Seeton won't mind—you'll have seen a lot worse in life classes, I dare say." She smiled. "Then what I'd like is for you to take a proper look at him—and I'd like him to look at your picture of the birdman so he can tell us who he is. For all we know, he—I mean Castringham—is a private detective trailing the bird bloke for divorce purposes. Softly, softly has to be our watchword. Foxon—don't introduce yourself as a detective sergeant, he'll see from your identification you aren't. Demote yourself for the sake of convenience, will you?"

"It was fun while it lasted." Foxon sighed melodramatically, and headed from the bar.

He trod gently up the stairs, aware that the hotel had other guests and live-in staff still asleep. He hoped Mr Castringham wasn't hard of hearing: he didn't want to disturb the peace and quiet any more than he needed.

He tapped on the door; waited until his quick ear caught the rustle of sheets, the creak of springs; then repeated that brisk, official rat-tat.

The springs creaked again. A human groan—a mutter—a voice telling him to go away.

He tapped even harder. "Mr Castringham?" he called softly. He wouldn't say who he was until the door was open. Hotel guests look with suspicion on other guests who've had midnight visits from the forces of law and order. "Mr Castringham, I'd like to talk to you. Can you spare a moment?"

A drowsy curse. If he'd heard correctly, it was a word Foxon didn't know. He filed it for further investigation. Rustling sheets, creaking springs, padding feet.

The door opened a crack: a bleary eye, a stubbled face, tousled hair. "Wass madder?"

Foxon produced his official card. "Mr Castringham, I'm a police officer and—"

"The hell you are!" The door was flung open, and Foxon could see his face properly. Miss Seeton's well-built man wasn't smoking a cigar; but there was no doubt he was of an excellent build. His pyjama jacket gaped to show muscle-thickened neck, and a broad chest covered by a tangle of dark hair. "What the **blinking blank** do you want?"

So sudden had been the change from sleepiness to full alert that Foxon took a backward step or two before recollecting himself, and once more showing his ID card. "I'm a police officer, Mr Castringham. There's been a spot of bother and—"

Castringham grabbed him by the lapels of his jacket. Foxon winced, less from alarm than for the sound of ripped fabric. "It's nothing to do with me," snarled Mr Castringham, shaking the younger man with a vigour that suggested the rest cure had been a success. "Go away! I don't care how much bother there's been, keep me out of it!"

He let go of Foxon, glared at him, and as the startled detective opened his mouth to register a protest cursed him roundly, then cursed again and threw a punch. Dropping his ID Foxon staggered back, but rallied quickly and waded in. He had no idea what was happening, or why, but two could play at this game.

In the event the game was joined by several others. It took the athleticism of the all-american Smith, the barrel-humping strength of landlord Mountfitchet, and Brinton's judicious application of avoirdupois—he sat down on top of the struggle, allowing out from under only those who were clearly on the side of the law—to subdue the unpredictable and ferocious Mr Castringham enough for PC Potter to produce his handcuffs, and apply them.

By next morning the news was all over the village. Guests had woken, wanting to know the reason for the rumpus; Doris heard all the commotion and appeared downstairs wearing a hurried scarf over pink sponge curlers, asking if she should telephone Ned Potter. She'd been surprised to find what seemed like half the Kent constabulary already present.

The voice of Mr Castringham was raised in more vocabulary-enhancing protest as he was led away on the charge of assaulting a police officer—more than one police officer—in the execution of his (or their) duty, and resisting arrest.

"I'd like to have done him for affray, and if any of the guests had come in on his side I would've, because legally it takes two," said Brinton, once the patrol car had departed for Ashford and the cells. "Young Smith accidentally hit me as well as chummie, but I doubt if that counts as two different assaults by two different people. Anyway, I'm letting him off with a caution." He grimaced amiably at the bruised but triumphant Bram, then grew serious. "They're only preliminary charges, but I want the blighter off balance for a while. Never mind I've a strong feeling there's more to come—he could have done Foxon a lot of damage, if we hadn't been here." Foxon had been despatched to escort Miss Seeton home with promises of fruit cake and the use of her little sewing kit. With his hands rather bruised he might find even temporary repairs awkward. "The lad's a good lad. If a bloke he's only trying to talk to decides to do him over, in my book that bloke's got something to hide."

"Hisself, for a start," said Charley Mountfitchet. Charley, with the assistance of Miss Seeton, had administered first aid all round, and offered strong tea with a dash of something in it for shock as they awaited the patrol car from Ashford. At least (Brinton grumbled) there would be enough spare men to cope with the prisoner, seeing that those three cars from the motorway were out of action. "Seemed strange all along," said Charley, "he'd come for a rest. Didn't act ill at all, to my mind, though it's none o' my business what guests get up to so long's they don't disturb other folks."

Disturbed guests became early risers. Continental breakfasts were offered by a Doris with immaculate curls, who promised something more substantial once the kitchen had fully woken. Potter went home; Bram went to bed; Brinton, thanking Mr Mountfitchet formally and promising to let him know the outcome, went across to Sweetbriars to collect Foxon.

"And I'll drive," he told his weary sergeant. "I don't like the look of you at all. That jacket doesn't help, of course—"

"Miss Seeton's been very kind, sir."

"—but I suppose the dry cleaners can do something with it, though goodness knows why they'd want to. Just give me the receipt once it's sorted. That'll give me time to indent for a pair of sunglasses."

Miss Seeton, apparently none the worse for her adventures, beamed upon the two and offered tea and toast, if they would care for it, to sustain them on their journey to Ashford. Brinton had said he'd be back, now that Sergeant (emphasised) Foxon wasn't likely to be driving for a while, at a more civilised hour for her statement.

"And if anything gives you the idea for a drawing as well, I'd be interested," he ended, before heading with his wounded subordinate into the dawn.

Miss Seeton wasn't sure if this last had been a firm instruction to a colleague, to be acted upon at once, or whether she might be allowed to catch up on a little sleep first. And she hadn't done her yoga exercises. After the concert last night there had of course been no time, and this morning one could hardly leave poor Tim Foxon to repair those ripped seams, though he'd put a brave face on things and said he was fine, thank you. At least she'd been able to cobble the pieces together; the jacket was wearable, unwieldy though her stitches undoubtedly were in such thick fabric. Really, a most disgraceful show of violence …

Violence. Yes indeed. She contemplated the sketch she had, without realising, drawn of a Punch and Judy show. The man who'd hit her on the head was Punch, and the man who'd hit poor Sergeant Foxon was Judy. The baby, its features hidden by an enormous cap with elaborate bows, much goffering, and lacy frills, lay in Judy's arms looking like a long, fat sausage in a shawl. The startled policeman wore under his helmet the face of Timothy Foxon.

Well, Punch and Judy weren't noted for peaceable behaviour, although as a child one had laughed heartily rather than disapprove the violence; but that man had done his best, by all accounts, to hurt poor Tim a great deal, entirely without provocation. Miss Seeton did not approve of bullying. Even if one *had* been woken from a deep sleep at an unsocial hour, it was the duty of all conscientious citizens to assist the police when asked to do so—which is why she had opened her sketchbook rather than go to bed …

It was the doorbell that roused her as she wondered about another cup of tea, so very refreshing. Perhaps a little too late now to go to bed; she would instead have an early night.

She went to answer the door. On the step stood Sir George and Lady Colveden.

"Miss Seeton, we heard the news and wanted to make sure you were all right," said her ladyship. "George spoke with Superintendent Brinton, who told him what happened, but we thought we should see for ourselves."

Miss Seeton looked shocked. "Do come in, but—oh, dear, that means they can't have gone home to bed yet. At my age loss of sleep isn't as important as it can be for the young, and of course there is my yoga—so helpful—and then, one grew accustomed during the Blitz to disturbed nights, and learned to adapt. I was about to make myself a cup of tea." She'd been on the point of going upstairs first for a wash and brush-up, but it would hardly be good manners to say so. "Won't you join me?"

"I'll make the tea," said Lady Colveden, with the assurance of an old friend. "You and George can have a peaceful chat. He'll tell you what the superintendent had to say."

"Said he was taking young Foxon to his lodgings and going home himself." Sir George regarded Miss Seeton with quiet admiration. A little pale, perhaps; looked a bit rumpled—but she didn't seem bothered. He pondered previous alarums and excursions. Nothing ever seemed to bother her, he amended quietly. Remarkable.

"Said he'd be along to see you later, but didn't feel he ought to be on the road just at present, with his eyes popping out, poor chap. You too, of course," he added quickly. Miss Seeton smiled and demurred: really, she been very lucky, when one took everything into consideration. As long as the bird-watcher didn't come back to bother her again she felt she should consider the matter safely over. Apart from her hat, the loss of which she regretted.

"We'll go into Brettenden tomorrow," promised Lady Colveden, bringing in the tea tray, "and see what Monica Mary has to offer. I'm sure the police would be happy to pay."

"Hmm." Sir George knew what the popular local milliner charged for some of her creations. Meg's hat for Nigel's wedding had almost bankrupted him. "Hmm. Brinton will know, of course, but ..." He coughed. "Unstable chap—chaps. Both of them. Good job it wasn't the one from the George who was keen on birds." Not that he or Brinton believed either of the two strangers had the least interest in birds: that was Miss Seeton's interpretation, and she always preferred to see the best in people. "Hat or no hat, he could have done you a lot of harm, m'dear. Even young Foxon's pretty shaken up, Brinton told me, at being hit as hard as he was."

Miss Seeton murmured in distress. Sir George, receiving a fierce look from his wife, made haste to reassure his hostess. "He's young. At that age they bounce back. Been promoted, too. That will help." He saw her smile and relax. "Thing is," he went on, "Brinton can't get a handle on the blighter. Won't say a word, not even to ask for a lawyer." He fingered his moustache. "Something odd there. Brinton said it was catching, and if anyone else tried the same trick he wouldn't answer for the consequences. No idea what he meant, but what he asked me was—"

There came a bang at the kitchen door, a clatter in the passage. Martha Bloomer stalked into the room to stand with hands on hips, glaring at her employer. "What have you been up to now, Miss Emily? I've only just heard. And why aren't you safely in bed and asleep catching up, instead of being bothered by people who ought to know better?" She glared at another of her employers, and Lady Colveden blushed. "Never mind your nonsense," as Miss Seeton began to explain, "I'm going to run you a nice hot bath right now, and if you're not upstairs inside five minutes I'll come and fetch you. The very idea!"

Lady Colveden looked at her husband. "Perhaps we'd better try again later," she said. "Martha does seem cross."

"I'm afraid that's my fault," began Miss Seeton, but her apology was waved away.

"We all know how devoted the Bloomers are to you, Miss Seeton, and we understand." Her ladyship directed another look towards her husband, who again was stroking his moustache. "But if we could just ask you—what Superintendent Brinton asked George—if by any chance you'd had time to jot down any impressions of what happened last night …"

Footsteps were heard descending the stairs. Miss Seeton jumped guiltily to her feet. "It seems foolish, I know, and I can't see how it could possibly help, but—Punch and Judy," she gasped as Martha reappeared to seize her by the arm, and pull. "I'm afraid that was all I could think of, but if Mr Brinton should find it of interest …" With her free arm she waved towards her open sketchbook. "Yes, Martha dear, I am coming." And she was gone.

The Colvedens tiptoed to the bureau where lay Miss Seeton's drawing. Sir George took a deep breath—glanced towards the ceiling whence came sounds of scolding, apology, and finally splashing as Miss Seeton climbed into her bath—hesitated still.

Martha came back down the stairs and popped her head round the sitting room door. "I'm making her a hot-water bottle, and I'll thank you to leave her in peace for a while, poor thing. She could have caught her death in that nasty cold tomb. Birdwatchers, indeed!" And she marched off to the kitchen.

"God bless America," murmured the chastened Sir George. "But Brinton did ask me. Miss Seeton herself said he might find it of interest. Better take just this top sheet along with us and I can—good Gad!"

He had torn off the Punch and Judy sketch Miss Seeton described without paying much attention as Martha was so clearly on the prowl. Now he stopped in his tracks.

And stared.

Lady Colveden was worried. "George, what's the matter? You look as if you've had a shock. You know Martha's not really …"

He shook his head. He waved the drawing.

"I know this chap," he said.

Chapter Thirteen

The British army trains its soldiers well. Major-General Sir George Colveden did not forget his training, and experience as a magistrate had trained his judgement still further. He knew when something was important, and when it could wait; and made decisions accordingly. Brinton, concerned about driving when short of sleep, had asked if he'd be kind enough to retrieve and deliver to Ashford any sketches Miss Seeton might produce in the aftermath of last night's drama. Sir George went one step further, and wouldn't make the handover unless it was to Brinton himself. He knew how paperwork could be lost for ever in a busy office, no matter how much care was taken.

Desk Sergeant Mutford, at first upset that the word of a Holdfast Brother wasn't trusted, came to admire the baronet's steadfast position, his refusal to allow Brinton's sleep to be interrupted. Sir George didn't want the poor chap, tired as he was, driving under a bus: he'd wait. He sat down. Mutford, thwarted but approving, organised tea.

The baronet was on his third mug when Brinton at last appeared, to see the glint in Sir George's eye, the envelope in his hand. "Come to my office," he invited. "Oh—just one moment, Sir George—Mutford, is anybody singing?"

"No, sir."

"Damn," said Brinton as he led Sir George towards his office. "Half the cells are full of people who either won't say anything except No Comment, or who won't say anything at all. The bloke who clobbered Foxon is the worst. Talk about the strong, silent type—that man scores ten out of ten on both counts. Won't even talk to the duty solicitor."

He waved Sir George to the visitor's chair. "You've got something? Miss Seeton's done the trick again? I can't always make out what she means, but if you can—"

"Certainly can." Sir George passed the sketch across the desk. "No idea who Punch might be, but Judy—I know him."

"You do? You can give us a line on Castringham? Sir George, you're a wonder—and so's Miss Seeton, of course."

Sir George frowned. "That what he's been calling himself?" Brinton looked at him. "His name's Castleford—or rather, it is in London. Same club, in a manner of speaking. Dry rot and builders, lodgers in the Trip—that's my club—from the Gallimaufry on the other side of the square." He fingered his moustache. "May belong to the In and Out as well, though I can't say I've noticed him there." He chuckled. "Mind you, I never noticed the Buzzard—Admiral Leighton—before he came to live in Plummergen, and he's been a member as long as I have. Naval and Military, y'see."

"You know this man as Castleford? What else do you know about him?"

Sir George's moustache was subjected to a judicious stroking. "Don't care to talk out of turn. Laws of slander, and so on. But this is a privileged occasion." Brinton assured him that what he said wouldn't go (in any identifiable way) beyond the four walls of his office.

"Hmm. Well. Wouldn't like to hang a man on hearsay, you understand." He coughed. "Rumours. People get the wrong end of the stick far too often, but—some sort of scandal about him. I'm not saying he was cashiered," hurriedly, "but it's my belief he was asked—a very strong hint, at least—to resign his commission."

"You mean he was an army officer?"

Sadly, the major-general agreed. "Major. Calls himself one, at all events. The Buzzard might have a better idea, being a bachelor." Brinton looked puzzled. "No home ties," said Sir George. "Sociable chap. Goes up to Town rather more than I do, these days."

"If we could find someone who served with him …"

Sir George frowned. "The Army List? Hmmm. Club library should have a complete set, although …" Then he smiled. "Like Ernest Worthing. Meg made me see that once, and I had to laugh. The cloakroom at Victoria Station—the Brighton line. Oscar Wilde was a bright spark, all right. May have been a pansy, but good luck to him. Takes all sorts to make a garden—Kipling, y'know. England is a garden and so on, though Meg told me he died in France once he was out of jug—not that Castleford went to prison, as far as I recall." Frowning again, he contemplated Punch and Judy, the Baby and the Policeman on Brinton's desk. Assault and battery. Cudgels. Fighting. Violence.

"Dynamite!" he remembered. "Poaching in Scotland somewhere—private loch full of salmon, absentee landlord. Ghillie bribed to turn a blind eye. They dropped sticks of the stuff in the water and knocked out all the fish. Float to the surface and just scoop 'em up. The Buzzard tells me it works the same way sweeping mines at sea. Blow one up and, bingo, fresh fish for all the crew, except that this chap Castleford was selling them. Reason they kicked him out of the Army was, he'd pinched the explosive from the firing range where he was stationed." He hesitated, grasping after an elusive thought. No, he couldn't catch it. "His sergeant helped him, I believe."

"Poaching," Brinton said thoughtfully. "Poaching ..." The Oracle's murder victim had been a poacher. The crime was still, as far as he knew, unsolved. And wasn't there some suggestion the killing—the beheading—might have been carried out by someone who knew what he was doing? Someone with military training? "Sir George, I'm going to talk to Chief Superintendent Delphick. I think he might be interested in Punch and Judy and I ought to let him see this picture as soon as possible."

Sir George demurred. "Didn't exactly give me permission, y'know. Martha hustled her off before we could agree officially, as you might say."

"You forget the wonders of modern technology. We curse it, of course, but it's not all nonsense. When it works, it earns its keep. There's some clever gizmo that sends pictures down a telephone wire. That's what I'm going to do with Miss Seeton's latest, and I want to warn the Oracle it's on its way." Brinton grinned. "You wouldn't hand the original over to Mutford in case it disappeared in the system, would you?" Sir George grinned back at him, nodding. "Same here," said Brinton. "If I warn him to expect a copy of this doodle at the Yard within the next half-hour, he can send that young giant of his who married your doctor's daughter to their end of the contraption to collect the thing in person."

Now that he'd played his part and things were starting to happen, Sir George was about to take his leave, but Brinton paused in mid-telephone stretch and shook his head. "Don't rush off just yet, please. Delphick might want to ask you for details. After all, you've talked to the old girl more recently than either of us."

Sir George, reluctant to poke his nose in, was gratified to be asked to stay. He subsided happily back on the visitor's chair and listened to Brinton's end of the conversation.

The first exchange was brief. Delphick expressed a definite interest in the new sketch. Sergeant Ranger was elsewhere, pursuing a new line of enquiry: Brinton wasn't wrong, they were getting nowhere with the Beheaded Poacher investigation and Bob had had a sudden idea that the chief superintendent felt didn't work, but shouldn't be suppressed without trying. Delphick would go himself to stand guard over the Yard's gizmo to receive Miss Seeton's sketch in person. He asked to speak with Sir George, who was able to reassure him that his tame art consultant seemed to be in excellent condition, considering all she'd gone through. He gave details. Delphick chuckled over Martha's strong-arm tactics and the bath. He then thanked Sir George, promising to call back once he'd been able to study the Punch and Judy picture.

"And the Army List," he added before signing off. Sir George was relieved. He hadn't really cared for the notion of consulting the Triptolemus Club library—too much risk of gossip—but it had been the only place he could think of. Delphick said the Yard had a collection of reference books that might be consulted by any serving officer.

As soon as Brinton replaced the telephone on its cradle, it rang again. The superintendent rolled his eyes. "Excuse me, Sir George." He picked up the receiver, listened, and rolled his eyes still more. "Just one moment—please," he told the telephone through gritted teeth, then covered the mouthpiece with his hand.

"It's one of the legal eagles, wanting to bend my ear. I can get rid of him soon enough, but I want Punch and Judy on their way. Look, Sir George, Foxon's not here, but Mutford knows you. Would you mind taking this—" he took the sketch from his desk— "along to him and making sure it goes to Delphick at the Yard, pronto? I'd go myself, but this blighter—"

Sir George, that firm (but far less aggressive) legal eagle, indicated his willingness to co-operate and accepted the sheet of paper from the harassed Brinton's hand. "I'll bring it straight back," he mimed, and left the superintendent to argue in peace.

Fascinated by the whole procedure, Sir George stayed after the picture's safe despatch to discuss the workings of the machine with a uniformed officer who swore he was the only man in Ashford to understand it properly. A cross between a Photostat and a telex with additional frills, it appeared. Dots, dashes, technical jiggery-pokery … "Fascinating," said Sir George again. "By the way, what happens if you aren't here?"

"Ah," said the self-professed expert, with a wink and a grin "Well …" He shrugged.

Sir George shot him a quick look. Once more he winked. "Overtime, and plenty of it."

"Indeed." Sir George nodded slowly, then took himself and the sketch back to Brinton, wondering how far he should be concerned. Did it count as interference if he suggested that paying a man overtime only worked if he was able come into the station? Suppose he took a holiday abroad? Suppose he were to be run over by a bus?

"Suppose," said Brinton gently, "he was pulling your leg. We've two or three more lads who did the training, though I admit he's the best we've got for gadgets, but …"

"Of course." Sir George grinned. "I did wonder. Met a few like him in my army days. Corporals, mostly. The privates don't dare cheek you and the sergeants have more sense."

"We're not the army, we're the police. HM Forces all right—but a very different force, behaving in a very different way. I'll have a word."

"Nonsense, m'dear chap, just an over-developed sense of humour. Officers are always fair game—and I let him know I didn't believe him. Not as if he was rude, exactly. Can't call a wink or two dumb insolence, can you?"

"Last April Fools' Day," reminisced Brinton, "that same bright lad did something to the walkie-talkie network that had Sergeant Mutford spitting feathers. Perhaps I should—"

The telephone rang. "Er—Foxon?" It took a moment to change mental tack from his expectations of Scotland Yard. "Woken up at last? … You're where? … But nobody told me you'd been in for a pool car … Motorbike? That promotion's gone to your head … Oh, have you. And you'll be on your way straight back with them? … Make it snappy. I've talked to the Oracle and he'll be calling me at any minute … Tobacco? … Drive carefully, then!"

He looked at Sir George, and sighed. "On the strength of his promotion, my new sergeant paid the deposit on some fancy motorbike and took himself along to Plummergen to get the statements we didn't get last night. And it sounds as if they could be … interesting."

The wildest of horses couldn't have dragged Sir George away now. Brinton asked if he'd like another cup of tea while they waited. Would Sir George excuse him while he did his best to clear part of the undergrowth of his current caseload? There were more of Miss Seeton's sketches to consult. They hadn't made a lot of sense the first time he'd looked at them, but in light of recent events ... The Ashford bank robbery might, or might not, have some relation to the Ecclesham affair; the scrap yard connection might or might not be pure coincidence. Foxon, blast the boy, said it was a copycat case and called them the Gridlockers. He might be right. If they hadn't been caught, they'd have tried the same trick again, he felt sure. A pity they'd been so quick to send for their lawyers: dumb insolence wasn't the word. The police were stuck. And now this Castringham, Castleford bloke struck equally dumb. Perhaps Sir George would give his opinion?

"Looks a jolly type," was Sir George's view of Moby Dick in the pony cart, with the scrap dealer ringing his bell. "Reminds me a bit of the totter who came round our way when I was a nipper. Goldfish, good heavens, yes. But this other chap ..."

"Foxon says MissEss talked about when she was a nipper, too," said Brinton. "Rang the bell once, and never forgot. Maybe that's all it means—but the other chap. Yes?"

"That trident," began Sir George.

Once more they were interrupted by the telephone. "Foxon?" snapped Brinton.

"Delphick. I've had a few thoughts about Punch and Judy, Chris. Bob Ranger has returned—no joy, sadly—and he's also been thinking. We cast our minds back to that witchcraft and fake religion business in your part of the world a few years ago ..."

"Nuscience," grunted Brinton. "I've got Sir George with me, by the way." One of the victims in that case had been a distant cousin to the Colvedens, although nobody had much lamented the death of Aunt Bray. "Should he be listening on Foxon's extension?"

"Where is Foxon?" enquired the Oracle. Brinton explained. Delphick's smile was audible. "Please convey our heartiest congratulations. He'll remain with you, I take it?"

"It does seem I'm stuck with him," said Brinton. "Likes his lodgings, he tells me." He did his best to sound aggrieved, but his listeners weren't fooled.

"No doubt he'll marry the landlady's daughter. Free bed and board for life." Delphick coughed. "Talking of females, it was Judy and the Baby who caught our particular fancy. As Miss Seeton's Policeman bears a likeness to one Detective Sergeant Foxon, so Judy closely resembles a certain Major Castleford—" Sir George, on the extension, muffled a cry; Brinton sat bolt upright— "kicked out of the army for removing rather more of their stock of explosive than anyone wishing to build a modest rockery in his garden should require." They could again hear the smile in Delphick's voice. "I would draw to your attention, gentlemen, the fact that both the major, and the sergeant who received the order of the boot around the same time, were stationed at the firing ranges near Lydd."

"Lydd?" The old war-horse scented another clue. "Lyddite!" he cried.

"Lyddite," agreed the Oracle. "An explosive based on picric acid, invented at Lydd—which is, you will recall, not a hundred miles from Romney Marsh."

"Local paper posts an official notice every time firing's scheduled," said Sir George.

"It was Bob, the proud father, who was so struck by the Baby. Not only do its wrappings make it resemble a sausage— or a cigar—but the headgear is most worthy of remark, with an excess of furbelows and twiddly bits putting peculiar emphasis on the infant's, ah, cap." He coughed again. "Wasn't it at Judy's Gap that the customs boat waited for the Nuscience crowd to make their escape from the Secret Place?"

"The old smugglers' tunnel," groaned Brinton. "Dates from Napoleonic times, and buried in the sand dunes. Customary Excuses thought they could find the seaward end to trace back and find where Miss Seeton tumbled into the thing ..."

"It is our contention," said the Oracle, "that Punch and Judy are somehow linked with the tobacco-smuggling case and the murder with which we have become involved—"

"Tobacco!" cried Brinton. "MissEss mentioned last night there'd been a smell of tobacco in that damned stone coffin the bird bloke shoved her into. The American, Smith, who fished her out apparently told Foxon the same. It's a shaky connection, Oracle, but somehow it all hangs together. This Castleford we've got locked up here arrived in Plummergen because he's involved with the tobacco smuggling—dammit, she's even sketched him with a massive cigar in his mouth! Of course. They lost their previous route when they killed the poacher, and switched to bringing the stuff in through Judy's Gap just the way the old timers did. But you'd need local knowledge for that. And if he was stationed at Lydd ..."

"Bob and I will be with you as soon as we can," Delphick promised.

As farewells were exchanged Foxon arrived, with the statements he'd collected and a nonchalant air. He greeted Sir George, and received congratulations on his promotion with a modest smile.

"Stop playing about, laddie. What've you got for us? The Oracle's on his way down," Brinton warned him.

"I've no idea what it means, but Miss Seeton's been drawing again." Foxon wasted no time on Bram Smith's statement: the words seemed straightforward enough, and could wait. When it came to Miss Seeton's sketches, the sooner dealt with the better.

"Yet another bell," said Brinton, looking back at the Moby-Dick-and-pony sketch with the necklace of bells round the whale's middle, and the handbell in the smiling totter's hand. In the new sketch she had drawn one large bell, with a graceful bird, pure white in colour, a worm dangling from its bill, perched on the handle. Sir George viewed it with interest.

"Not the European Roller we had all the fuss about," he observed. "Young Lily Hosigg called that a back-to-front kingfisher—red and blue, rather than blue and red. This little chap could be an albino blackbird, I suppose." He shook his head. "Not too many about. Don't live long. Other birds mob them, poor things."

"Miss Seeton told me she's been reading up on exotic birds," said Foxon. "The Roller got her interested, and Mrs Ongar from the Rye sanctuary lent her a couple of books. She said she thought it could be a bell-bird, sir, from South America. She said that's not a worm, it's a wattle. Like chickens only different, she said."

Brinton frowned. "South America? Hardly likely to turn up here, then. She drew this in response to you asking her about last night?"

"With a bit of encouragement, sir. But it's got me stumped."

The other two were likewise stumped. "Change of subject," said Brinton. "There's still the scrap dealer sketches—Sir George, you were starting to say something about

Neptune's trident when the phone rang and we were distracted. Care to start again?" He glared at the telephone, daring it to ring.

"Thought at first it was no more than a length of pipe with a—a twiddly bit on top." Sir George was happy to borrow from Delphick. "Then I thought, some kind of road sign." The superintendent and his sergeant exchanged glances. "More of these new Common Market regulations, no doubt." Sir George laughed. "With the kid goat as well, I expected the thing to warn about cattle crossing, though of course we're mostly sheep around the Marsh."

"We need another word with Kidman and Gallop," said Brinton. "And to think I did such a good job of fending off that lawyer. I could've asked him—still, we know where they live, the blighters, if they're the ones behind all this trouble."

"Behind some of the trouble, sir," Foxon politely amended. "I doubt if it was any of them knocking Miss Seeton on the head and hiding her in the smuggler's phony tomb."

Brinton grinned. "As they were in the cells at the relevant time, so do I. It might have been another of 'em we haven't yet caught, but—Punch, now. You're sure you don't recognise him, Sir George?"

"Sorry, old chap. Only Judy—your Castringham, my Castleford. But …"

Brinton sat up. "Yes?" With Foxon, he'd have barked an order to spit it out, but with a visitor who was not only a general, but also a magistrate, he bowed to superior rank.

"About Castleford," said Sir George slowly. "Occurs to me he relied on that sergeant of his rather a lot—as people do," he added, directing an affable nod towards Foxon. "Backbone of the regiment, a good sergeant. The Army List doesn't include other ranks—officers only—but if Delphick's done his homework properly, which knowing him he has, he should be able to tell you what the army records have told him about Castleford's lot in general."

Brinton glanced at the clock. "They can't be here yet. Ranger doesn't drive the way you do, Foxon." Foxon tried to look hurt. "Never mind your nonsense for now, laddie." He pondered. "Miss Seeton told us the pair of 'em were dodging each other up and down The Street in the dark. We thought it might have been about divorce, didn't we? Softly, softly, I said. Well, we don't think that any more."

"You bet we don't," Foxon chimed in. Sir George nodded.

Brinton opened his desk for a peppermint and offered the packet to his guest who, with another nod, took one. Brinton inserted his own mint and, as he continued to ponder, offered one to Foxon. There was a thoughtful, aromatic silence.

"We could," said Brinton at last, "have a preliminary word with Castringham—we know your real name, we know a lot more besides—but that sort of thing can backfire. It *might* unsettle him into spilling all the beans—or it might encourage him to start yelling for the lawyer he refused when we first arrested him."

"Swings and roundabouts," sympathised Sir George, as Brinton sank back into a silence that was now calculating, and Foxon frowned judiciously. "Glad I haven't got your job, I must say. Magistrates need to consider both sides before making a decision, but at least we start off with the facts. This is a dashed sight more difficult. No facts beyond a bruise or two on your sergeant, here—" another affable nod— "and giving a false name, though that might be harder to pin on him unless it's for criminal purposes. Have to identify the crime, first. Wish you the very best of luck."

Brinton wondered if he should for safety's sake ask the baronet to observe the prisoner through the Judas window of his cell door, but Sir George's original identification from Miss Seeton's drawing had been definite. It wasn't the kind of evidence to offer in court, but Sir George was right. They were short on facts. Delphick had also said it was Castleford, but that (so far) was hearsay. When he arrived he would bring photographs, a physical description, perhaps even fingerprints with him. When he arrived. Until then, Castleford would just have to wait … and so would they.

Sir George was once more making a move. "Leave you to it, old chap. Let me know what happens, if you can. Every faith in you. Delphick too, of course."

"And Miss Seeton," Foxon reminded him with a grin. "And me," he added softly.

Brinton glared at him; and Sir George took his leave.

There were other crimes to deal with, more paperwork to address, as they waited for the Yard to arrive. Before plunging into routine matters Brinton gave Superintendent Furneux the latest on the scrap metal investigation, saying it looked as if they'd narrowed it down, but he didn't want to send his man off to make an arrest, or even to ask more questions, until the rather more serious matter of an unprovoked attack on a police officer, a possible outbreak of smuggling, and a definite murder had been resolved.

"Your blonde is out of Intensive Care," was the main news from Sussex. Foxon, who during the previous twenty-four eventful hours had understandably forgotten all about the glamorous Phoebe, was glad to hear of the lady's improvement and hoped it would continue. Furneux told him this seemed probable, and returned to the scrap metal thefts and—as an afterthought—the Ashford Gridlockers bank robbery. Brinton amiably cursed both his friend (for making stupid jokes) and his sergeant (for having thought up the name in the first place). He said he'd let him know what happened next. After the Yard had been.

When Delphick and his sergeant at last appeared, the two Ashford men greeted them with enthusiasm. There may well be virtue in reducing a paperwork backlog; no doubt there is satisfaction in making procrastinated decisions when there is time for clear, unhurried thought: but these activities lack excitement. Only the likes of Desk Sergeant Mutford could regard a full out-tray, a half empty in-tray and properly regimented files as an acceptable use of police resources when a particular case seems on the point of breaking, but requires the presence of others …

The greeting was enthusiastic, but brief. Brinton demanded to know what the visitors had brought with them from London.

"Photocopies of files, mostly from army records but also from the police in Scotland." Delphick tossed a cardboard folder on Brinton's desk. "The latter had to be wired down to us, thereby losing a little in clarity. In summary, however, if your Castringham is the man we think, he's an enterprising character, though not as enterprising as Sergeant Bell, who—"

"Who?" cried Brinton and Foxon as one. Delphick and Bob looked startled.

"Matthew Bell: the sergeant whose presence the army decided it must forgo at the same time it dispensed with the services of Major Castleford. You look surprised. I thought from our previous conversation that you knew all about the salmon poaching in Scotland, and the theft of explosives from the firing range at Lydd."

"About it—them—yes, but by no means all." As Delphick retrieved the Yard file and began leafing through its contents, Brinton scrabbled among such papers as he hadn't consigned either to his out-tray, or the filing cabinet. "It's your girl-friend with the sketchbook," he said in triumph, "who knew *all* about it. Look."

He laid a selection of those special drawings across his desk. "She may have got her cases muddled a bit, but if the old girl wasn't telling us to keep our eyes open for a bloke called Bell I'll—I'll bump Foxon up to inspector within the week."

Delphick and Bob studied merry Moby Dick with his chiming necklace, the totter with his hand-bell and the white bird that had caught Sir George's attention. Brinton identified it to the visitors, feeling rather smug. Ornithology wasn't one of the Oracle's particular interests. It was comforting to be able, for once, to know something the Yard man didn't.

"Yes," Delphick said, his finger marking the file he still held. "I'd say you're right."

"Miss Seeton's right," Brinton amended. "Dammit, Oracle, he hit her on the head! People aren't generally wrong about someone who treats 'em like that."

"Not generally, no." Delphick held the file open for inspection. One look made Brinton's triumph complete.

"Unless he's got an identical twin that mugshot's him, sure enough. Bell—Mr Punch—whatever you call him, she's spot on as usual. Any fingerprints'll be a bonus."

"The army records make no mention of a twin, or even of a brother. They list an aunt as his next of kin—no parents, siblings, wife, or children. Curiously, the Scottish police files give his name and address—a different address from the aunt—and his solicitor as next of kin, suggesting that by then he had no close personal ties. A deliberate choice, one must suppose. Having blotted his copybook in so spectacular a manner, he chose to cut himself off almost entirely from his past before embarking on what a distaste for melodrama prevents one calling 'a life of crime'—after all, we have no idea beyond educated guesswork what he might have been doing after the affair in Scotland—but I fancy 'a different life' would be a fair summary."

"Your *almost entirely* meaning Major Castleford."

Delphick once more hunted through the file, then displayed the appropriate page. There was no doubting the identity of the man in the photo; fingerprint confirmation came as an anti-climax. "Castleford, like Bell, would appear to be a solitary individual," Delphick observed. "In his case the next of kin is listed as his bank. I wonder what they were up to, during the missing years? Did they spend them together?"

"Looks like it, else why the mutual cover-up?" said Brinton. "Could be there's a hundred unsolved crimes just waiting to be solved once we get a statement from the blighters. Can't think why they didn't change their names altogether."

"Matthew Bell might have done," said Foxon.

"He might, but MissEss says he didn't."

Foxon altered tack. "Major Castleford would've found it awkward to change if he wanted to go on belonging to clubs in London. People would recognise him. He could try saying he'd come into money and had to take his benefactor's name to get his inheritance, but he probably relied on the scandal dying down after a few years. Even Sir George wasn't sure of the details." He warmed to his theme. Brinton and Delphick regarded him with interest; Bob, with surprise. "I've no idea how gentlemen's clubs work, but perhaps he used membership to—to make connections, sir, or learn things that might come in useful for—for whatever he wanted to get up to next, if being kicked out of the army turned him into some sort of … establishment career criminal."

"Raffles," said Delphick. "Well, well. The sprightly wardrobe and idiosyncratic sense of colour shelter a romantic soul. Sergeant Foxon, you have hidden depths."

Brinton snorted. "The major might be a career criminal who finds it useful to keep his name, but that won't be how it works with other ranks." He grinned an evil grin at the two younger men. "Sergeant is a pretty humble rank."

Foxon grinned back, and Bob, when he caught up, smiled as well. But he was thinking.

"The army records show Matthew Bell was an expert in unarmed combat," he said slowly. "He didn't kill the poacher—if it *was* him—in an amateur panic, the way we wondered—he just reverted to his training, only he was a bit rusty. Misjudged the strength required—the thickness of the wire—or is it thinness that matters?" He frowned. "Anyway, he found Isaiah Gawdy out with his snares in the middle of the night, seeing what he shouldn't have seen, and …" He spread expressive hands.

"I wonder why he didn't just hit him on the head, the way he did Miss Seeton?"

Chapter Fourteen

It was Delphick who answered. "You have that the wrong way round, Bob. I think you should ask why he didn't kill Miss Seeton the way he did the poacher. My answer would be one word: herself. The man may be a trained killer reverting to type, but the inference from the records is that he was an orphan, taken in and raised by an aunt of whom he may or may not have been fond. Miss Seeton, as has been noted over the years, is everyone's idea of an aunt. You've adopted her as such yourself." Bob nodded. Foxon said nothing. The Oracle smiled.

"Aunt Emily Dorothea Seeton is, like her millions of sisters, England's backbone, mainstay and personification. You can't have forgotten her accidental performance at the Paris Casino where every other female wore nothing on stage but spangles, while she had tweeds and a Union Jack wrapper—no, I thought not," as Bob grinned. Neither of them had seen it, but they'd heard about it from a journalist friend who'd been present and had dined out on the story for years.

"Good grief. When was this?" demanded Brinton, who'd never heard anything at all. Foxon could only stare.

"Another time, Chris. Miss Seeton is also," the oration continued, "a retired teacher, accustomed to quelling unruly pupils with a single look; and, perhaps most important of all, she is an innocent. You said she was convinced her intruder was an over-keen twitcher wanting to know where the rare bird had gone: in the end, he probably came to believe that such was indeed her conviction. He stunned her to ensure her silence while he did whatever he had already planned to do, whatever that might be—removing smuggled stock, at a guess—and left her where she was sure to be found before too long. Who knows? That twinge of conscience might shorten his eventual sentence by a year or two."

"Not if MissEss has her way." Brinton was grinning. "You should've heard how she carried on about her titfer. Lady Colveden's taking her to that posh hat place in Brettenden today. Will the Yard field that particular expense, or must we?"

"Perhaps we should first make sure our theories are correct." Once more the Oracle consulted files, photographs, sketches. "Remember, Castleford is our only positive identification: fingerprints don't lie. Even identical twins differ in that particular respect. But there are such things as doppelgangers, and so far we have only Miss Seeton's drawing and its resemblance—admittedly, an extremely close resemblance—to a photo on which to base the working hypothesis that her Mr Punch assailant is Matthew Bell."

"She's drawn a lot of bells around the place," Brinton reminded him.

"Indeed she has, but I suggest we need more than campanology and what might be mere coincidence before we trouble the aunt's local force with an official request to pop round to her house and see if her long-lost nephew has made an unexpected appearance. A blank sheet of paper, some sharp scissors, and a window should resolve the problem …"

Watched by his fascinated colleagues he held the Punch and Judy sketch against the glass, covered it with a second sheet of paper and drew round Punch's face, omitting the cap, the quiff and the frilled collar to leave nothing visible but the features.

"Punch because he hit her, no doubt," he said, then sat down with the paper and snipped neatly round the outline. He placed one sheet on top of the other and asked where the nearest photocopier might be.

Armed with the blocked-off likeness of Mr Punch, Delphick and Brinton, with Bob and Foxon two respectful paces to the rear, proceeded to the largest interview room. "Get him worried," gloated Brinton. "So many of us."

"Didn't worry him too much before, sir." Foxon rubbed his bruises in a marked manner.

"Young Ranger can sit on him this time." Bob uttered a protest; Delphick chuckled. The previous night's fracas at the George and Dragon had been described in some detail. The oracular comment on the benefits of lapsed diets had been ignored.

"What I meant," continued the dignified Brinton, "was that he'll worry how much we've actually got on him, with a chief super coming down from the Yard for a chat. With any luck, that might be all it takes."

It took rather more than that.

The man who called himself Castringham had been brought from his cell to the interview room by police officers who studiously addressed him by that name.

"Ah, Major Castleford," was Brinton's greeting. "Do sit down. Let me introduce Chief Superintendent Delphick, from Scotland Yard."

Left, right. Invisible blows, and unexpected. The prisoner froze.

For less than five seconds. "My name's Castringham. Mister—" with emphasis on the civilian title— "William Richard Castringham." He sat down, and folded his arms.

"Your fingerprints say it isn't."

"It is not," put in Delphick, "an offence to change one's name, even temporarily, unless it is with criminal or fraudulent intent." The prisoner's eyes, narrowing, turned to him. "It does, however, seem both curious and unnecessary for a man to adopt a pseudonym just to stay in a small hotel in a small village where he is unknown—unless it is with criminal or fraudulent intent."

"I didn't want to be disturbed by anyone. I've been ill. I needed peace and quiet."

"You didn't get much of that last night," said Brinton. "Nobody did."

The silent Foxon stirred. Recognition dawned in the still-narrowed eyes. "When I'm woken from a deep sleep in the middle of the night by a total stranger making unreasonable demands I can't understand, it comes as a shock to the system. I told you, I'm in this part of the world for a rest cure. My nerves … I—I panicked. I apologise. Things look very different in daylight, after a night in the cells. If there's a fine I'm happy to pay it, but there's no more to the matter than that."

"You didn't want to be disturbed by anyone," echoed Delphick. "Or—recognised? The London club of which you are a temporary member has several permanent members who live in Plummergen."

"Not to mention Sergeant Bell, last seen playing chase-me-Charlie up and down The Street with you in the dark," added Brinton. A silent Delphick held out Mr Punch for the man's inspection—after which, it was a matter of routine questioning. Bob and Foxon took notes, as Brinton and Delphick shared the interrogation.

Major Wilton Reid Castleford had supervised—no, he wouldn't say established, but he wasn't prepared to name names for fear of reprisals—had been employed to supervise the bringing of tobacco products, duty free, from the Continent to England for repackaging—

"From Horatio to Pyramus y Thisbe," interposed Delphick. "Fraudulent purposes, as we have already agreed." Castleford seemed about to protest, but hesitated and then carried on. For repackaging and ... more profitable distribution. Smuggling if they preferred, but he preferred the term free enterprise.

"Or free trade, as they called it in Napoleonic times," said Delphick.

"Famous for smuggling, this part of the world," said Brinton.

Castleford gave vague details of dates and times of parachute drops, and agreed that the pick-up team—no, he considered *gang* unnecessarily pejorative—served also as the repackagers. He knew nothing about them: he'd rented a house to double as a workroom and left Matthew Bell to sort out everything else.

"Someone who had worked with you before, rather than a stranger. A relationship of long standing, it seems. Why alter an arrangement that brings results?" Delphick indicated, but did not open, the topmost folder of the pile they'd assembled. The bulky folder with the prominent label.

"Sergeant Bell and I have paid our debt to society," said Major Castleford, trying to sound lofty and principled. All four policemen regarded him in silence.

"But nevertheless found yourselves unemployable as a result," said Delphick at last. "For how long, and what exact pursuits—legal or illegal—you both undertook in order to make a living, do not at present concern us." Castleford shifted on his chair. Delphick nodded. "Not, I repeat, at present. We are more concerned with last night's attack—"

"I panicked!" snapped the major. "I told you!"

"—on an elderly woman, in her own home, by Sergeant Bell. Was this on your orders?"

"What? I knew about—" Castleford broke off, just too late.

Delphick pounced. "You knew about the unlucky poacher he garrotted, but you didn't know that he had broken into an old lady's cottage, bashed her over the head, tied her up and left her senseless in a two-hundred-year-old stone sarcophagus in Plummergen churchyard, abandoning her to whatever passer-by might be brought there by fate. Or," he added coldly, "might not."

"Or not in time to help the poor old soul," growled Brinton. The note-takers noted with silent amusement these remarks. Anything less like the tragic, feeble figure conjured up by their superiors than Miss Seeton they found it hard to imagine.

"I knew nothing of this!" Castleford, sensing not only professional curiosity but also an intensity of feeling that unsettled him, stared from one accuser to the other. Both stared back, Delphick wearing a quizzical expression while Brinton continued to scowl.

"Yes, I did know about the poacher," conceded the major. "Bell telephoned me in Town to say there had been … an incident and he feared that during subsequent investigations the original hideaway could be discovered. I found a new place for them on the outskirts of the village where—where you found me …"

"You knew about the farmhouse being empty because you overheard people chatting in the club," supplied Brinton. "You knew about the easy route from Judy's Gap on the coast because you were stationed at Lydd."

"As was Sergeant Bell," said Delphick. "Tell us about him. For instance, did he approve the perhaps inconvenient change from air drop to sea landing?"

Again the man hesitated. "It was no more his place to approve or disapprove changes of plan than—than it was mine."

"Only obeying orders," said Brinton. "We've heard that before." *And why don't I believe you? Because I believe you're the big boss of the whole shebang, doing your best to kid us you're among the lowest of the low. Fear of reprisals, indeed!*

"Why were you chasing each other up and down The Street?" the chief superintendent wanted to know. "If he was such a trusted subordinate? You were spotted trying to avoid one another. Were you making sure your tame thug carried out his attack on the old lady to your complete satisfaction?"

"I tell you I know nothing of any such attack," insisted Major Castleford.

"Ah, yes." Delphick's tone held the same disbelief that Brinton's silent thoughts had already expressed. "Did you authorise the near-beheading of Isaiah Gawdy?"

"Certainly not!" His eyes shifted. He breathed heavily. They all waited. "I was growing … uneasy about Bell," he eventually brought out. "After the death of that poacher I felt he was less … reliable than he'd been in the past. Now you tell me he assaulted an elderly woman. In his right mind he would never have done such a thing. He was devoted to the aunt who brought him up, as she was to him."

Delphick and Brinton made mental notes that a search for her missing nephew should be promptly requested from her local police force. Sergeants Foxon and Ranger, thinking the same, wrote notes in shorthand.

"We hadn't—that is, the system that had been set up and proved its worth didn't seem to be working as well as it once had," continued the major. "There was far less money coming in than we would have expected. I began to suspect—it was suggested to me that somebody might be creaming off a regular percentage of the profits by delivering short once the goods had been repackaged for sale. If that person was Bell, I wanted to catch him in the act, so I came down to Kent and checked into the nearest hotel to his farmhouse HQ, keeping out of everyone's way by saying I needed to be left alone for reasons of health. I kept intermittent watch on the farmhouse, on who came out and where they went …"

"And then the school concert got in everyone's way." Brinton, two days later, was winding up the case—all the cases—over the telephone with Delphick. Their sidekicks, as usual, were licensed eavesdroppers. "Bell had lost a lot of sleep shifting his loot to that tomb in his spare time—"

"Which could explain his first encounter with Miss Seeton," said Delphick.

"And with me, sir," chirped Foxon, whose bruises were fading.

"Shuttup," came Brinton's automatic response. "As I was saying—he'd filled the tomb with stolen smokes and wanted the whole lot back once he knew they'd be moving house again. With The Street crawling with kids—you know what sharp eyes they've got—he had no chance to get out of the farmhouse up at the Common and back down into the village until they were all safely in bed. The rest of the time, he was scaring people off by playing the ghost in white satin camouflage he'd pinched from that film star."

"A waste of expensive bed-linen," sighed the Oracle.

"Bed? The woman's never in it. Potter says she genuinely has trouble sleeping, and wanders about at all hours in her nightie. Must have driven Bell crazy."

"One would have supposed," said Delphick, "that her presence, dressed always in white and no doubt wringing her hands at the same time, would have served him well in reinforcing the ghost rumours when he wasn't doing the job himself."

"Temperamental, these actresses. Never knew when he might run into her bump, did he? If she'd spotted him, she might've asked awkward questions. And if he'd bumped her off the way he did your man Gawdy, he'd have had the police *and* half the world's press crowding into Plummergen, asking even more awkward questions."

There was a pause for contemplation of the different publicity likely to be generated by the murder of a movie legend, as opposed to that of a poacher. Or the assault and kidnap of a retired art teacher.

Brinton resumed his narrative. "So, come the night he planned to shift the loot he wore everyday camouflage so nobody would see him. If he'd still been a ghost—well, there's safety in numbers, and plenty of people about. Someone might have tried a—a physical exorcism and rumbled the whole business. And *then* he spots Castleford trying to avoid Admiral Leighton, who's escorting Miss Seeton home after the concert."

"And army training kicked in," said Delphick.

"Right back in," agreed Brinton. "Both of the blighters. Hence all the hide-and-seeking spotted by MissEss. An artist's eye's as good as any trained forces, if you ask me."

A further contemplative silence.

"She had that scrap dealer bang to rights, too," said Foxon. He'd gone with Brinton to interview Kidman, who had been so sure they'd come about the brass fender "for Auntie's sitting room fire" that he hadn't thought it necessary to hide his second set of books. These, kept under the name of Gallop, contained a far more accurate representation of his affairs than those he routinely produced for inspection as required by law. The legal books had to be bound, kept exclusively for the purpose, and retained for two years after the last entry; as they were. The truthful (rather than honest) loose-leaf books held full details of people whose nicknames and cryptic addresses demanded translation. Brinton had been quick to demand one.

"Sang like a canary," gloated Brinton now.

"Don't you mean a European Roller, sir?" Foxon was irrepressible.

Brinton ignored him. "At least we know who was responsible for landing that blonde in Intensive Care. The accident wasn't intentional, I'll give the blighters that, but Harry Furneux says it'll be a while before they walk off with council property again."

"Or people's garden gates." Foxon remembered his grandmother.

Delphick intervened hastily. "What is the latest on the young woman? She was heading for a job interview, as I recall. Is she well enough yet to try again?"

"No need, sir." Foxon had resumed watch on the progress of Phoebe Stanley. "She's been signed up by some posh model agency in London that saw her photo in the paper and sent someone down to take a look at her. And they liked what they saw."

He sounded disappointed. Bob Ranger, married man, laughed. "You've missed your chance there, Tim."

"Never say die," said Foxon.

"And the European Roller?" enquired Delphick. "I trust that it is likewise still in the land of the living."

"I gave Miss Seeton a lift to the bird sanctuary to sketch it closer up, sir," said Foxon. "Mrs Ongar says once the feathers've grown back, it'll be fine."

A stunned silence from the London end. Brinton sighed. Promotion hadn't sobered his young sidekick the way he'd thought it might.

"Miss Seeton—" there was an element of control in Delphick's voice— "rode pillion on your motorbike?"

Bob made a choking noise.

"We went in a police car, sir." Foxon was reproachful. "Mr Brinton sent me to Plummergen to get additional statements from Mr Smith and Miss Seeton and—well, it's only a few miles to Rye and I thought it was the least I could do. So I did it."

"Ah," said Delphick. "A natural misunderstanding. The very idea of Bob's adopted aunt in leathers and a crash helmet disrupts one's usual thought processes."

"Yes, sir, but aunts can be tougher than you think." Bob and the chief superintendent had read with interest the reports from those officers who had gone to the former home of Matthew Bell. Miss Campanula Bell had proved surprisingly expert in delaying tactics, and needed much persuasion before she would allow her property to be searched. They'd got him in the end, but it had been a lively occasion. The old lady had now been bailed on her own recognisance, and the nephew was locked in a cell.

Customs and Excise sent investigators to the two addresses Brinton, thanks to Major Castleford, had eventually been able to supply. Another team examined the files of estate and letting agents deduced by clever cross-referencing against the original agency used by the major to find the first, suitably discreet, property rented for the pick-up and repackaging gang. One or two names led to further identification of suspects.

"All in all," concluded Brinton, "not so dusty. The Ecclesham bank lot are beyond anyone's reach, but we've got the Ashford gang sorted. Funny, how they crumpled the way they did. All these legal bods know one another, of course. I reckon when Castleford began yelling for help the word got round ..." He chuckled. "Poor old Block will have to wait for his pipe-cutters back, though. They're evidence. Mutford says he's not happy."

"It's hard to please everyone," Delphick consoled his friend.

"So Customs've got a lead on the tobacco smuggling, and a killer's been caught. The only thing that's not sorted is the scarecrow business, and everyone knows who's responsible." Brinton sighed. "I've told Potter to turn a blind eye if the Watch Men are a bit spirited on some dark night in the near future …"

"Unless," prompted Foxon, "Miss Seeton gets involved."

Miss Seeton put the finishing touches to her watercolour of the European Roller. Mrs Ongar and the rest would have photographs; she had only her talent—such as it was—with paper, pencil, and brush. Not, perhaps, worth framing; this was one for her portfolio, a memento of a little adventure that began when Dulcie Rose Hosigg invited her to see the big blue birdie in her garden, and ended when Mr Foxon—Tim—had taken her to see the poor thing recuperating at the Wounded Wings sanctuary. So privileged an opportunity; so close a view. The twitchers and other visitors were all gone, but how exciting it had been while they were there. And how very kind people were.

She picked up her pad and began to doodle. The school concert wasn't so long ago. A gratifyingly large audience, thanks to the Roller. Such generous contributions. "Five and twenty ponies," she sang to herself. A little girl with Dulcie's face clutched an extravagant doll, and peeped out through frills and furbelows as Lily smiled beside her.

Miss Seeton mused further on Kipling. Mr Smith—again, how very kind—had taken her to Bateman's. They played quotation games together. He recited "Gunga Din" and Jack Crabbe was as impressed as herself …

A man appeared, with a bald head, a large moustache and gold-rim-bespectacled eyes. In his mouth was an elegant cigar. As they spiralled upwards, wisps of soft grey took on a supple, beguiling female form …

"A woman," murmured Miss Seeton, "is only a woman—but a good Cigar is a Smoke."

Also Available

Lucky Miss Seeton! A modest Premium Bond win means a whole week in legendary Glastonbury.

By coincidence, a kidnapped Heir to an industrial family may be hidden around there and Chief Superintendent Delphick has asked the ex-art teacher to create some of her famous, insightful sketches.

Even he is nonplussed by the resulting images of capering sheep in straitjackets, flashing false teeth!

Serene amidst every kind of skulduggery, this eccentric English spinster steps in where Scotland Yard stumbles, armed with nothing more than her sketchpad and umbrella.

About the Miss Seeton series

Retired art teacher Miss Seeton steps in where Scotland Yard stumbles. Armed with only her sketch pad and umbrella, she is every inch an eccentric English spinster and at every turn the most lovable and unlikely master of detection.

Further titles in the series—

Picture Miss Seeton
A night at the opera strikes a chord of danger
when Miss Seeton witnesses a murder . . . and paints
a portrait of the killer.

Miss Seeton Draws the Line
Miss Seeton is enlisted by Scotland Yard when her
paintings of a little girl turn the young subject into a
model for murder.

Witch Miss Seeton
Double, double, toil and trouble sweep through
the village when Miss Seeton goes undercover . . .
to investigate a local witches' coven!

Miss Seeton Sings
Miss Seeton boards the wrong plane and lands
amidst a gang of European counterfeiters. One
false note, and her new destination
is deadly indeed.

Odds on Miss Seeton
Miss Seeton in diamonds and furs at the roulette table?
It's all a clever disguise for the high-rolling spinster . . . but
the game of money and murder is all too real.

Miss Seeton, By Appointment
Miss Seeton is off to Buckingham Palace on a secret
mission—but to foil a jewel heist, she must risk losing the
Queen's head . . . and her own neck!

Advantage, Miss Seeton
Miss Seeton's summer outing to a tennis match serves up more than expected when Britain's up-and-coming female tennis star is hounded by mysterious death threats.

Miss Seeton at the Helm
Miss Seeton takes a whirlwind cruise to the Mediterranean—bound for disaster. A murder on board leads the seafaring sleuth into some very stormy waters.

Miss Seeton Cracks the Case
It's highway robbery for the innocent passengers of a motor coach tour. When Miss Seeton sketches the roadside bandits, she becomes a moving target herself.

Miss Seeton Paints the Town
The Best Kept Village Competition inspires Miss Seeton's most unusual artwork—a burning cottage—and clears the smoke of suspicion in a series of local fires.

Hands Up, Miss Seeton
The gentle Miss Seeton? A thief? A preposterous notion—until she's accused of helping a pickpocket . . . and stumbles into a nest of crime.

Miss Seeton by Moonlight
Scotland Yard borrows one of Miss Seeton's paintings to bait an art thief . . . when suddenly *a second* thief strikes.

Miss Seeton Rocks the Cradle
It takes all of Miss Seeton's best instincts—maternal and otherwise—to solve a crime that's hardly child's play.

Miss Seeton Goes to Bat
Miss Seeton's in on the action when a cricket game leads to mayhem in the village of Plummergen . . . and gives her a shot at smashing Britain's most baffling burglary ring.

Miss Seeton Plants Suspicion
Miss Seeton was tending her garden when a local youth was arrested for murder. Now she has to find out who's really at the root of the crime.

Starring Miss Seeton
Miss Seeton's playing a backstage role in the village's annual Christmas pantomime. But the real drama is behind the scenes . . . when the next act turns out to be murder!

Miss Seeton Undercover
The village is abuzz, as a TV crew searches for a rare apple, the Plummergen Peculier—while police hunt a murderous thief . . . and with Miss Seeton at the centre of it all.

Miss Seeton Rules
Royalty comes to Plummergen, and the villagers are plotting a grand impression. But when Princess Georgina goes missing, Miss Seeton herself has questions to answer.

Sold to Miss Seeton
Miss Seeton accidentally buys a mysterious antique box at auction . . . and finds herself crossing paths with some very dangerous characters!

Sweet Miss Seeton
Miss Seeton is stalked by a confectionary sculptor, just as a spate of suspicious deaths among the village's elderly residents calls for her attention.

Bonjour, Miss Seeton
After a trip to explore the French countryside, a case of murder awaits Miss Seeton back in the village . . . and a shocking revelation.

Miss Seeton's Finest Hour
War-time England, and a young Miss Emily Seeton's suspicious sketches call her loyalty into question—until she is recruited to uncover a case of sabotage.

Miss Seeton Quilts the Village
Miss Seeton lends her talents to the village scheme to create a giant quilted tapestry. But her intuitive sketches reveal a startlingly different perspective, involving murder.

Miss Seeton Flies High
On a week away in legendary Glastonbury, Miss Seeton's artistic talents are called upon to help solve a mysterious kidnapping.

About Heron Carvic and Hamilton Crane

The Miss Seeton series was created by Heron Carvic; and continued after his death first by Peter Martin writing as Hampton Charles, and later by Sarah J. Mason under the pseudonym Hamilton Crane.

Heron Carvic was an actor and writer, most recognisable today for his voice portrayal of the character Gandalf in the first BBC Radio broadcast version of *The Hobbit*, and appearances in several television productions, including early series of *The Avengers* and *Dr Who*.

Born Geoffrey Richard William Harris in 1913, he held several early jobs including as an interior designer and florist, before developing a successful dramatic career and his public persona of Heron Carvic. He only started writing the Miss Seeton novels in the 1960s, after using her in a short story. Heron Carvic died in a car accident in Kent in 1980.

Hamilton Crane is the pseudonym used by Sarah J. Mason when writing 16 sequels and one prequel to the Miss Seeton series. She has also written detective fiction under her own name, but should not be confused with the Sarah Mason (no middle initial) who writes a rather different kind of book.

After half a century in Hertfordshire (if we ignore four years in Scotland and one in New Zealand), Sarah J. Mason now lives in Somerset—within easy reach of the beautiful city of Wells, and just far enough from Glastonbury to avoid the annual traffic jams.

Note from the Publisher

While he was alive, series creator Heron Carvic had tremendous fun imagining Emily Seeton and the supporting cast of characters.

In an enjoyable 1977 essay Carvic recalled how, after having first used her in three short stories, "Miss Seeton upped and demanded a book"—and that if "she wanted to satirize detective novels in general and elderly lady detectives in particular, he would let her have her head . . . "

You can now **read one of those first Miss Seeton short stories** and **Heron Carvic's essay in full**, as well as receive updates on further releases in the series, by signing up at farragobooks.com/miss-seeton-signup